FRANKIE & DOT

ROSIE RADCLIFFE

The Book Guild Ltd

First published in Great Britain in 2024 by
The Book Guild Ltd
Unit E2 Airfield Business Park,
Harrison Road, Market Harborough,
Leicestershire. LE16 7UL
Tel: 0116 2792299
www.bookguild.co.uk
Email: info@bookguild.co.uk
X: @bookguild

Typeset in 10.5 Adobe Garamond Pro

Printed and bound in Great Britain by 4edge Limited

ISBN 978 1835740 781

British Library Cataloguing in Publication Data.
A catalogue record for this book is available from the British Library.

For Jeff, who always believed in me

ONE

The woman looking back at me from the mirror was drop-dead gorgeous, even if on the shady side of forty. A lot of work by a whole team of people had gone into producing my appearance – hair, nails, frock, diamonds glittering in my ears – no detail or expense spared for an important political dinner.

The taffeta skirt of my new dress rustled against the silk of my lace-topped stockings as I sashayed downstairs and into the antique-filled living room of our Georgian London townhouse. Even to jaded eyes my husband looked so handsome in full evening dress, with his carefully maintained grey hair styled in a floppy Hugh Grant look. A "silver fox" as one of my friends had called him. He leaned against the marble fireplace, cut-glass tumbler of whisky in one hand, and I smiled at him, anticipating admiration.

Henry took one look and frowned, saying, 'Bloody hell, Francesca, I can't take you out dressed like a tart with your tits on display. They'll fall out or something; you'll have to go and change.'

He turned away to refresh his drink, the conversation clearly over from his point of view. Too deflated and stunned to argue, I was halfway back up the elegant staircase when my brain did something it's never done before (but absolutely should have) and said, *enough – fuck this shit*. Up in our bedroom I kicked off the Jimmy Choo heels and let the beautiful dark blue dress drop to the floor, before climbing into bed in my undies (also silk, Parisian, wasted on Henry), and in a strange state of calm reached for the TV remote.

The doorbell rang, and from below Henry called, 'Come *on*, woman, the ministerial car is here.'

I didn't move or answer, so he stormed up the stairs to find me watching a car-chase film in bed.

'What are you even *thinking*?' he shouted, his face scarlet with the rage he was careful never to allow friends or colleagues to see. Only me. 'Don't you understand how important this dinner is to my career?'

'Yes, I do, because you've banged on about it long enough.' I tried to maintain a cool exterior and calm voice, flicking through the channels in an attempt to control my shaking hands. 'But the thing is, I don't care about the dinner or your career. I'm done.'

Henry stared at me like I'd lost the plot, unable to process the words coming out of my mouth. I added a few more for good measure.

'I can't, won't, live this life anymore. You may as well get used to doing things by yourself. I'm leaving you.'

Where had this courage come from? I was proud of myself for standing up to him, instead of always giving way and allowing him to dictate our life.

Dear Henry completely lost it – not a pretty sight – his face and neck almost purple with fury against the white of his formal dress shirt. I even worried he might have a heart attack.

'You ungrateful *bitch*. After everything I've done for you,' he hissed, stepping closer, spite twisting his face. Another ring of the doorbell.

2

'Just *go*, Henry.' My ability to stay calm was fraying at the edges.

'If this is an attempt to sabotage my career as some kind of petty revenge, you're not getting away with it.' His voice rose, becoming shrill. 'I've worked too hard all these years, arse licking the right people, and now when I'm *this* close to everything I've dreamed of, you decide to leave me?'

I stared back at him, stony-faced. 'I should have done it years ago when you were first unfaithful. And how many times since?'

That shut him up. Henry ran one hand through his hair, messing up the elegant arrangement of his "cool-as-fuck" look. He spluttered a bit more but only managed to bluster, 'Haven't I been good to you, given you everything?'

Such a cliché. Next, he'd be saying I didn't understand him.

I leaned back against the goose-down pillows. 'Oh yes, everything except the love you promised me when we made our vows in church. I'm not a fool, Henry. Your current liaison has been going on for at least ten years. You don't give a damn about me, as long as I turn up to be appropriately decorative as and when required, glad-handing the punters, the rising-star political couple. I'm not going to do it anymore. End of story.'

Henry started shouting, but I turned up the TV volume and met his angry ranting about ingratitude and disloyalty in silence. Inside was a cold kernel of fear, though he'd never been violent towards me. His preferred methods of control were sarcasm and ugly moods that lasted days. The doorbell rang again, a longer more insistent ring this time, while I lay there pretending to be engrossed in a programme about lionesses in a matriarchal society. About then it began to register in his tiny brain that short of dragging me out of the bed he'd *have* to go to the dinner alone. With an uncanny resemblance to a kid having an epic tantrum, he stormed out of the room, shouting back over his shoulder, 'You'll be sorry you did this!'

Hearing the front door slam, I turned off the TV. My threat to leave had been no more than angry words, intended to hurt him after being told I looked like a tart. Now, out of nowhere, a voice in my head was going, *why the hell not?* Unhappiness was something I'd got used to over many years, the unvarying background music to an outwardly successful and privileged life. I saw with new clarity that none of it was worth the price I'd paid. Slumping back against the pillows, the understanding dropped into my brain that it was *easy*. I could just walk away; in fact, why hadn't I done it sooner?

Ten minutes later, I'd packed some essentials into a hard-shell suitcase and dressed in more sensible clothes – jeans topped with my favourite Chanel jacket. Then I left Henry, our Bayswater home, the constituency, all of it; boom, done. I don't remember if I thought about it at all in that moment but must have imagined coming back later for the rest of my things. Any embryonic dreams of a new life didn't include the possibility I'd never see them again.

*

On a tide of adrenalin, I drove my Mini aimlessly through the streets while I tried to figure out where to go. A hotel just for a day or two? In the end, I headed to Felicity's house, blithely confident that after her experience of a messy divorce, she'd understand and offer temporary refuge. I should have phoned first.

'Um, Francesca, it's not really convenient,' she said, standing in the doorway of her pretty mews house wearing a designer top and Gucci loafers, looking at me and my suitcase doubtfully. 'I've got a new boyfriend now, and he…'

'It's fine,' I said stiffly, in that way you do when it isn't. 'I'll go to a hotel then. Thanks anyway.'

'No, wait,' she said, holding out a hand. 'Sorry, please don't be like that. You can stay tonight, of course you can. He isn't here right now but when he comes back later tomorrow, you'll have to make other arrangements.'

'Thanks,' I said, hitting planet reality with a thump and feeling about as welcome as a dog turd on the doorstep. 'Only tonight, then I'll find somewhere else.'

She didn't engage in any more conversation, only showed me upstairs to a luxurious designer guest room. Lying there with Felicity's French flax sheets cool against my skin, the first chill prickles of doubt began to creep in. Looming in front of me were the realities of life without the cushion of Henry's inherited wealth. Sod it; I'd burnt my bridges but would have my revenge on Henry for the wasted years somehow. Waking from tangled anxiety dreams, I heard Felicity in the kitchen around 8.00am, so got dressed in yesterday's clothes and went downstairs with my case, with every expectation of being asked to leave immediately.

She was making us pancakes for breakfast and gave me a wry smile.

'Sweetheart, I'm sorry for the cool welcome last night. It was… unexpected, you do understand? This thing with Carlos is new and exciting…'

'And you don't want a random friend in need messing things up. Awkward, right?' I finished for her.

'You must be thinking I'm crazy, taking up with a Spanish toyboy? I know it can't last,' she said, 'but while it does, I'm making the most of it. He's younger than me and the sex is so damn good, he does this thing…'

Such details were something I absolutely could *not* listen to. Putting down my coffee cup, I groaned, 'Felicity, don't even go there. I'm practically a born-again virgin. It's been so long I've forgotten what you do.'

'A gorgeous woman like you? Don't tell me Henry isn't interested? He'd have to be completely numb in the trouser department.'

I stopped smiling and met her eyes across the table. Why pretend not to know Henry was gay? All our friends knew; most of them before I did.

'You are kidding, right?' I said. 'OK, I may have been the absolute last person to work it out, but it was eventually obvious even to me that the wife and child thing was only window dressing for him. He's been having an affair with his constituency agent for years.'

She'd put a plate of fluffy American-style pancakes on the table but got up to fiddle unnecessarily with a bottle of maple syrup. It was obvious she'd heard all the rumours; so much for being a good friend and taking the trouble to enlighten me.

'Ah,' I said. 'You knew then.'

When had she and I stopped being close friends, the kind who chat most days and tell each other everything? A taste of ashes in my mouth came with the sudden knowledge that it might have been my fault. When her own marriage spectacularly imploded the year before, I hadn't always supported her the way I should have. Henry hadn't wanted a tearful presence in our house at unexpected hours and insisted I kept her at arm's length. Too late, I appreciated how desperate and lonely she must have been. Now our roles were reversed, and it was my turn to be the needy friend. Karma, I suppose. At least I'd worked out a kind of plan while lying awake in the early morning.

'Well,' I said, pushing my empty plate away with a bright and resolute "better-get-on-with-it" smile. 'Henry will soon figure out this is more than a hissy fit because I won't be going back to repent of my sins.'

'Ah, I see.' Felicity smiled knowingly. 'You really are serious about this.'

'Yes, so swift and direct action is required and there are some things I need to get from your local high street this morning. I don't want to leave my suitcase visible in the Mini, so can it stay here in your hall? Then I'll come back to collect my stuff and be out of your way.'

'No problem. I've got nothing on this morning, so you go shopping,' she said, with an enthusiasm which had been absent the night before. 'Then you can tell me the whole story about what happened with Henry and how you came to leave.'

Felicity's smart area included several high-end shops for the comfortably off residents of her upmarket London suburb. Suppressing all feelings of guilt at spending Henry's money, I put the joint credit card to good use and swiftly acquired a fancy new phone and an equally top-of-the-range laptop. These were the basic necessities of a new life, continuing the small-scale editing and proof-reading business I ran to give me something real to do. It wouldn't bring in enough to live on, so the bottom line was that I'd need to get a job. Knowing this brought out all the demons of fear and doubt as I walked back to the house. Could I even do this; would anyone employ me? I hadn't had a proper job in years (constituency work or sitting on committees didn't count), not since Justin's birth.

Back at Felicity's, an appreciative grin spread across her face at the sight of my purchases. I laughed with her; it was going to be OK – her enthusiasm for giving Henry the finger helped to banish my immediate doubts. She even helped me take the laptop and phone out of the packaging so I could put everything into one suitcase and be able to carry it all.

'I'll get rid of these boxes for you,' she said. 'They can go out with my recycling later, but right now I want to hear *everything*.'

Over coffee, I related the unsavoury story of my unexpected rebellion; the line that had finally been crossed after twenty years. When I got to the part about Henry's impotent fury, she cackled.

'God, Frankie, I can so picture his face; wish I'd been a fly on the wall. He always was a pompous arse, and it serves him right.'

'I am going to make him pay, drag him though the divorce courts unless he cooperates to protect his precious reputation. You know, I lay awake last night remembering how it used to be love's young dream, for me at least. Justin was the best thing to come out of it, but he's an adult now and all I can see is that the twenty-plus years invested in Henry's career was a total waste of my youth.'

'No, Frankie, stop right there,' insisted Felicity. 'Don't go chucking out the good stuff along with the bad – though I did the same at first. My therapist says every experience helps form the person we become, and one day you'll even be grateful for all of it – especially in the new independent life you're planning.' She grinned at me. 'I can recommend life after divorce.'

'I'll take encouragement from your example then, but can I impose on you for an hour or so longer?' I asked, getting up to put the Emma Bridgewater mugs in the dishwasher. 'Coming back from the shops I spotted a sign for a room in a shared house. It's not far from here, so I called the number and I've got an appointment to view it in half an hour. Can you hang onto my stuff while I go and see the place?'

'A shared house? Francesca, no, you'd hate it.'

She was right, and the houses nearer the shops were smaller and less desirable, but cheaper. I planned to take the car, wanting to look like someone who could afford a decent address.

'I have to start somewhere, and it won't be for long – only until I can negotiate a generous divorce settlement from Henry.'

The Mini was parked down the street from the house, shaded by a beech tree from the summer sun. As I walked towards it, my head began to explode with excitement and possibility as I indulged in visions of my new life as an independent woman.

A police car was double parked on the street, the Day-Glo yellow and blue of the checked sides looking thoroughly out of place in this conservation area where tasteful, heritage colours were a requirement. Two officers were pointing in my direction as I drew level with the Mini, and they got out, clearly intent on speaking to me. My absolute first thought was for my son. He'd had a terrible accident, been attacked, stabbed or something. I braced myself for what must be coming.

'Mrs Wilton?' enquired one.

'What's happened? Oh God, is he all right?'

'Don't give us any of your bullshit,' said the other. 'Francesca Wilton, I am arresting you on suspicion of arson. Do you understand?'

TWO

The judge stared down with a stern, cold expression, leaning forward from his high seat. None of it felt real, the wood-panelled courtroom a film set full of actors. Nothing to do with *me*.

'Francesca Dorothea Wilton, the jury has reached a unanimous verdict, and there is no doubt in my mind as to your guilt. Your motives were those of bitterness and revenge because you discovered your husband's affair. You have shown no remorse whatsoever and persistently denied the truth of your attempt to burn down the marital home. In so doing, you placed Mr Wilton's life in severe jeopardy and such actions can only warrant a custodial sentence,' he told me.

My whole body trembled, disbelief the primary emotion in a tidal wave of despair and fear. During the trial, my husband had lied with creative and brilliant conviction, and the rapt jury had lapped it up. All I could do was watch and listen in open-mouthed horror. His super-expensive barrister had expertly dismantled my flimsy defence, making me sound like the evil wife from hell; bitter and twisted. After this, everyone in court viewed me as some kind of monster, and the jury drew the inevitable and, to them, obvious conclusions.

His Honour Judge Philpot had more sharp and condemnatory remarks, but much of what he said went past me because the word "custodial" had got stuck in my brain. Until that moment, my naive faith in the justice system had been more or less intact. I'd believed that people who were telling the truth wouldn't be convicted, or that reasonable doubt would indicate a suspended sentence and probation. My knees turned to water and only a few of his remaining words registered – like the bit about me being fortunate the charge hadn't been attempted murder.

The other part I heard all too clearly was when the judge said, 'Therefore, having been convicted of a heinous crime, I see no alternative but to make an example of you and send you to prison for four years. Take her down.'

There was a stir in the room, a murmur of assent and satisfaction that I was guilty as hell. Propelled by two officers down the steps towards the cells, I was suddenly nauseous, cold, then hot, and the last thing I remember after that was the doctor asking me if I could hear him.

*

I served less than two years in the end, with the time I'd spent on remand knocked off. There are always people who believe life inside is cushy, and prisoners have it way too easy with televisions and internet access. Believe me, because I *know*, that is total and utter bollocks. Being in prison leaves scars, only some of them are visible, and all of them run soul deep. The mixed aromas of cabbage, bleach and sweat still trigger an indelible memory of things I'd rather not revisit. Only my furious, slow-burning anger kept me going. That and plotting the hideous revenge Henry had coming to him.

Resident at His Majesty's Prison Enderton, I learnt the hard way to keep my head down. For someone brought up as I'd been, those early weeks were not so much a rude awakening as a total tsunami of culture shock. Even the months I'd spent on remand had not been any kind of preparation for the realities of existing alongside hundreds of other women, all of whom were angry, including me. There were times when I was so low and overwhelmed it seemed utterly impossible to survive, and the staff had me on suicide watch for a while.

Who knew that the menstrual cycles of a group of women incarcerated together will eventually synchronise? Once a month the whole prison became a seething cauldron of rage and hormones. For so many reasons, those first weeks were undiluted hell, a living nightmare. My two cell mates dismissed me from day one as "posh" and bullied me mercilessly on the assumption that I looked down on them. They made my life a misery, but the worst were the ones who spat in my food at the dinner queue, or jostled my arm so that I dropped the tray. After a beating in the showers which put me in the hospital wing, I became hyper-vigilant about the ever-present threat of violence.

Not all the inmates live on the wings, although that's where everyone starts off. There are also houses at Enderton; small separate blocks each home to around sixteen women, offering a more relaxed regime. Everyone, including me, wanted to move out into one. Tracy from Liverpool who'd recently been demoted from such a house moaned endlessly about being sent back to a cell on the landings.

'One tiny bit of weed and the way they went on you'd think I'd shot the governor,' she told the lunch table I happened to be at. We all exchanged covert glances as she went on and on about it, pretending to be concentrating on that day's offering of spam fritters with something they claimed was coleslaw. Not that you could easily ignore a loud and disgruntled scouser.

'Wasn't expecting a search, was I? When they found my tiny stash, hardly enough for a joint, I was hauled out of there so fast me feet never touched. Fuck 'em all.'

So, when some weeks later, a prison officer came to find me and said, 'Get your stuff, we're moving you off the wing and into one of the houses,' a light shone in my darkness akin to the Miracle of Lourdes. I sobbed with the relief of being separated from my tormentors, so overcome that the officer even gave me a friendly hug.

'You'll do OK,' she said, as she helped me gather my few possessions into a bin bag. 'I know it's hard for someone like you. You gotta learn to be strong and stand up for yourself. You can't survive inside if your heart and mind are still stuck on the outside. Let it go, stick it all in a box for opening later, when you get out.'

Wise words, and I set off to follow her with a glad heart, hauling my stuff and jolted out of my depression by this unexpected change. Walking out of the cell block into the open air, I even allowed myself to hope for better things. Then we got to my new quarters, where Fat Sal was informed that I was to be her roommate. She was unimpressed. Very. Her body was shaped like a barrel, wide in the middle with small breasts, almost no bum and strong muscular arms. The short grey hair looked like she'd slept in it, and she shot me a look of disgust.

Once the prison officer left, she gave it to me straight in her strong northern accent.

'I'm not gonna babysit some wet behind the ears, posh kid, so you better learn fast,' she told me. 'Put your things there and leave mine alone. We're stuck with each other, so you'd better not get on the wrong side of me. Yeah, and keep your bloody opinions to yourself.'

I was scared of her at first, but it was brilliant being off the wing and not living in hourly fear of gang violence, so I set out to be the best roommate ever. It worked, up to a point. Trained by the nuns at school to keep my space tidy, I took on jobs like emptying the bin without being asked and making both beds if necessary. Proper hospital corners – the nuns taught us that too.

The main meal in prison was at lunchtime, then only sandwiches and snacks later. When it was our turn on the rota to put out the food for what everyone called "tea", the two of us worked side by side unloading the trolley sent over from the kitchens. Sal had been a cook in her former life, so she'd been put straight to work in the catering department.

'Call this crap fit for human consumption?' she said in disgust. 'Yeah, I prepared some of it, but they don't give us the budget to do anything decent. God knows what this margarine stuff is made of, but in my book it doesn't even count as a food product.'

This provided an opening to make Sal laugh by telling her about the fancy canapes at political events, and some of the people I'd met.

'Lavinia Sondheim might be a great TV host but she's horrible and rude to staff like waiters,' I said, sniffing doubtfully at what I thought might be meat-paste sandwiches. 'Talk about drink like a fish too, the way she hoovered down champagne you'd have thought world supplies were about to run out.'

Sal chuckled, nicking a crisp from the bowl she was setting out.

'The one who does that chat show? Always gives the idea she's so sweet and caring, right? I don't drink much but give me a gin and orange any day over that champagne stuff. Overrated if you ask me.'

'I used to like my gin with elderflower, ever tried that?'

'No but it sounds like something my missus might fancy; I'll tell her about it on our next phone call.'

There were pictures of her wife on the wall above the bed – a black woman with laughing eyes and a wide smile. They were clearly crazy about each other, which caused a pang of envy. It had been a long time since I'd felt cherished and special.

When everyone came in for their meal, Sal complained about the skinny helpings and reached for more crumpets, slathering them in the dubious stuff which did duty for butter. You ended up being able to taste it for hours after.

'Not going low fat then, Sal?' said a stick-thin girl called Marlene. 'Bad for you, that crap is. I never touch it.'

Sal shut her up with one look. 'Now listen, if you want to call me fat go right ahead if you're up for it but hear this: my weight is not a problem to be solved,' she told the whole table. 'If my missus considers me to be bloody gorgeous then nobody else's judgemental opinion is required,' she said. 'Wanna argue about it?'

Nobody did.

Later, in our room, one of the officers came round with the post (I rarely got any). Sal opened a pale blue envelope and squinted hopefully at the letter inside. She sat on her bed holding it, head bowed, leaving me unsure what to do or how to react.

Then she leaned forward and passed it across the space between the beds saying, 'Frankie, do me a favour, and read this – I've put me glasses down somewhere and can't see a bloody thing without them.'

I'd never seen her wear specs, ever, and a quick scan of the first page showed it to be from her wife.

It dawned on me then that she couldn't read.

'It's kind of… personal. Are you sure?'

Sal nodded mutely, daring me to pity her. 'Chloe, who was my roommate before used to read them to me. She got out last month. My missus knows I like getting actual letters, same as other people.'

I went and sat beside her on the bed, holding the pages where she could see them, tracing the words with my finger and keeping my voice matter of fact. She didn't need my sympathy but maybe I could *help*.

After this, during the long hours incarcerated in our room, I taught her to read and she taught me how to survive.

'Now hear this,' she said in another speech to the assembled inmates of our house one lunchtime. 'I got sent down for GBH, right? OK then, anyone who has a pop at Frankie will have me to reckon with.'

'Your new girlfriend, Sal?'

'Nope, but she's my buddy now and off limits. You clear about that?'

'Yeah, or else what?' jeered another woman.

'Listen, you,' said Sal. 'After years of him knocking me about, I threw my bastard partner out of the house. All that lifting heavy pans came in handy, and he got a dislocated jaw, concussion and two broken arms, so if you want some too you got it.'

Nobody took her up on this offer.

I never managed to equate the woman I came to know so well with victimhood, but one night in the anonymous darkness of our room she told me more about Jason.

'I couldn't stand it no more, Frankie; he'd have killed me if I didn't do something. It were a living nightmare until I cracked and went to see Buster, who runs the local law centre. She helped me get Jason legally evicted from my boarding house, then we changed the locks and took him to court. When he got sent down, Buster moved in and the rest is history. God, I love my woman. She put me back together and when Jason turned up again a few years later I told him straight I wouldn't be putting up with any more of his crap. Hurt him more than I meant to, but he got the message.'

'So how come you got sent to jail? Shouldn't it have been a suspended sentence because otherwise it's victim-blaming?'

'Ah well,' her voice from the bed close to mine held tinges of regret. 'The bugger sued me for assault after the beating I gave him, didn't he? You should have seen my Buster – mad as a box of frogs because of what I said in court. I told the judge damn right I'd intended to hurt Jason, payback time and he had it coming. Buster was livid because me doing time meant she had to take on the cooking at our boarding house,' Sal told me. 'She says the residents can't wait for me to come back; they miss my fish and chips.'

'I used to cook; it was a real pleasure to me.'

'Fancy cordon bleu stuff, right?' I tried to protest but she went on. 'It's chuffing hilarious that a posh woman like you got done for setting fire to your house.'

'But I didn't do *anything*. It had to have been my husband who started the fire, and I told them that in court, but nobody believed a word I said.'

Sal only laughed even harder. 'Yeah, well maybe you didn't do it, but the bastard deserved it so you probably *should* have, right?'

'As if. Those units were hand-built and painted pale blue, special order from Germany, a thing of beauty and a joy forever. Now, I *would* have burnt Henry's study upstairs, where he had all his precious stuff – public-school trophies and photos taken with celebrities. One day I'm going to make him pay for his lies because he got the insurance and guess who got the prison sentence? And for something I didn't even do!'

Even though I knew she believed me, Sal took zero notice of my protests, ever after referring to me as The Arsonist, and this soubriquet had stuck.

*

Serving time is something you just have to get through, putting one foot in front of the other until it's done. The unvarying routine of prison life helped, plodding along, ticking off the days. With the end at last in sight, a sick dread came over me whenever I thought about Sal's release date, a month ahead of my own. I lost weight because food didn't appeal, and the fear of coping alone without her protection and support made me go cold all over. Even worse, it was impossible to tell her how I was feeling, because she was so excited and happy to be going home.

Then Sal heard from Buster via their weekly phone call that one of their long-term lodgers had gone into a nursing home following a devastating stroke.

I was sitting on my bed repairing a well-worn T-shirt when she came bouncing in to tell me about it.

'Poor old sod, he were such a nice man. But, Frankie, this is great news! Seeing as you've got nowhere else to go, his room has obviously got your name on it because you'll be needing a place to stay, right?'

I was dumbstruck because this was an answer to all my anxieties about where I might end up once released.

'It's not exactly your home turf so no hard feelings if it's not what you want. I wouldn't wanna live down south, but you might. Ain't gonna lie, St Annes is a dead ordinary place,' Sal told me. 'But way better than a bloody hostel would be. The Lancashire coast isn't fancy, but lots of fresh air and stuff.'

'Are you serious?' I looked into her homely face and couldn't quite take in this generous offer, which required very little in the way of reflection. 'You know what, Sal, a long time ago I realised there wouldn't be any point in attempting to go back to London, or the "friends" I've never heard from since the guilty verdict.'

'What about your old dad; wouldn't he take you in?'

I actually growled. 'Father was so ashamed of my conviction, he felt compelled to move somewhere he wasn't known and could start over. I'm not going to get any help from his direction.'

'There you go then, come and stay with us.'

For the longest time I'd kept most of my tears locked inside – in prison you daren't show any weakness – but I cried then, overwhelmed with sheer relief at having somewhere to go with at least one friendly face.

'God, Sal, I've been dreading life here without you.'

'You'll do grand,' she said, gathering me into a clumsy hug. 'The lasses here all think the world of you now, the way you help them with letters and legal stuff. And it's only a few weeks before you're out too. So, is that a yes to the room?'

'You are a lifesaver, and I would *love* to come to St Annes,' I told her, closing the door on my past life with a resounding clang. 'But will Buster be OK about this? It's no small thing to take in a random stranger fresh out of jail.'

'I've told her all about you; used up a whole bloody phone card doing it. Don't worry, she gets it – you helped me, so now we help you. You'll get on fine with the other residents – it's only us, Auntie Dot and young Angus up in his attic.'

'I've always wanted to live at the seaside,' I said with a watery smile. 'I can be anonymous there, and you're sure it isn't an expensive place to live?'

I literally couldn't find the words to tell my friend how grateful I was, and when I tried, she only said, 'Ah get over yourself, silly cow, it's no bloody palace.'

'Thanks, Sal, you have no idea what a difference this makes. It's like a miracle.'

'Don't be so bloody daft,' she said.

When I went to tell the resettlement officer at HMP

Enderton I wouldn't be needing a hostel place after all, she was pleased for me but realistic.

'Frankie,' she said, moving pens around the battle-scarred surface of her desk. 'I'm not going to bother dressing up the harsh realities of life after prison. It's great you have a place to stay with a friend but getting a job can be tough when you've got a criminal record. However, since you're presentable and intelligent, I figure you'll find something, even if it's not what you're used to.'

I understood very well that my new existence wouldn't remotely resemble the metropolitan life I had before. Another thing Henry owed me for.

'Don't worry, my sights will be set appropriately low,' I assured the officer. 'St Annes might only be a northern seaside town in winter, but I can probably do waitress or bar work while trying to build up my online business again.'

*

A bitter February wind howled around the prison on the morning of my release on licence. The person who stepped through the gates was not the same one who'd gone in; how could she be? A lot of core beliefs such as faith, trust, hope and confidence had taken a severe beating. I hoped to find them again one day, but the woman who emerged was a faint shadow of my former self, thin and pale, outwardly robust enough but inwardly frail.

The staff on the gate said a cheery goodbye and good luck, then slammed the door behind me. I stood outside wearing jeans, a T-shirt, trainers and the Chanel jacket I'd gone to court in, not nearly warm enough to keep out the cold. The only things I owned were a bin bag of well-washed sportswear and a designer handbag containing my travel warrant and a small cash grant. Very small.

I'd written to Felicity in London, hoping she'd kept the suitcase I'd never been able to reclaim. The sniffy note she sent by return said yes it remained in her loft and she would courier it to Sal's address in St Annes on the condition that I never contacted her again. Apparently, a criminal record stretches friendship a bit thin.

Safely on the train, the clickety-clack rhythm of the rails was soothing my jangled nerves as I sipped rubbish coffee from a Styrofoam cup. I had a book to read but instead observed my fellow passengers and the view from the window with all the delight of someone seeing the world afresh. It was like going from black and white to technicolour. After grey concrete walls and wire fences, the colours in the landscape struck me as incredibly fresh and vivid, even the winter grass somehow greener.

St Annes on Sea has the kind of tiny station you don't imagine existing anymore – what would once have been called a "halt" – picture-postcard cute with bright tubs of winter flowering pansies and hanging baskets. I almost didn't recognise Sal until she cannoned down the platform towards me.

'It's The Arsonist; you made it!' she crowed, wrapping me in a huge hug, so enthusiastic she almost knocked me over. It took time to fully appreciate the short curly hair dyed a vivid shade of fuchsia pink from its previous grey. Teamed with a turquoise padded duvet coat, bright patterned leggings, and electric-blue Doc Marten boots, it was an altogether different style from the prison persona I'd been used to. The warmth of her welcome made me feel a whole lot better, even if I remained sensitive about being labelled an arsonist loudly and in public. In prison, the name had been mildly amusing, but out in the world it sounded kind of awkward and a lot less funny.

'Hey, Fatso,' I said.

'You've cut your hair.' Sal leaned back to study me properly.

'One of the girls did it in exchange for writing a statement for her lawyer,' I said. 'It's an awful cliché but it was an act of rebellion because Henry always preferred it long. I'm embracing the grey bits too.'

'Get you,' said Sal. 'It looks good; short suits you. Come on then.' she heaved my bin bag over her shoulder. 'Let's get you home where it's warm, you look about frozen. On this coast you'll be needing a proper big coat.'

She wasn't wrong; the wind off the sea bit into me sharp and cold after the warm fug of the train, and gulls protested noisily in the sky as they battled to make any kind of forward progress. Detritus from a chip shop blew around the pavements, and the few hardy souls foolish enough to venture out kept their heads down against the arctic blast. The blessedly short walk to the house took us over the railway bridge, past a selection of small individual shops which London estate agents might have bigged up as having a "quaint village feel". We turned by a church advertising a weekly coffee morning and good-as-new shop, into the residential area of Norcross Road.

Sal came to a halt outside the faded glory of a Victorian semi built over four floors, including a basement, and said with a flourish, 'Ta-da, this is it. Welcome home.'

The house had a few steps up to the front door and handsome bay windows but, like many of its neighbours, had been built of soot-stained, ugly yellow brick. A weather-beaten sign outside proclaimed "Sea View, High-Class Boarding House", but both it and the house had seen better days.

As I took in the sign, Sal said, 'This really was a high-class establishment once, back when St Annes used to be a proper upmarket resort, somewhere you came on the train for your holidays. Me and Buster live in the basement flat, I were born in the same bedroom I sleep in now.'

Sal set off down the stone steps, hauling my bin bag.

'But can you see the sea from here?' I asked, puzzled by the sign. There hadn't been so much as a glimpse of coastal vistas so far, only the tang of ozone on the wind.

'No, you daft cow, it's only the name; it's always been called that. I suppose if you stood on the roof... but the shore is back the other way. You'll find it when you explore the town. Come on in.'

The generous-sized sitting room she led me into was full of light.

'Londoners would call this a "garden apartment", very desirable,' I told her.

'There is a bit of garden, out back where it's level,' said Sal doubtfully. 'Only a patch of grass and in summer some geraniums in tubs. Buster does them.'

The room's central feature was a 1950s fireplace of brown mottled tile, with its elderly gas fire and an assortment of mismatched furniture all very much more shabby than chic. An ordinary but cosy and comfortable home – somewhere to kick your shoes off and not worry about coasters when you put a coffee mug down, or the occasional stain on the rug. A huge monster of a marmalade cat lay curled up on an armchair and opened one green eye to examine me. Unimpressed, he fixed me with an impenetrable stare before going back to sleep.

'That's our Spike,' said Sal. 'I hope you're fond of cats because he pretty much runs the place and will make himself at home in your room unless you keep the door shut, though he'll find a way.'

Much as I'd looked forward to my release, the reality of starting over from nothing was beginning to creep up on me. I had no idea how to navigate this new world, a whole planet away from my London life. I'd have to start fending for myself sharpish or be a burden in Sal's busy life.

'Come through and I'll make us a butty for lunch,' she said over her shoulder.

The narrow galley kitchen was fitted with stainless-steel cabinets, a large worktable and an impressive range cooker. Catering-size pans were shelved above, and utensils hung from a metal rack suspended from the ceiling.

'Got all this professional catering stuff when a caff over the bridge went bust,' said Sal, with evident pride in her domain. 'I cook for the whole house, so Uncle Al put it in for me ten years back and it's still going strong even if he isn't.'

After ham sandwiches with English mustard on thick slices of white bread which Sal described as "doorstops", she showed me around the rest of their flat. A comfortable double bedroom in shades of lilac, and a bathroom with an old-fashioned green suite.

'Pampas, that colour is,' Sal told me. 'It were the mutt's nuts back in the '80s.'

'But shouldn't you be at work today?'

'Nah, took the day off so's I could see to you,' said Sal, plonking her bulk down on the shapeless sofa. 'Bit of a shock to the system when you first get out, innit? Lucky my mates who run the pub were glad to have me back, but they can manage for one day, and it's not as if Mondays are busy. I generally do the lunchtime trade and leave by 3.00pm to come home and get the boarders' dinner on. You'll soon see how it all works.'

After the initial excitement of getting out, I was beginning to feel overwhelmed and ready to lie down and hide in a blanket fort. Sal knew me well enough to understand about putting a brave face on things.

'It'll be OK, Frankie, you'll see,' she said with gruff affection. 'St Annes is nuthen special but it's all right; people are friendly too. Not fancy the way it must be in London, I suppose, but give me this place any day.'

I couldn't ever tell my generous friend how much part of me longed for the easy, city existence I'd once had. Coffee shops and bistros, lunch with friends, multiplex cinemas, museums and galleries, even the tube trains with their particular smell of soot. No regrets about Henry, obviously, or any of the political stuff, but I'd made myself a promise that one day I'd have that metropolitan life again. And Henry's head on a plate.

'Snap out of it, love, no point moping,' said Sal. 'See starting over as an adventure, and you'll do grand. Come on, I'll give you the guided tour; your room is on the top floor, and I've already lugged your case up there. It got here a few days ago.'

I followed her up the internal stairs from the basement to where they emerged at the back of the hall. The main floor consisted of a large living room at the front, with bold striped wallpaper, a large dark red sofa, and a couple of armchairs. Beyond this space, the wall had been knocked through to a dining area where the residents took their meals at a large table topped with a red polka-dot plastic cloth.

'Buster leaves for the law centre early, and I start food preparation in the pub kitchen at 9.00am. I've never offered lunch because of working at the pub, so how it works is you see to your own breakfast, and I cook a proper dinner,' said Sal. 'Cereals in plastic containers on the sideboard there, milk in the fridge and some pre-packed supermarket sandwiches. Found out Angus were having bars of chocolate and those instant noodle things between meals, and I told him it wouldn't do, so I get the butties in for him. Auntie Dot sometimes has them too, when she's in the mood, and you can help yourself as well if you want – write what you take on the clipboard by the fridge, then I get more in, and we settle up later.'

Also supplied was a catering-sized jar of improbably red, sticky jam and thick sliced white bread to put in the industrial toaster, a sturdy commercial appliance similar to the ones we'd used in prison.

Sal was checking the levels in the cereal containers. 'Stock up on a good breakfast to get you through the day. You can have snacks in your room, but no cooking allowed – fire hazard. Oops sorry, shouldn't mention that.'

She cackled at her own hilarity, but I was experiencing a sense of humour failure.

'OK then,' Sal continued with a cough. 'Everyone clears up after themselves, and the dirty crockery and cutlery gets stacked in the dishwasher downstairs in the kitchen. Auntie Dot is usually the last one down in the morning, so she takes on the job of switching the machine on and setting the table for dinner.'

Trying to take in all these instructions, I must have been looking at bit lost because Sal said, 'Buck up, love – get out into the town tomorrow and explore a bit. Mebbe search out a decent coat too, spend some of the generous grant you were given?'

'But all I've got is £47,' I protested. 'I'll have to be careful with it.'

'Don't be daft, proper winter clothes aren't a luxury, and you're not used to the cold being a soft southerner. You might find some interview gear too – presentable and clean will do. There's that appointment with probation coming up, and then you should get the benefits process underway; start it online. But give yourself a breather for today at least.'

Our tour moved on into the hall, where a once elegant staircase sported a startlingly bright traditional red Axminster stair runner.

'Job lot from a warehouse, this carpet. Cheap as chips, grand quality and built to take heavy traffic. It were meant for a Hammond hotel, but the developers went tits up. Their loss, our gain.'

Looking closely, you could just find a crest built into the pattern which had a large H among the garish swirls.

'Tell me about the other residents,' I said as we climbed the stairs with my bin bag.

'Right then, Auntie Dot has this whole floor above to herself, and up another level under the roof there's Angus the computer whizz kid, next to the bathroom you'll be sharing. This room at the front is yours.'

I'd been expecting something small and basic, but Sal opened the door onto a large space under the eaves, its sloping ceilings bringing back vivid memories of my childhood bedroom. I've always had a thing about attics and this one had a modern VELUX skylight as well as a dormer window in the gable which, between them, let in lots of light. I was already mentally adding some cushions to the small window seat, which would make it an inviting place to sit.

The black vintage cast-iron double bed frame had brass knobs in need of a polish, but the duvet and pillows were plump and welcoming in their plain-white covers. Going by the smell of paint, the pale blue walls had been freshly decorated and a balding upholstered armchair sat by the small gas fire tucked into the original black metal surround. A faded rug covered the floorboards by the bed, and an oversized Victorian wardrobe with a matching chest of drawers stood against the opposite wall. I didn't possess enough clothes to fill either one, let alone both.

'Is it OK for you?' asked Sal, a hint of anxiety in her voice.

'It's perfect,' I told her with genuine enthusiasm. 'And so much space, I can't believe it.'

'You clean your own room, including the bathroom, and there's a launderette a few streets away. It's a bit bare right now since Mr Hammond moved out, but you'll soon make it home. Plenty of charity shops in town, and the local auction house always has loads of interesting stuff. Me and Buster go bargain hunting every chance we get.'

'Honestly, I love it. All I need is a table to use as a desk.'

'There might be something out in one of the garages – I'll have a rummage when there's a minute. Oh, and the gas for the fire is on a coin meter if it gets cold,' said Sal. 'The boiler in the basement heats the whole house, but not very well. Our flat gets cosy and since heat rises, Angus always says he's warm enough up here, but then his room is like a dark cave and anyway, he's a bloke. Auntie Dot feels the cold more at her age, so uses her gas fire as much as she needs to but pays us a stonking good rent for the privilege.'

This jolted me out of my imaginings of how I'd make the room pretty and more personal.

'But, Sal, what am I going to do about paying you?' This had been worrying me because there'd be a delay of weeks before any benefit payments arrived. 'I've got some jewellery to sell but after buying a disgusting coffee on the train, all I've got for now is what's left of the cash grant the resettlement officer gave me.'

'Don't worry – we'll get it all sorted down the job centre. You'll get housing benefit, same as Mr Hammond.'

'There are other things I could sell – my handbag is vintage designer, and they handed back my wedding and engagement rings when I was released. I'm wearing them for safety but on my right hand.' I flashed the jewellery at my new landlady in an attempt to convince her of my financial probity.

HMP Enderton had also returned the diamond stud earrings I'd been wearing when arrested; a twentieth wedding anniversary gift from my husband, which I hoped would also bring in some money I could live on in the short-term.

Taking Sal's hands in mine, I said 'I *can't* let you and Buster support me financially; it wouldn't be right.'

Sal pulled a face at me. 'How many times do I have to say it, you daft cow? There's plenty of time to worry about rent when you've either sold your jewellery, got a job or benefits,' she said. 'Now shut up about it and let's get you settled in.'

The sight of my suitcase at the end of the bed was encouraging; Felicity's courier had shrink-wrapped it for transit, a cellophane version of the mummy's return. I hoped the hard shell had protected the contents, always assuming I could manage to hack my way into it.

'Brought some scissors,' said Sal, reading my mind and producing kitchen shears from her pocket. 'This thing is bloody heavy – got all your valuables in it?'

'Yes, at least, maybe,' I told her. 'If not, I'm screwed, because working from home as an editor won't be an option.'

Sal made short work of the wrapping and put the case on the bed. Removing the top layer of summer clothing, relief flooded through me at the sight of the polystyrene packing pieces shielding the laptop. I'd wrapped it in clothes and a towel too, tucking the phone bought at the same time in among the layers. This wouldn't be much use until I could afford a SIM-only contract.

'All the clothes in here are summer weight,' I said with a sigh. 'The jeans are OK, and there's a couple of useful cardigans, but apart from the undies and shoes not much else for winter temperatures. Never mind, I've still got this bin bag of crappy tracksuits.'

We both laughed, but something cold came and settled in my stomach. In all my sheltered forty-three years, I'd never previously experienced being out in the world with no money or resources at my back. I slumped down on the bed, overwhelmed by my new and fragile existence.

Sal wrapped me in a hug. 'I've been there, remember. You cry if you need to.'

'But I *don't* cry,' I sobbed into her shoulder. 'My dad always taught me girls had to be tough to survive in a man's world.'

'The old fekker was right there, at least,' said Sal, 'but nobody can be strong all the time. We're all allowed a wobble now and then, and you *will* make it, Frankie, it's gonna get better, I promise.'

'Only when Henry goes down for perjury and my name is cleared. Let's see how *he* likes prison food.'

The major flaw in this optimistic statement was that my solicitor had said an appeal against my conviction would require new evidence, and I didn't have any. Not a damn thing.

THREE

By the time I went down for dinner in response to Sal's enthusiastic pounding of the gong, my few possessions were unpacked. I'd also got my head back on straight from its ever so slightly panicky state. The newly reclaimed electronics were plugged in to charge, and I'd changed out of my posh jacket into jeans and a navy sweatshirt. Some red lipstick found lurking at the bottom of my handbag bolstered my courage; a ritzy brand I'd always used but wouldn't be able to afford anymore.

The smell of Indian spices hit me before I'd made it halfway down the stairs, and I was all but drooling in anticipation. Sal came into the hall, saying, 'Frankie, come and meet the gang,' then added in an undertone, 'don't talk directly to Angus or look straight at him, else he'll freak out and leave, but it'll be OK once he's used to you.'

Angus wasn't the only one shying like a nervous pony, but I managed a smile as the assembled residents surveyed me with unabashed interest. The black woman with ultra-short natural hair was Sal's wife. Admiring her fluffy pink sweater and huge gold hoop earrings, I wished my own appearance could be half as stylish and a lot less boring.

'Hi,' she said, 'I'm Barbara, but everyone calls me Buster. I've heard a lot about you, Frankie.' Friendly but cool; the jury appeared to be out in terms of her opinion of me.

A diminutive sixty-something woman with a sharp penetrating gaze wearing a jazzy scarf as a kind of turban greeted me with a big smile, showing off improbable teeth.

'Hello, dear, I believe you prefer to be called Frankie rather than Francesca? I'm Auntie Dot, welcome to Sea View. Come and sit by me.' The cultured voice with no trace of a northern accent suggested she might be another exile.

'And Angus down at the end there,' added Sal. As instructed, I tried hard not to meet his eyes directly, only raising a hand in vague greeting. My overall impression was of a lanky, blond young man with the thin, sensitive hands of a pianist.

Sal served up rice and fragrant chicken curry, padded out with lots of veggies. After two years of institutional stodge, the flavours made my brain explode in joyous appreciation.

'Buster got me an Indian cookbook and I've been working through it,' said Sal. 'Being able to read opens up the whole bloody world.'

'You could read a little bit before, so don't put yourself down, Sal,' said Auntie Dot. 'But we've all benefited from your culinary explorations. This coconut naan bread is fantastic.'

'I make it in a frying pan, not having one of them tandoor thingies handy, and so cheap to do.' Sal beamed with pleasure. 'And it's not true that I could read, I only pretended to. I could do some letters and recognise words on packaging such as tea and coffee, flour and so on, but it took Frankie to get I might be dyslexic, same as her son.'

'You have a son?' said Dot. 'How old is he?'

A sensitive subject for me. 'Justin is twenty-two now, and must have finished uni, but I haven't seen or heard from him since my arrest. My letters to him at our London address were ignored, and then Henry had his lawyer send me a cease-and-desist instruction not to write again.'

'Ouch, that's got to hurt,' observed Buster, her expression softening.

'We weren't exactly super close,' I admitted sadly. My adorable little boy had grown up to become every bit as arrogant and entitled as his father, and then an elite boarding school had finished the job. 'But it's how I understood about dyslexia, from Justin's early struggles, so I recognised the issues Sal had with reading.'

'Buster tried but she couldn't understand why I didn't get it. Frankie did, and it only changed my whole bloody life,' Sal told the room at large, dishing up more chicken to Angus who'd already cleared his plate. 'She was amazing, got the prison authorities to fix me up with a specialist tutor bloke who officially diagnosed the problem, and then she helped with all the homework he set. Before, the rest of the world used a code I couldn't crack, but gradually everything made sense. By the time I got out, I were reading anything I could get my hands on.'

'She hasn't stopped since,' said Buster. 'Thirsty for knowledge with a phenomenal memory for everything she's read.'

Sal ran a hand through the wild pink hair. 'The memory thing is practice. When you can't read, you hide it by training yourself to remember stuff. In prison, I got started with some novels too. A lot of them are plain daft, and they never have any gay or black people – it's like we don't exist.'

'An astute observation,' said Auntie Dot, pushing her plate away with a contented sigh.

Angus startled me by commenting from the end of the table in a soft voice. 'I get it about learning to read, and Sal finding it mysterious and challenging. Computer code can be like that at first – then one day it starts to make sense and whole universes open up.'

'Bang on, love. Unlocking words were the same,' said Sal. 'Lucky break for me going to jail – turned out well, in my case. I owe Frankie a *lot* for all the help she gave me.'

'Sal, you don't owe me anything,' I said, blushing. 'I was glad to help.'

'Well, now it's my turn to give you a leg up,' she said, in a voice which told me again she wouldn't be argued with. 'Let's crack on and get these plates sided away. Anyone for kheer? It's Indian rice pudden.'

*

I surfaced in the morning when a scratching noise made its way through my brain fog. It was Spike wanting to be let in and he promptly made himself at home at the end of the bed. I love cats and didn't mind at all; he'd be someone to talk to and maybe, when he trusted me more, to snuggle up with. In great need of warmth and comfort, human or animal, I'd take whatever I could get.

Having charged up the laptop the previous day, it came as a severe blow to be met with the black screen of doom when I switched it on. The indicator lights glowed, but it didn't boot up. Dammit, the thing was brand new (if you didn't count sitting in a suitcase for two years) and had been state of the art back then. Sal had said Angus was a computer geek, so he might be someone who could diagnose the problem, but I didn't quite feel comfortable asking. Nothing to be done but leave it for the time being and go and explore the town.

As I headed back over the railway bridge into town, the sky was pewter grey, and the vicious wind cut through the thick fleece tracksuit I'd added over my normal clothes. Henry or

34

Felicity would have sneered at the way I was dressed, but they weren't the ones braving the wintry conditions and a wind off the sea. Cresting the hill, a sharp gust took my breath away as the wicked chill found its way inside right to my skin. I pulled the sleeves of my top down to cover my blue hands, and even with two pairs of socks making my trainers pinch tight, my feet were already cold.

Speeding up to jogging pace, the wide main street lay ahead, intersected by a busy road. Not many people had braved the raw blustery day, but running was improving things. I turned left and pounded around a whole block until my breath came in gasps, but at least I'd warmed up and the exposed skin tingled. More than that, my body came alive in a whole new way, as if the part of me that prison had made numb was rushing to the surface and joyously exploding. Only then, like a kid visiting an enticing row of sweet shops, did I dive into the nearest charity shop.

Embarrassment and something like shame had stopped me from admitting to Sal I'd never ventured inside one before. My husband had always been scathing about other people's "revolting old junk". It turned out Henry was dead wrong, as on so many other subjects, though I soon discovered all the shops smelled the same, vaguely musty with an undertone of sweat and even the occasional barely masked hint of cigarettes. The things people gave away came as a surprise, and in minutes I took my first purchase to the till, a travel kettle and a pair of mugs for only £3.

'This is such a bargain, are you sure the price is right??'

'Oh yes, love,' the elderly volunteer assured me. 'And it definitely works because electricals are always tested, but nobody wants holiday items in winter. Here I'll throw in a handful of teaspoons too, we've got hundreds of these cheap tinny ones in the back.'

In the next shop, I went straight to a rack of coats and pounced on a red fabric number, knee length, the hood trimmed in improbable fluffy grey fake fur. My fashionista ex-friends would have dismissed this chain store offering as "naff", but the wool was warm and thick, and the colour cheered me up. At the counter, a basket contained gloves for £1, so I grabbed a pair of those too. Job done, as Sal would say.

Coming out of one shop, I thought for a wild moment I was looking at Henry. The silver hair and the camel overcoat brought an unexpected jolt of fear, then the man turned to reveal a red, weather-beaten face and the bulbous nose of a drinker. Standing rooted to the pavement, it was a shock how much the encounter affected me. Did Henry already know my whereabouts? Would he even care anymore? It seemed unlikely but didn't stop me feeling threatened and just a touch nauseous.

My final purchase wasn't strictly necessary, reckless even, but completely irresistible to someone starved of colour and beauty. The large patchwork quilt had been handmade in an assortment of blue fabrics, now soft and faded from frequent washing. Far from being a problem that only enhanced the appeal, and it smelled fresh though extensive repairs were needed. Labelled £10 and reduced to £7, it simply had to be mine, even if awkward and bulky to carry. I set off for Sea View with a sense of pride and unbelievably only a total of £21 lighter, though I did stop to buy a large bar of chocolate with which I hoped to bribe Angus to investigate the computer. I'd have to take any work I could get for now, but my long-term goal was to build up the editing jobs to a point where it would earn me a modest living. First, the recalcitrant technology had to be persuaded to work.

Auntie Dot must have been listening out for my return because the minute I tottered up the stairs with my haul of goodies, I found her waiting on the landing outside her door.

'Ah, The Arsonist, you've been shopping. Would you care to join me for coffee?'

Burdened with kettle, quilt and coat, I said, 'Yes please, but let me put these things away upstairs first.'

'Absolutely not,' commanded Dot. 'I want to see your purchases. You will soon discover that I am incurably nosy.'

Dot wore another bright scarf, orange and pink this time, wrapped turban-style around her head, and ushered me into a large room with the same footprint as the floor below. It had a matching bay window, high ceilings and an elegant fireplace in which stood a log-burning stove. You had to look carefully to tell it ran on gas rather than wood; there were even a few genuine logs stacked to one side for effect. Coffee and sandalwood scented the room which held antique furniture and oriental rugs. The window treatment shrieked "no expense spared", designer fabric puddling on the floor in graceful folds, the kind of interior I'd once taken for granted.

As a resident of Sea View, I'd half expected Auntie Dot to be eking out a modest existence on a slender pension, but the evidence of her flat said otherwise. Something didn't add up and my new friend was undoubtedly more than she seemed.

Two deep armchairs sat invitingly by the fire, and she all but pushed me into one of these, exclaiming over my quilt.

'I can see why you bagged this – what a treasure.'

'It is lovely, isn't it? Easy enough to stitch back up where the patches have separated.'

Dot glanced at the price tag. 'Once mended this would fetch a fortune in a smart antique shop; you could sell it on at a profit.'

I stroked the soft folds and everything in me rebelled against the idea of parting with my find.

'No, because it represents something important. Most of the very few things I now own are well used and utilitarian, and nothing in prison was any better, but this is *beautiful*. I've missed the way some objects bring such pleasure. I need that feeling more than any price it might bring.'

A smile of recognition spread across Auntie Dot's face. 'As I suspected, a woman of discernment. We're going to get along splendidly.'

While she had her back to me, busying herself with the high-end bean-to-cup coffee machine housed in an antique cupboard, I scanned the room. The only other modern item was the Apple computer standing on an inlaid desk, and there were a couple of good paintings, but most of the walls were occupied by bookcases, jammed floor to ceiling with an eclectic range of volumes. Shrugging off my sweatshirt top – the stove kept the room almost too warm – I wandered across to study them. Dot wasn't the only curious one.

'I look at people's books too,' she said over her shoulder.

'You read Arabic?' I asked, taking out a large tome which dealt with Islamic architecture, impenetrable to me apart from the astounding photographs.

'Better than I speak it – my accent isn't altogether convincing.'

As I put the book back, she handed me a bone china mug, Royal Worcester with a gold rim. I recognised the design, which further indicated Auntie Dot's residence at Sea View had nothing to do with being reduced to penury.

'God, *proper* coffee,' I said, inhaling the fragrant steam. 'Robusta not Arabica?'

'Yes,' said Auntie Dot with approval. 'I lived in the Middle East for a time, and learnt to appreciate my coffee strong, but I'm from London originally.'

I wanted to enquire how someone like her came to be living in St Annes but refrained from asking impertinent questions. It didn't stop Dot, though.

'Come and tell me all about yourself,' she said as we sat down, and somewhat to my surprise, I did. She wanted chapter and verse, from growing up in the Home Counties, convent boarding school, my mother's death and, of course, my husband.

'So, you aren't an arsonist at all, though you'd have been perfectly justified. Henry sounds like a self-centred prick,' observed Auntie Dot with dry precision. 'Why did you stay with him so long?'

I'd asked myself the same question a lot in the past couple of years.

'When we got married, I was very young and madly in love. Henry was heart-stoppingly handsome, and still is,' I said, cupping my hands around the fragile mug. 'Then Justin came along just over a year later and I had this perfect life, believed myself the luckiest girl in the world. It took me ten years to realise that for him it constituted a marriage of convenience because he's gay. By then I had a… comfortable life, a gorgeous little boy, friends, a beautiful home and almost everything you could want. Does it make me sound mercenary that I decided to settle for what I had?'

'A practical decision, if not an altogether wise one,' observed my new neighbour.

'Also, his family money cushioned our life, and I had almost nothing of my own.'

'Then you showed great courage in deciding to leave it all behind.' The sharp intelligence in her face made me wonder if she'd been a head teacher or something, she had the air of someone accustomed to command.

'Well, even after twenty years I obviously didn't understand Henry at all,' I said sadly. 'He perjured himself in spectacular fashion, and I'd never have believed him capable of it.'

'There must have been a lot at stake. A sudden desperate and violent act, destroying parts of his own home, but which would also elicit sympathy for him as a victim and wronged husband,' said Dot, putting her empty cup down. 'It is evident you've had a difficult time, but as a brave person you will find a way to begin again. I had to do it myself, so can assure you all it takes is time and determination.'

'God, I hope you're right,' I said. 'Right now, I don't feel very brave. I'm only out on licence and terrified of messing up and being sent back to prison.'

Dot dismissed this with a wave of her hand. 'But that is the nature of courage. As those T-shirts say, "feel the fear and do it anyway", or something of the sort. Anyway, such anxiety is surely groundless – it's not as if you're going to breach your licence conditions by robbing a bank or setting fire to something.'

The crammed bookcases reminded me of another purchase I'd intended to make.

'Dammit, I meant to buy some reading material – the last charity shop I went in had paperbacks at three for £1, but then I got all emotional about the quilt and forgot.'

'Let me lend you something – I keep most of my fiction in the bedroom,' said Dot.

'You don't have a copy of *Pride and Prejudice*, do you? I've so been wanting to read it again.'

Auntie Dot grinned; looking years younger as her whole face lit up.

'The literary equivalent of comfort food, isn't it? I certainly do have a copy, which you are welcome to borrow. I'm confident you aren't someone who will fail to return it, and you'd better take *Persuasion* while we're about it.'

'That is my second-favourite Jane Austen – yours too?'

'Absolutely,' she said, disappearing along the landing to return shortly with the two volumes, which I slipped into the jute bag holding my kettle.

'Is there anything else I can help you with, my dear?'

'Not unless you're a technology wizard,' I said, struggling to keep hold of everything, and explained about the rescued laptop refusing to start. 'My expertise with electrics doesn't extend to computers.'

'You want Angus for anything technology related,' she said, 'he takes care of mine, and we all piggy-back on his super-fast broadband connection. Of course, he's not used to you yet, which is tricky for him, so I'd suggest approaching him with a note under his door asking if he can help. He can only ignore it or say no.'

I needed to get back online sharpish. The construction of a whole new life might depend on it, not to mention the research I'd need to do if I was to garner evidence for an appeal. I wasn't lying down under what had happened to me. Frankie Douglas was out in the world again and fighting back, so Henry Wilton had better watch out!

FOUR

In those fragile early days of freedom, my emotional stability level was that of a small child. Even minor setbacks seemed overwhelming, and the black screen of the laptop a personal, malicious insult from an evil piece of technology. Being powerless is such a horrible feeling and my skin flushed hot as I gritted my teeth in frustration. It would have satisfied my inner rage to throw the damn thing at the wall, but the machine was too important a part of my plans. With no money to take the laptop to a local repair shop, Dot's suggestion of Angus as computer saviour appeared to be the only avenue open to me. I lay on my bed and did some deep breathing in search of inner calm, then used the back of a flyer advertising takeaway pizza to write him a message.

> *Hi Angus,*
>   *My laptop won't boot up. The lights are on, but nobody seems to be home.*
>   *Can you help?*
>   *Frankie*

I pushed this and the bar of chocolate under his door on my way downstairs for dinner. Most of the doors in the old house

42

had a sizeable gap at the bottom, though Dot's were fitted with shiny brass draught excluder brushes. Another item for the to-do list when funds allowed. Later, with the heavyweight Spike curled up on my feet, I got myself tucked up under the duvet and restitched quilt to renew my long-standing friendship with Jane Austen. I only found the sheet of paper under my door as I stumbled to the bathroom before bed.

It read: *What make and model of laptop? PS I prefer dark chocolate. A.*

Carefully noting the required information on the bottom of the sheet, I pushed it back under his door on my way to breakfast the next morning. Angus didn't acknowledge my presence at the table, so I did the same and ignored him. Then I went out to buy myself a jar of halfway decent instant coffee and some more chocolate for him. On my return, there was another note.

'*Leave laptop on landing. A.*'

I did so, putting the bar of dark chocolate on top, before setting off to attend a meeting with the probation officer, Tony Norton.

The bus trip to Blackpool afforded occasional glimpses of the sea – unimpressive, brown and dirty-looking, not unlike the Thames in London but with a bigger sky. The offices were in a dreary concrete block at the end of a run of shops, some of them boarded up. I was shown into an area divided into half-glassed cubicles which featured metal furniture in standard government shades of grey – more than a little bleak and not exactly designed to cheer up the newly released ex-con. No attempt had been made to personalise the room beyond a potted plant, which appeared to be close to death.

Tony sat well back from the desk to accommodate a sprawling paunch and studied me carefully before saying, 'Nice to meet you, Frankie. This is a routine first appointment, to set out how we proceed from here.'

The uncomfortable back of the chair forced me to sit bolt upright and not lean or slouch. The hard seat offered no ease or comfort, and I wondered if this was deliberate to ensure clients were paying attention. Before leaving prison, I'd been made aware of the standard licence conditions of my early release – keep in regular contact, search for work, sign up for benefits, behave myself, stay within the law and continue to reside at the approved address unless or until I moved on.

Tony proceeded to go through all of this again, giving me time to observe my supervisor while he talked at me. Middle-aged and flabby, he had combed strands of hair across a balding scalp which were held rigid by some artificial means. I'd cobbled together an "interview outfit" with my best black trainers and tried to appear sensible and cooperative.

Reaching the end of his spiel, Tony said, 'You should be clear that your landlady can take no formal part in the rehabilitation process, other than on a friendship basis. She's also a client but sees a different officer. Is your accommodation OK?'

'I have a large bedsit at the top of the house, and it's great,' I told him. 'In time a few bits and pieces will make it feel more personal, but I'm enjoying the quiet after prison, and everyone at Sea View has been so welcoming. It's a good start.' Strange how my voice wobbled at bit at the end there.

Tony studied me over the top of his bifocals. 'It's all a bit much at the beginning, isn't it? A bright girl like you will cope, you've got more mental and emotional resources than many of my clients but cut yourself some slack in these early days. Keep us informed about how you get on at the job centre – check in by email or with a phone call for now, and I'll see you in two weeks.'

'It might have to be snail mail until I can get my phone and laptop sorted out,' I told him.

Armed with information leaflets about claiming benefits, I headed back on the bus ahead of the threatening clouds which were gathering over the muddy grey sea. Being out of prison and genuinely free filled me with a bubble of quiet joy, even if hedged about with conditions and requirements to keep out of trouble.

Back at home, I continued my long-standing friendship with Miss Elizabeth Bennett while waiting for Sal to get back from work at 3.30pm, when we were going out to register me at the job centre. I'd heard nothing good about navigating the welfare system, but at least I didn't have to go on my own. Arriving downstairs, I found Sal ending a phone call, and she turned to me with a smile as bright as her lime-green stripey jumper.

'Fantastic news, Frankie! Buster says to put the job centre visit on hold for now – there's some work available through a contact of hers if you want it.'

'Do I ever? Did she say what kind of job – no, it doesn't matter, I'll do anything legal.'

'She had a client due, so couldn't talk, but says the guy's desperate and doesn't care about you having been in prison.'

Feeling excited to have "prospects", I helped Sal with the evening's food preparation (the least I could do when not paying rent). As I worked, my mind kept indulging in speculation over what kind of job it might be. Office work could require a whole new wardrobe.

I'd finished peeling and chopping the last of the carrots when Buster got home. In a smart navy suit and pearl stud earrings she was every inch the professional woman. Disappearing into the bedroom to change, she came back as her usual self in a shirt, leggings, warm polka-dot sweater and sporting her trademark off-duty gold hoop earrings.

'It's been quite the day,' she said, accepting the mug of tea Sal put into her hand. No bone china here, but a sturdy ceramic number with an image of the famous tower and the words "A Present from Blackpool".

'Tough one, love?' asked her wife.

Buster grinned. 'No, the opposite. Radnor Housing backed down and agreed Mr Sergeant's flat should be classified as unfit, given the mould and rats. He'll soon be on his way to a new property, removals all paid for, but with the option of going back to his old place once remedial works are complete. If he wants to, of course. I wouldn't.'

'Well done,' said Sal, plonking a congratulatory kiss on the top of Buster's head. 'Some landlords get away with renting out any crappy old slum because people are desperate.'

Sal went to put the shepherd's pie in the oven, and I set the carrots ready to boil while Buster leaned against the kitchen door with a sigh of satisfaction as she drank the strong, brown tea.

'The day started badly when I realised the office hadn't been cleaned and the bins were full,' she told us. 'I got onto the company to ask why and found Jim half out of his mind because three of his best workers have gone back to Poland, leaving him short-staffed. So, when I said I might know someone wanting work, he didn't care about you being in prison, as long as you're fit, strong and up to the job.'

With a sinking heart, I asked, 'So, what does it involve?'

'It's a contract cleaning company; they do offices, schools, you name it, but best of all the work is local, so no bus fares to find. Split shifts, unfortunately, which nobody much wants to do. Normal hours are Monday to Friday, 6.00am to 10.00am, doing offices in central St Annes, then 4.00pm to 6.00pm at the high school. Optional weekend work if you want the overtime. Minimum wage at first, a week's trial, and see how you get on.'

'Sounds great,' said Sal, turning to me. 'No weekend hours unless you want them, and a free space in the day where you can do your editing stuff or whatever. It's perfect for you.'

Buster studied me as she took another long draught of restorative tea. 'I'm not sure Frankie agrees. You had something different in mind?'

Sal's face was suddenly flint, and she fixed me with a laser stare. 'Is that right? It's OK for you to clean your own house, but not someplace else?'

Her tone challenged my undoubted snobbery, and I blushed.

'I said I'd do anything, so lead me to it.' My attempts at a cheerful face weren't fooling anyone.

'Oh, I get it,' Buster instantly identified the issue. 'You had a daily, right?'

Guilty as charged: I hadn't cleaned my own house in years or done the ironing. But we'd all had to share the domestic work in prison, so why resist the idea now? These women had opened their home to give me a safe place to stay, were supporting me financially, and I absolutely couldn't turn my nose up at a job. Any job.

Putting my shoulders back, I said, 'Yes, you're right, but this is no time to be picky, right? Buster, thank you so much, it's a huge relief not to have to navigate the benefits system.'

'Don't celebrate yet,' said Buster. 'You won't get paid until the end of the month. If you want the job, Jim will give you a formal offer in writing when you start on Monday. Probation will be OK with it because he's had ex-offenders before.'

'Great,' I told them, with as much enthusiasm as I could manage.

'Atta girl,' said Sal.

*

By Friday morning the laptop reappeared outside my door with another note.

'Only a loose connection. Did it get dropped or something?

47

Have set you up with some basic software and Wi-Fi, plus free virus protection. Could do you a memory upgrade too? I've got the necessary parts.

Angus.'

The suitcase had most likely received some rough handling in transit, despite being labelled fragile, so I'd been lucky any resulting damage hadn't been worse. The paint-spattered table Sal had produced from the garage was not a thing of beauty but would work as a desk for now until I found time to renovate it. The next few hours were spent setting up my screen, getting a new email address and stalking Henry online. Yeah, not exactly the best idea but I was burning with anger at what he'd done to me, and only the prospect of one day exacting a horrible revenge kept me going.

The search results made me hot and nauseous, especially the photos of Henry wining and dining with celebrities. Most of them also featured Jerry Marchant, the long-time constituency agent and now partner who'd been shagging my husband for years. Fierce anger bubbled up from deep inside at the wasted years I'd spent glad-handing the voters and opening fetes. A piece reporting Henry's recent promotion to minister for the environment made me laugh, but only at the bitter irony. He'd never given a shit about green issues and couldn't even be arsed to put things into our recycling.

I shared these reflections with Auntie Dot on Sunday, as we sat in her comfortable flat having a sandwich lunch and coffee together.

'I'm sorry not to be able to invite you upstairs to mine, but all I've got is instant coffee, two mugs, one of which I've already chipped, and the only armchair is a bit wonky. Hopefully Sal can lend me a screwdriver to fix it.'

'There's plenty of time to make home improvements and, in the meantime, don't feel guilty about enjoying my hospitality. I do make excellent coffee and anyway, I enjoy our little chats.'

'Have you heard about my new job?'

'Yes indeed,' she said, her tone dry, leaving me to guess what might have been said about my reaction to this employment opportunity. 'It may not be your career path of choice, but it's a place to start.'

Polishing off my cheese and pickle sandwich I said, 'I've got another plan to help with short-term cash flow. Sal says if I go into Lytham there's a jeweller who deals in second-hand items. I'm hoping they might buy the diamond stud earrings Henry got me as a wedding anniversary present.'

'I know the shop you mean; we'll go together. Don't be disappointed by the price you're offered,' advised Dot. 'It's a buyer's market and they'll be wanting to make a substantial profit on the deal. You'll get less than half what they're worth.'

'My internet research suggested the same, but since I had to cough up to get the bus to Blackpool for the probation meeting, the sum of my assets is currently £18.42. It should at least be worth the bus fare into Lytham, whatever the jeweller is willing to offer, and I've got to keep going any way I can until my first payday.'

Thinking about the pictures of Henry I'd seen provided a sudden image of chandeliers and gilt mirrors, the diamonds sparkling in my ears along with the antique necklace which had once belonged to Henry's mother. Silk rustling against my skin and the twitter of conversation at a political shindig, all of this taken for granted as my rightful place in the world. I'd never imagined losing it, or the woman I now saw in Dot's gilt mirror. Too thin, with no make-up and pasty grey skin, desperation in her eyes.

*

On Monday morning, I got up in the darkness before the bloody birds. Fortified by two rounds of toast and a sugar boost from the red jam, I wrapped up in my new warm coat and set off for the offices we'd be cleaning. Striding through the side streets following the directions Sal had provided, I passed an eclectic array of shops and eateries, way more interesting than the High Street, with its many bargain chains, charity outlets and empty units.

The offices were in a modern concrete block above a small supermarket. Waiting in the car park was a minibus proclaiming "Morley's Contract Cleaning", with half a dozen people standing beside it.

'Bloody hell, it's Little Red Riding Hood,' said a woman with a badger stripe of dark brown at the roots of her bleached-blonde hair. I flinched when she said, 'Jim, please say she's not with us?'

The man with a clipboard, lots of piercings and a shaved head said, 'Leave off, Doreen, be grateful I found someone. You must be Frankie? Right then, you're crew number four with Doreen and Shannon here. Protective clothing.' He held out a polyester tabard and a pair of rubber gloves. 'Shannon's in charge and she'll show you the ropes. Back at the end of the shift and I'll give you a proper employment offer letter then if these two say you'll do.'

As we rode up in the lift, Shannon, a plump woman with almost no neck and around my age surveyed me without optimism.

'Say what you like about immigrants, them Poles could graft, but they went home so now we've got you. You'd better not be afraid of hard work.'

'Show me what to do. I won't let you down,' I said, determined not to get off on the wrong foot.

'You sound *posh*,' said Doreen accusingly. She must not

have noticed the well-washed grey tracksuit I'd chosen as work clothes. Nothing upmarket about my appearance.

'Sure you're up for this?' Shannon asked with a hard glare.

I'd had more than enough experience of inverse snobbery while in prison, but by superhuman effort managed to keep my mouth shut. I *needed* this job. Unloading cleaning equipment from the landing cupboard, Shannon said, 'Right, here's how it works. We've got three hours clear to do the office floors then once the staff begin to arrive, we move onto toilets and kitchens. Got it? First job emptying bins and for fuck's sake wear the gloves – the bitches who work here toss out all kinds of crap they're not supposed to, so try not to touch anything.'

Nobody had mentioned handling hazardous waste as part of the deal.

'Me and Doreen will crack on with the desks and booths, then when you've done the bins follow us with the vacuum cleaner. Be sure to go under the desks and *don't* fall behind, we got to keep moving and if we run over our time there's trouble.'

The two women swung into action like the professional team they were, and I had to push myself hard to keep up the pace they set. By 9.00am I'd been reduced to a sweaty wreck, every muscle protesting, but I *had* kept up as we moved onto the next stage.

'Bring a water bottle tomorrow,' advised Doreen, watching as I stuck my head under a kitchen tap and drank thirstily. 'Take sips to keep you going, then you won't need to pee so much. Do the bins but don't touch the sanitary containers – they ain't in our contract.'

As the office workers began to trickle in, I couldn't help noticing that our presence went unacknowledged; we were either invisible or not considered worthy of attention. The management who inhabited the private offices were all men – no surprises there. The glass ceiling appeared to be fully functional in this establishment, which had to be obvious to the mainly female employees. Maybe it was only a job for them too, except they got better pay and conditions.

By the time we returned to the car park, I was aching all over and ready to sleep till lunchtime. Then Shannon shamed me by saying, 'You off to do the pub now, Doreen? See you at the school later.'

'Doreen has another job?' I said in disbelief, as she disappeared towards the main street.

'And three teenage boys to feed,' said Shannon, with the look of someone who had seen too much and expected very little. 'Her husband left, so what choice does she have? Cleans at the Dog and Duck after this, then back home to do her own housework until we start the classrooms later.'

'My friend Sal is the cook at that pub.'

'What, Fat Sal? Why didn't you say so before? She's a good 'un.'

'She certainly is,' I said, before collecting Jim's letter and heading home.

Let's not dress it up, that first week was undiluted hell. I only got through it by having a nap when I got home from the offices; I'd never have made it to the late-afternoon school shift otherwise. The muscles of my back and legs ached non-stop, having not been required for heavy use in a long time but now called into active service. Some people paid good money for a workout of that standard: I certainly had in the past. As the days passed, I learnt how to pace myself better, and something must have been said about Sal because Doreen's hostility lessened, particularly once I'd proved I could and did keep up. Only sheer bloody-mindedness kept me going, and a fierce determination to prove the "posh" woman could do her bit.

*

It was bliss to sleep in on Saturday morning, but I managed to be up, dressed and wearing my red lipstick when Dot knocked on my door for our trip to Lytham. It took me a minute to recognise her; the blonde wig came as a surprise, as she hadn't been hiding such a hairstyle under her usual scarves and turbans. I'd also never seen her wear glasses before either, let alone chunky tortoiseshell ones.

Auntie Dot chuckled at my startled expression. 'It's fun to ring the changes,' she said. 'We'll take the car, even if parking will be a nightmare.'

'You have a car?'

'My Mini's name is Miriam, and since, like me, she is well past the first flush of youth, I keep her in the garage when not in use.'

Miriam turned out to be a classic, at least twenty years old; British racing green, with cream leather seats piped in black.

'My Mini was called Dolly,' I said. 'A pale blue special edition with a matching velour interior: I bloody loved her, used to drive around sometimes for the sheer joy of it.'

'We clearly share similar tastes,' said Dot. 'Shame about your car. I know they say it's better to have loved and lost, but that's awful bullshit.'

The morning shone bright but cold, and Dot drove *fast*, getting us along the coast to Lytham in under ten minutes. The town didn't have the wide main street of St Annes but possessed a singular charm of its own, including a pedestrianised town square lined with eateries, and any number of interesting higher-end shops. Visibly more prosperous in subtle ways, I spotted a lot of people in designer clothes with expensive accessories and an astonishing number of fancy cars which wouldn't have been out of place in Bayswater. For a small northern coastal town, it had a continental vibe I appreciated.

'Nice, isn't it?' said Dot, swerving expertly into an on-street parking space the instant the previous occupant had left it. 'I'm told St Annes used to be the preferred resort years ago, but now Lytham is the place to be. Lots of well-off older people.'

I wanted to ask why she didn't live there herself, and Dot understood immediately where my mind had been going.

'What I have at Sea View suits me very well,' she said. 'In fact, in many ways it's perfect. I've never been keen on cooking, except when necessary for basic survival, and there aren't many places which provide meals where I can have all my things around me. Not old and infirm enough for Sunset Towers yet, and even when I am, I will resist residential care with every fibre of my being. Probably join Exit or something. Institutional food and bloody bingo are not my jam.'

'How long have you lived at Sea View?' I asked.

'Almost seven years now, and I've no plans to leave unless it's in a box.'

'Don't you miss London? Theatres and all those museums and galleries?'

Auntie Dot locked the car before answering, having first collected a walking stick from the back seat; I'd never seen her use one before.

'I did at first, but virtually everything is accessible online these days. My retirement originally began in a remote part of scenic Scotland – fabulous views but too quiet and very dull. It might suit some, but I prefer to be around people and amenities. Come on, the jeweller you want is across the road.'

A window display of vintage rings suggested I'd come to the right place, so when the two of us went inside my confidence ran high. Coming out again a few minutes later my entire body was shaking with rage.

'Right,' said Dot, steering me along the pavement with a firm grip on my arm. 'You need strong coffee and probably chocolate, which always makes things better. There's a decent place down here.'

I barely registered the Italian-style coffee house she ushered me into. Through gritted teeth, I said, 'Henry Wilton is going to *die* for this.'

'He only has the power to make you feel bad if you allow it to happen,' Dot said, leading me to a low table with comfortably worn leather armchairs. 'It's just a setback, and you already knew he was a lying toad, so why be surprised by further evidence of his perfidy?'

'But... fucking fakes!' I spluttered. 'He told me they were diamonds *and* that the stones were a good investment.'

'As I recall, you were aware by then of the long-standing affair with his agent?'

'Yes but...'

'Frankie, do not let this throw you off balance,' she said, pausing to ask the waitress to bring us coffee and chocolate fudge cake. 'Before today, you had less than £20, and now you've got quite a bit more.'

I tried, but the discovery of Henry's deception was like acid pouring through my veins.

'Yeah, scrap value for the platinum in the earrings and my wedding ring,' I said bitterly.

'And the offer of a lot more if you want to sell your engagement ring. He did say those stones were the genuine article, and art-deco style is very popular these days.'

'I'm keeping that as my insurance policy in case I'm ever really up against it,' I said.

'And you aren't now?'

The cake arrived and Auntie Dot tucked in with enthusiasm. When she urged me to try it, I took a tentative bite and found it layered with amazing subtle flavours.

'Fabulous, isn't it? Proper cake forks too, which makes this one of my favourite watering holes, and the coffee is excellent.'

The sugar hit did make things marginally less awful, but not much. I'd been sucker punched and it wasn't a nice feeling.

'The truth is, I'd been counting on the earrings realising enough money to pay Sal and Buster some rent to be going on with. I feel bad that it's not going to happen.'

'You know they're OK with that; how many times do they have to say so before you believe it?'

She was right. Good friends had my back, and it's not as if I was facing eviction or anything; I had a job and some measure of security. This and the cake and coffee were assisting my recovery nicely when I became aware of scrutiny, with that sixth sense you feel when you're being watched.

'Why is that woman over there staring?' I said, intensely uncomfortable under her intent gaze. Perhaps Henry had sent her to spy on me or was that paranoia on my part.

'What? Where?' Dot's voice grew sharp.

'Shh, she's coming over. Do I look weird or something?' I'd shed my tracksuit in favour of a variation on the interview clothes, teamed with the Chanel jacket. Even so, these were far from being up to Lytham standards.

The woman tottered over on vertiginous heels; I recognised the upmarket brand, having owned a similar pair myself. They'd hurt my feet.

'Oh God, I'm so sorry, this is positively rude of me, and I don't mean to interrupt,' she said.

I still wasn't used to the way people felt able to approach or talk to you in the north; it wasn't *done* in London.

'The thing is, your handbag... it *is* real, isn't it, not a copy? No, I can see it's genuine, how cool is that? Sorry, you must be thinking I'm some kind of crazy person, but you have no idea how long I've been searching for one of these.'

She wore an expensive leather coat teamed with a permatan and huge false eyelashes. Most of her face didn't move except when she talked, making it anybody's guess how old she must be.

'Yes, it's vintage, from the 1980s I believe,' I said, bemused by this conversation.

'And in *such* good condition. You can find this design sometimes but not in the crocodile finish. It's been well cared for; I can see that.'

Another present from Henry; not a particular favourite but it just happened to be the bag I'd been using when arrested, and therefore the only one I now possessed.

'You wouldn't – God this is pushing my luck – but would you consider selling? I've wanted one of these for *so* long... I could give you £500 for it?'

I was stunned into silence by this offer, which she took for hesitation over the price.

'OK, maybe that's a bit low; I'll give you £600 – I can get cash for you from my bank, it's just up the street.'

Determined to be honest, I said, 'The shoulder strap is missing, and there are some marks on the inside lining.'

Dot leaned forward. 'She'll take £650 in cash.'

'Seriously? Oh my God, this is *epic*! Please don't go anywhere, I can't believe it. My name is Paris and I'll be back in a mo.' She was out of the door as fast as her heels would allow, and I turned an astonished face to Auntie Dot.

She grinned in satisfaction. 'It appears "God is a very present help trouble" and don't you dare turn down a good offer.'

Paris must have been better at walking in those shoes than me because she returned as promised with the crisp new notes in the time it took me to finish my cake and coffee. Dot produced a cloth shopping bag into which I tipped my modest possessions, before handing over the object of desire.

'I can't thank you enough,' gushed Paris, her face hardly moving. 'You've made my day, I feel *so* lucky, this is awesome.' She tottered off in a state of high excitement, waving goodbye, and stroking the bag like the precious treasure she clearly considered it to be.

Dot finished her coffee and ordered more, while I sat there in a state of shock, unable to believe the serendipity of this encounter.

'Bloody hell, did that just happen?' I asked.

'Be grateful,' advised Dot, smirking as if she'd engineered the whole thing. 'Now you can go shopping for some necessities.'

The list of items I needed but hadn't yet been able to afford would have run to several pages. I settled for more underwear and pyjamas in a sale and Dot found a filter coffee machine marked down by 70% because of being last year's model and the box ever so slightly trashed.

'No, I can't, even though it is a bargain. I need to give Sal at least half of this money as rent. It's only fair.'

'Then I insist on buying this for you,' Dot informed me. 'No arguments, it is my pleasure, and proper coffee is one of life's necessities. Call it a housewarming present.'

My other purchases included a good as new faux-leather rucksack from a charity shop – much more practical to carry my stuff than the designer bag had been. I also blew money on my favourite lipstick brand, telling myself it was an investment in my mental health and well-being.

I tried to thank Dot for her help, but she brushed my

efforts aside. 'Haven't had so much fun in years,' she said. 'It is truly more blessed to give than receive. You didn't *mind* parting with the bag, did you? I did rather force you into it.'

'Absolutely not,' I told her. 'I'm more than happy to get rid of anything which reminds me of Henry. He is fucking *history*.'

FIVE

Over dinner (always fish and chips on a Saturday night), Dot regaled everyone with the story of pushy Paris and the sale of my bag.

Fat Sal couldn't stop laughing. 'Seriously?' she said with a fruity chuckle. 'More bloody money than sense; you fell on your feet there, Frankie.'

'Dot did the negotiating, not me,' I protested. 'Anyway, the bag was Hermes and had serious rarity value.'

Sal was having none of it. 'People who fall for the label thing are bloody fools,' she said.

Centuries on from my Bayswater days, I was inclined to agree and had grown up enough to understand that such status-symbol possessions were nice to have but genuinely irrelevant. This fresh insight left me feeling like an ignorant teenager who was finally growing up; *not* a comfortable experience at forty-three.

After dinner, I knocked on the sitting room door of the basement flat and tried to give Sal £300 for rent.

'Don't be daft,' she said, refusing to accept the envelope I offered. 'You need that money to get on your feet.'

'Take it', urged Buster from the armchair, who was wearing the scrumptious pink jumper again. 'Then we can get the damn light switch in the kitchen fixed, and you can see what you're doing again.'

Sal made a growling noise. 'Works when it wants to, but never when you most need it. Every time I decide to get someone in the damn thing behaves itself again. It'll go weeks without so much as a blink, and *then* decide to go on strike, just that one switch. Lucky the cooker is gas, but I had to do the fish and chips by torchlight.'

'Could be a loose connection,' I said. 'Want me to fix it?'

Buster frowned. 'We'd better get someone properly qualified in.'

'I *am* qualified,' I told her. 'Did City & Guilds Domestic Electricals course in prison.'

'I'd forgotten about that!' said Sal. 'Frankie were bored out of her tree and took the only class on offer which sounded useful.'

'It passed the time,' I said, 'though I'm not harbouring any ambitions to take my very basic skills further. Have you got a screwdriver?'

After some rummaging under the sink, the object Buster produced had multiple heads stored in the handle, and Sal showed me the master switchboard for the power.

'It's this one, and it don't cut off the whole house, only the flat. Had it done when the kitchen were put in,' Sal told me.

The problem turned out to be a simple fix, well within my abilities.

Buster grinned at Sal then back at me and gave her verdict. 'She'll do.' High praise, from Sal's expression.

'And what about the money? Please let me give you this as an interim payment?'

'All right, but the deal here is we charge what people can afford,' said Sal. 'Auntie Dot pays us a cracking good rent, and since Angus makes a comfortable living from the computer business he runs up in his cave, he's on market rates too. The old chap who had your room before only had his pension, and housing benefit kicked in for him.'

'I'll get paid soon,' I insisted. 'You must let me at least cover my keep, or it wouldn't be fair.'

'OK then, but tell you what, when we see what your take-home is we'll figure something regular out,' offered Buster.

*

As March came in, wild and wet, my first wages went into the new bank account I'd opened with the balance of Paris's cash. This windfall had also allowed me to set up a sim-only contract for my two-year-old phone. Back in business, I emailed the new number to my dad and Justin, though only the latter responded with a quick text. Another step forward.

I came home from work one morning and, as I changed into a clean top, noticed how muscular my arms had become. Standing in front of the mirror, the woman I saw was lean and strong. I'd got into the rhythm of the team and built up my stamina to the point where I no longer needed a nap to recover from the early shift. In the afternoon high-school sessions I'd soon discovered the little darlings continued to decorate their desks with dried snot and chewing gum, requiring more rubber gloves. And the graffiti!

'Bloody hell,' I said to Doreen, 'at their age, I'd never have been able to draw such anatomically correct illustrations. Having had a very limited sex life before Henry, I probably couldn't even now.'

Doreen cackled, bending down for a closer inspection of the artwork. 'You're forgetting this lot have access to internet porn. Don't do them much good, the lads expect all women's tits to be round the way implants are. And then they worry about not being hung like donkeys, same as the fellas in the films.'

Shannon snorted. 'Yeah, and wasn't your boy Jake blown away to discover women have body hair too? Kids always believe they know everything, but they'll learn.'

On Shannon's say-so, I'd been made permanent staff and put on a slightly higher hourly rate. Not enough to make a massive difference in terms of take-home pay, but it mattered to give the job my best shot. Buster's challenge still stung. There was also a warm glow of satisfaction that my colleagues valued me. They continued the teasing about being "posh". I couldn't explain to them how much that had been and still was only a veneer of sophistication. Even with a cultured accent, the real me was every bit as fragile and ordinary as anyone else. Possibly more.

My dad remained in "never darken my door again" mode. It hurt when he didn't respond to my new phone number, but perhaps he didn't know how to text. I bought a pad of paper and handwrote a letter to him, believing the effort would be appreciated. He had old-fashioned ideas about such things.

Dear Dad,

> *Hope you are keeping well. Justin tells me you have had some painful sciatica and I do hope it has now settled down. This is to confirm my contact information and to tell you I'm building a new life here, making friends and have a job now. I'm ready to put the past behind me and hope you might feel able to do the same. It would be so nice to be in regular contact again.*

> *Your daughter,*
> *Francesca*

His reply came within days. My heart leapt when I saw the familiar black handwriting and my mouth was dry as I opened the heavy cream envelope. Hope died as I read the short missive.

Dear Francesca,

Thank you for this information, and I note you are now using your maiden name again. You must understand how very let down I feel by your shameful criminal conduct, but you remain my daughter, so I owe you a duty. Justin is a good boy and calls me every week but needs his mother as he and Henry don't appear to be getting on very well.

I am glad you have a place to live and a job and, of course, I wish you well, but after what has happened cannot feel we have very much to say to one another.

Yours,

Father

This response was like having a bucket of cold water thrown over me. Yes, it was unrealistic to think his attitude might have softened in two years, but the feeling of loss was unexpected. Hot tears I'd never expected to shed fell onto the paper, smudging the ink. Was I still such a child, longing for Daddy to kiss and make things better? His answer shouldn't have come as a surprise – our relationship had always been stiff and formal, particularly after my mother's death and the years at boarding school.

Even though we'd never been close, it had stung deep when Dad chose to believe the worst of me. He'd attended some of the court case and managed to accept all of Henry's lies as gospel truth – what with him being a man and therefore a reliable e.g. non-hormonal witness. Since Justin had been away at university at the time of the fire, couldn't my dad even *consider* the possibility that my flimsy-sounding defence was the truth, and Henry was responsible and not me?

At least Dad's rejection left no aching void since he'd never been very present in my life. What mattered was that my son and I were now in regular contact, and I heard all about the tensions with his father by email.

Hi, Mum,

My God, you wouldn't believe life around here. Jerry turned out to be some kind of clean-freak monster and insists on me doing housework. There's no choice about living at home because for now I'm only an unpaid intern at the law firm. Without Dad's monthly allowance, I wouldn't even be able to get to the office and I can't afford to meet the boys for a drink most of the time. Jerry won't do my laundry with theirs; he says it's time I behaved like an adult. The food he makes isn't great either, all healthy greens; I'd kill for some of your lemon drizzle cake.

Don't suppose you can spare some cash – life is tough right now.

Justin

Something inside me went cold, a touch of frost on our recovering relationship. I knew our son could be every bit as selfish as his father, but he hadn't even asked if I was OK, and to touch me for money was unbelievable! What kind of daily life did he imagine I was living? Stupid of me, but I put a couple of £20 notes for beer money in a brown envelope, posting it with a brief note explaining I couldn't do more because I only had a cleaning job.

Afterwards, I lay on my bed lost in memories of a beautiful blond child who'd flung his arms around my neck, saying "I love you, Mummy". Big mistake. Once I'd tapped into those feelings, everything I'd been holding back for so long burst to the surface. A wave of grief welled up from the depths of my soul, in great racking sobs which shook my whole body. With my face pressed into the pillow, I howled and wept for my little boy, for the broken, loveless marriage begun in such hope and joy on my part, all the injustices of recent years and everything I'd lost. Then that nasty little voice at the back of my head insisted it was all my own fault, it was me who'd ruined everything and now my life was over.

According to the psychologists, allowing yourself to fully experience and acknowledge feelings of grief is much healthier than locking it all away. I'd kept so much inside during the prison time, as a necessary coping mechanism, not daring to acknowledge the dark monster lurking in the corner. Once that demon broke free, I got lost for a time in a dark wasteland of grief and despair. It took a massive effort of will to kick myself in the metaphorical pants and tell my inner child to get over herself and face reality. Maybe it *did* do me good to let it all out, but it also made my head hurt.

'Come *on*, Frankie,' I said aloud. 'Never mind the past, you can build a new life. It's not like there's a choice.'

I'd blown my nose, taken painkillers and regained some control when I spotted the bar of milk chocolate I'd originally given Angus wrapped in a note he'd pushed under the door.

Don't cry. It gets better. A.

This simple act of human kindness only made me weep all over again, but this time my tears were appreciation for the people who'd helped me get this far from the prison gates. The sugar helped too; I ate the whole bar, obviously. It was possible to do this starting over thing, and I damn well would.

Downstairs at dinner, everyone carefully avoided mentioning my puffy red eyes and didn't ask questions. But then Auntie Dot, observing no such sensitivity guidelines, dragged me into her flat as I made my way back upstairs, pushed me into a comfortable chair by the stove and put a glass of gin into my hand.

'Sit there,' she commanded. 'OK, so what's making you look like a wet weekend?'

The drink had a ratio of gin to tonic high enough to make me cough and my arms and legs tingle. Under its influence, I gave her the long and winding version of my tale of woe.

By the time I meandered to a halt, Dot was giving me a stern headmistress glare.

'I'd tell you to pull yourself together, but I gather one isn't supposed to do so these days. Frankie, you cannot worry about your dad, Justin, Henry and his lover, or any of the former friends who were so quick to dump you. Now is the time to put *yourself* first and move on.'

'Some days it's only being so bloody furious that's keeping me going,' I said, blowing my nose on the tissue she held out.

'It's not doing anything of the sort,' said Dot, topping up my gin. 'Anger and resentment corrode the soul and eat away at you. Ask me how I know. Lay them down before such negativity destroys your essential self – you are *better* than this.'

'No, I'm not – every single part of me wants to remove Henry's testicles slowly and painfully with a blunt instrument.'

Dot grinned. 'While I might applaud the principle, or feel he richly deserves it, such an action would only get you sent straight back to prison. Hardly a desirable outcome,' she said, taking a large swallow of her drink. 'Frankie, I learnt from bitter personal experience that when life knocks you down all you can do is put yourself back together any way that works. The result may end up being a patchwork of things you never wanted but life is precious, so don't go wasting time hankering after what you can't have. Learn to want what you *do* have and appreciate every experience which comes your way. Previous generations would have called it "making the best of things", which sounds terribly prosaic but there's a lot of wisdom in some old sayings.'

'You did the same?' I asked. 'I get the impression something happened, and you had to retire suddenly?'

Auntie Dot went very still, and after a long pause she said, 'I don't talk about it but yes, you are correct. After every part of my old life had been comprehensively trashed, I didn't at first see any way to survive. But I made it through, and so will you.'

*

Something deep and important lay behind Dot's words, and I understood the truth of what she'd said about bitterness being toxic and poisoning me. From then on, I resolved to let go of everything to do with Henry, and what he'd done to me; sometimes I even succeeded. When signs of spring began to emerge and brave windswept daffodils bloomed in the municipal planters, I took walks along the shore on fine afternoons. The wide sea and sky were healing, softening the hard shell I'd been growing over my inmost self. Out there, walking the tideline with the gulls crying overhead, my troubles receded as small and unimportant. A process of finding and holding onto a fragile peace was just getting underway when something managed to destroy it all again.

My phone pinged with a text; these were usually work-related or from friends at Sea View, occasionally the doctor's surgery I'd registered at. I didn't immediately notice the lack of a caller ID, not even a number. Stupid of me to click on it, but you can't always be on high alert for potential scammers, trolls or lying husbands. I was walking home from the school shift at the time, trying to dodge a cold rain coming off the sea with the incoming tide. Pausing in a shop doorway, I opened the message, half expecting it to be Sal asking me to bring something from the shop. But it wasn't.

Henry says to keep your mouth shut. If you say anything he can get you sent back to prison. Got it?

Rooted to the wet pavement, I shivered then went even colder as rain trickled down my neck from the shop sign. It was the menace behind the words that threw me, and how had someone got my brand-new number? Anyhow, not being party to the details of Henry's current life beyond the stuff already in the public domain, how could I talk about it?

Back at Sea View, I put my sodden coat around a chair back to dry and went down to dinner (curry again) feeling lost and blown off course. Sal shot me some interrogative looks, and eventually Buster asked, 'You OK, Frankie? You're awfully quiet.'

'Yeah, sorry, bit of a headache,' I said, with perfect truth. Even Angus glanced briefly at me across the table, and he clearly didn't believe a word of this lame excuse either.

As soon as the meal ended, Dot turned to me. 'Perhaps you'd care to join me for coffee?' she said.

'No, I'd rather…'

Buster interrupted, 'Do what she says, Frankie, and don't argue.'

In Dot's flat, I turned down the offer of gin, but she then put a cup of coffee in my hand as fast as the machine could produce it.

'OK, no bullshit. You've been doing so well in recent weeks; what's happened?' she demanded.

I showed her the text.

'Bloody rude and extremely unpleasant,' was Dot's comment. 'I can see why you're upset, but what does it mean?'

'God knows,' I told her as the caffeine did its work and cleared my head. 'I have no idea what's going on, and don't know what I'm not supposed to talk about.'

'And the threat of going back to prison... clearly intended to frighten you.'

'It's done that all right and now I'm panicking. Henry has told so many lies already, and if he does it again the probation service might believe I've breached my licence conditions... Oh God, Dot, it's all happening again. He's got enough money to make things look bad for me if he chooses.'

My chest was tight as I came close to hyperventilating – in imminent danger of losing it. Dot remedied this by tipping a large slug of brandy into my coffee.

'Slow down and don't get ahead of yourself. Yes, with his ministerial contacts he probably could, but...'

'You're not... helping by telling me that,' I stuttered.

She fixed me with a stern glare. 'Frankie, slow down and *breathe*. The question you should be asking has to do with what you know and could tell because this sudden threat is the action of someone scared of what you might say.'

'He's scared of *me*? But these days the only information I have is what anyone can find out from the internet,' I protested.

'You've been googling him, haven't you? Don't be such a bloody idiot, what good does that do except make you feel bad?'

I tried to slow my breathing. 'It was only once, weeks ago when I first arrived and got the computer set up. Henry is a minister now and lives with his political agent, Jerry. Justin says their relationship is very tense and they row a lot.'

'Could it be something from before, while you were married?' Dot's sharp intelligence cut through the turmoil occupying my brain. 'You were well aware of his sexuality and the affairs,' she said, trying to put the pieces together. 'But that all came out even before your trial. So, what else? What *isn't* public knowledge?'

'Henry's fondness for the sadomasochistic side of sex, I suppose. Not with me, but there were some sickening photos on his computer… his taste ran to whips and tying people up. I know he went to parties held by some kind of group who were into such stuff, but these days, would anyone even care what he got up to in private? Public figures get away with all sorts,' I said doubtfully, the brandy warming me from the centre, loosening the muscles in my tight shoulders.

'I still have friends in London who are aware of the goings-on at Westminster. They could make some discreet enquiries.'

'No, for God's sake let's not stir anything up! I'll keep my head down, as instructed.' The panic threatened to rise again.

'Nothing will be done without your permission, I promise,' said Dot. 'But the offer stands if you ever change your mind.'

The whole episode left me feeling unnerved and threatened, and back in my room I talked to Spike about it as the cat made himself at home on my bed.

'I gave it my best shot,' I told him. 'Learning to be grateful, practise mindfulness, live in the moment and not waste energy on being angry. Now, out of nowhere the shit is hitting the fan again and I don't understand *why*.'

He climbed on my stomach and kneaded my chest with his huge paws. When I scratched under his chin, he rewarded me with a guttural, growly purr.

'You don't think I should be worried?' I asked. Spike made a "meh" noise and insisted I carry on the scratching.

'You may be right, and I'm overreacting,' I told him. 'But anything to do with being sent back to prison, especially without Sal's protection, is my absolute worst fear. I've even been having bad dreams about it.'

When the phone pinged again, I almost shot off the bed in alarm, upsetting Spike and demonstrating the state of my nerves. It turned out not to be a problem, but even *good* news; a second editing contract via the website I'd set up. An unpublished author inviting me to provide editorial feedback on his early chapters. Such work didn't pay a fortune, but it got my name out there, even if I wouldn't be getting rich on two editing jobs in six weeks. I also checked out my site, searching for tweaks to publicise my services better. Two reviews had come in: one from my first contract, commenting on the fast turnround and helpful suggestions. The second made me feel sick.

I've dealt with this person before and found her work sloppy. A free grammar checker would have picked up what she found. Definitely a waste of money.

Even before my conviction, I'd never had a client by the name of Penelope Ransome, so the whole thing was a fake. I'd take the "review" down, obviously, but it set me wondering if this could be Henry again, trying to undermine my efforts to start over. But why? The modest website I'd set up didn't get anywhere near the amount of traffic needed to attract clients, so wasn't an obvious target. It could have been the kind of random malicious trolls who would always be out there. If it hadn't been for the text message, I might not have worried, but now it was beginning to feel personally directed, leaving me gazing powerless into the face of a threat I didn't understand.

SIX

In the following days, I constantly reminded myself to focus on the good stuff and resist the downward spiral into despondency. A lot of effort went into cultivating a positive attitude and I liked to think the results were making me stronger, at least on my better days. I'd read somewhere about choosing to be half full rather than half empty, so I tried to stay with that and thought I was successfully projecting an upbeat image.

Then one grey morning, going up in the office lift, Shannon said, 'Something's bothering you, Frankie, you're too quiet – is it us? You do get that we're only kidding around, right?' She glanced at Doreen, whose face mirrored her concern.

'Oh God no, it's not you, honest.'

'Well, that's a relief – you're a good worker, and we wouldn't want to lose you,' Shannon told me.

Doreen couldn't resist adding, 'Even if you are posh.'

The moment passed in the rhythm of work, and I hoped they'd let it go. When we got to the bathroom part of our shift and the three of us worked side by side, cleaning the sinks, they jumped on me again.

Doreen asked, 'Is it some bloke upsetting you? They're usually the bloody problem, right?'

Since both were shockingly free with the most intimate details of their own lives at every opportunity, it felt like I owed them something.

'It's my ex,' I told them, scrubbing at a mark on the mirror, possibly lipstick. 'He's trying to make trouble and threatening me, but I'm not sure why.'

They knew the broad outline of what had happened to me. In sharp contrast to my former friendship circle, they'd also accepted without question that I wasn't guilty.

'Mebbe it's no more than spite – just because he can? Twisting the knife, like,' offered Shannon, adding a giant roll of toilet paper to a lockable dispenser.

'But it doesn't make sense. He's a well-off and powerful man, so what could I do to hurt him?' I said, giving the area a final wipe and moving onto the next. 'I got a text instructing me to keep my mouth shut, but I don't even understand what it is I'm not supposed to talk about, so why is he after me?'

One of the office workers came in, and there were no more opportunities to chat, but going down in the lift, Doreen startled me with a quick hug and Shannon said, 'Frankie, if you need help, anything, you just ask. OK?'

*

On the positive side, Justin continued to keep in touch, and it lifted my heart when an email from him pinged its arrival in my inbox.

Thanks for the cash, Mum, but not quite what I'd had in mind. Are you really doing a cleaning job or having me on? I mean, you went to university. The boss at my law firm isn't very impressed with me – said to buck my

ideas up and stop thinking the world owed me something.
What a knob.
     J

Definitely a half-empty moment, and no warm fuzzies from this particular communication. It was tempting to write back and tell him the boss had it right. Of course, I loved my boy, and always would, but it didn't blind me to the truth that he suffered from the arrogance of youth; an all-too-typical public-school kid, seeing himself as God's gift to the law on the back of a mediocre degree. At a guess he'd only got the internship because of his dad's connections.

When Buster and Sal offered to take me to the local auction house, I jumped at the chance of free entertainment (the people attending) and successfully bid £15 on a job lot consisting of a wooden rocking chair and a pile of rolled-up Indian dhurries for the floor. These were grubby and smelled kind of musty, so I gave them a good scrub out in the car park on the first available fine day. I also sanded down the chair before giving it two coats of leftover white paint which Sal produced from her hoard of Useful Stuff out in the garages.

My attic room became so much more welcoming for the personal touches I'd added, and I looked around one day realising it had begun to feel like *home*. It was a lightbulb moment that meant so much to an ex-con and former socialite. From a distance, the plastic plant in a white pot looked amazingly realistic – bought because I lacked confidence a real one would survive my casual efforts at maintenance. Our Bayswater cleaner had always watered the plants, along with so many other things she'd taken care of. It was becoming abundantly clear that I should have appreciated her more. Buster lent me her elderly sewing machine, and I cut down the large blue-and-white striped single curtain I'd bought into a new smaller pair for the dormer window. There was even enough fabric to run up some cushions as well. Taught by the nuns, I liked sewing and found it meditative.

But what I treasured most was my time out on the beach, razor clams and cockle shells under my searching feet, gulls crying overhead and the tangy air with its reek of seaweed. The space and freedom became something I couldn't do without, and the sands were normally deserted except for a few random dog walkers, all of us on nodding terms. It gave me a chance to think and breathe. Winter was over, and bright, milder days meant more people claimed space on the sand, so I had to learn to share like a proper grown-up. A couple of hardy family groups even set up camp with portable chairs behind a canvas windbreak, where the little kids could do the traditional bucket-and-spade thing.

The ice cream shops and slot machine arcades by the pier, locked and shuttered in the winter months, now showed signs of life and even got a fresh coat of paint in lurid pinks and greens. A renewed sense of hope and optimism lifted me as the days lengthened and everything bloomed and came to life around me. All this should have been enough to remind me of the old adage: if it can go wrong, it will.

Window shopping my way home from the early shift, I realised someone was following me. It took a while to be sure but whenever I looked back, there was the same youngish guy in sharp city-style clothes. The time spent watching detective series on the laptop hadn't been wasted, as I ducked into shops and side streets trying to lose him or prove I was imagining his pursuit. My grasp of evasive techniques must have been less than brilliant because, glancing back at the corner of Norcross Road, he was still behind me. Sudden fear made me cold all over and my body went into fight or flight mode, heart racing.

He halted at a safe distance and called out, 'Don't be afraid, Mrs Wilton, I only want to talk to you. Please.'

Spooked, I dived across the road into St Aidan's church hall, providing a moment's diversion and entertainment for the attendees at one of their regular coffee mornings. The female vicar in skinny jeans and a navy-blue sweatshirt with the church logo stood by the door to welcome people. She took one look at my panicked face and said, 'Are you OK? Can I help with something?'

'A man is following me,' I told her urgently, my breath coming in short gasps. 'Blond guy on the corner, in the chinos and brown brogues.'

'I see him,' she said, 'wouldn't say he's local, not in that jacket.'

The assembled clientele of elderly people had given me curious stares as I burst in, before going back to their custard creams and strong brown tea.

'You're one of Sal's residents, aren't you? Want me to get rid of him? His kind usually back off when challenged.'

My heart was beating fast. 'This may sound ridiculous, but I don't want him to see where I live.'

'And anyway, I'm not scary enough, right?'

Since the rest of her outfit included red canvas ankle boots, dangly earrings and a spotted scarf tied in a jaunty bow around her short grey hair, I had to agree.

'I'm Ellie,' she said. 'Fancy a cup of tea?'

'Frankie, but I don't drink tea…'

'Then let me make you a coffee and we'll see what he does.' She led the way to a surprisingly modern kitchen and produced a tin of powdered instant and a sturdy mug bearing the logo of a local builder.

In the safety of the church hall, my fears subsided and I began to feel a fool.

'You probably think I've lost the plot thinking someone might be following me?'

'Not at all,' said Ellie. 'As a single woman who gets around the town a fair bit visiting people, I have to be security conscious too. You did the right thing coming in here if you felt threatened.'

'Has he gone?' I asked as Ellie led me and my mug to a table near the door.

'He's standing there watching. Shall I call Auntie Dot to come and collect you in her car?' Surprise must have been written on my face because she said. 'Dot is an occasional attendee at Sunday service but always makes it clear she only comes for the ritual and music. An honest doubter and an awesome woman, I love her to bits.'

I picked a custard cream absently off the plate; these and the pink wafer biscuits always reminded me of convent school. Comforting in their way and helped with the vile taste of the cheap coffee.

'If it's OK with you, maybe I'll drink this and see if he goes away,' I told Ellie.

But he didn't and remained on the corner staring across the road.

'How's this for a suggestion? I'll go out and take his photo on my phone,' she said. 'Make it clear he's been spotted and provide evidence in case we need it.' She was soon back and showed me the picture, saying, 'He's not familiar or anything?'

'Absolutely not, and he's way too young to be interested in me – not exactly a typical sex pest.'

Ellie chuckled. 'Frankie, they don't all wear raincoats and shades.'

I flushed, 'Yeah, sorry, I have this bad habit of making instant judgements about people based on their appearance. I'm from London, it's what we do.'

'I can see why you might need to read people quickly in a big city and be ultra-cautious about personal safety. It's possible I might have scared him off by taking the picture but, just to be sure, why not ring Dot? I'd take you myself but can't leave my old dears.'

Dot arrived in Miriam the Mini within minutes of my call and parked around the back of the hall, out of sight. When I emerged from the kitchen door, far from laughing at my fears, she took them very seriously.

'Get into the back seat and crouch down. I'll drive around the block a few times to be sure.'

If I'd felt an idiot before, by the time we pulled into the car park at Sea View the sensation was even worse. I'd been cultivating a vision of myself as an adult woman, out in the world on my own and making a living. Turns out it was ridiculously easy to demolish my confidence and turn me back into a frightened child.

'Thanks, Dot,' I said, clambering awkwardly out of the two-door car. 'He scared me, and I didn't know what to do – it was Ellie who suggested calling you. Has he gone?'

Her phone pinged. 'No sign of him as we passed but Ellie just emailed me his picture,' she said as we went in the garden door, unseen from the street. 'Don't be too worried – a professional would have taken a lot more trouble to blend in, and you'd never have spotted the tail. Given your situation, maybe I'll ask a contact to check him out for me.'

'My situation?' I asked.

'Henry has already threatened to get you sent back to prison,' she said. 'Let's take the cautious approach. Of course, you might not have been the object of his interest – perhaps he has a thing for vicars?'

'No, I was definitely the target; he called me by name, or at least my old one,' I told her.

This encounter left me on high alert, tense and nervous with a degree of vigilance which had me suspecting every random stranger in the street. When I saw Henry outside a shop, I almost had a heart attack and my mouth went dry, but then the man turned and my breath whooshed out of my body with relief. Why would he even bother, of course it wasn't him, but it *might* have been. My imagination was supplying monsters round every corner ready to jump out at me. I stayed at home more and didn't even take my usual walks on the beach, but by Saturday morning there'd been no further sightings of the man who'd followed me, giving rise to hope that it had just been a passing encounter.

I was engaged in the therapeutic labour of sanding down the battered table when a text came from Auntie Dot saying: *Fancy an early lunch? Come down.*

With Sal's permission, the table was receiving a similar makeover to the rocking chair, now standing by the window with one of my cushions on it. My room had got a little bit dusty from the sandpapering, so I was glad to change my clothes and go downstairs to Dot's flat.

Her day's attire consisted of a chestnut bob wig, with Lennon-style gold-rimmed glasses.

'I've been into Lytham this morning and bought bagels, cream cheese and smoked salmon; far too much for just me.'

If part of me suspected she'd bought extra on purpose, I didn't mention it. Dot's kindness could be an embarrassment, meaning she sometimes brought me things she'd happened to "find". I'd stopped telling her about hunting for a particular item in case she produced one.

'God, this salmon is to die for,' I said, the flavour subtle and smoky with a silky texture.

'Fabulous, isn't it? Proper freshly made bagels too; the supermarket ones are like bricks. And full-fat cream cheese; I can't be doing with the skinny stuff.'

Once we'd seen off the bagels, Dot made us coffee, saying, 'I've been softening you up because I have a favour to ask before I deliver the good and bad news.'

'After that gorgeous food, your wish is my command,' I told her.

'I was hoping you'd say that because I've had a distress call from the vicar. One Saturday afternoon a month St Aidan's hosts the emergency food bank, as well as their regular weekly slot, and two of her most faithful helpers have gone to Tenerife on holiday. She needs volunteers to cover their absence, so I said we'd come.'

'Ah, you're press-ganging me,' I said.

'I knew you'd say yes,' Dot told me, mischief in her face.

'OK, so let's have the rest.'

'The good news is the man who followed you isn't a sinister hitman or anything.'

My jaw dropped. 'If you believe Henry might... well, he just *wouldn't*.'

Dot's eyes were unflinching. 'You don't know that, and he must have a lot at stake, why else bother to threaten you? Anyway, you're already well aware of how far he will go if pushed.'

An accurate statement, unfortunately. 'And the bad news?'

'Your stalker is a freelance reporter, almost certainly sniffing out a story about your "fall from grace" or something of the sort. The tabloids would lap up such stuff.'

My brain instantly supplied the headlines: "Former socialite broke and working as cleaner". Nice. Or maybe: "Minister's wife hits the skids".

'Oh God, I'll have to move away, won't I?'

It was unexpected to feel heartbroken at the prospect of losing something I'd only ever seen as short-term until I could get back to London life. Now there were friends in the north to leave behind, and a place which had woven strands of connection into my heart.

'No, Frankie, moving will *not* be necessary,' said Dot, leaning forward to take my hands, which I hadn't even realised were trembling. 'There's no point in running away, it would be much too easy to find you again and repeat the cycle. Nor can you hide out here at Sea View the way you've been doing all week.'

'Then what? My options appear to be limited,' I said, feeling like a cornered animal and with a strong preference for skulking in my den.

'Maybe your reporter would prefer to investigate Henry's sexual proclivities? It might well be a much better story, and my sources say he continues to indulge in "risky behaviour".'

'Bloody hell, Dot, how come you're well connected enough to be able to identify people *and* pick up Westminster gossip? Were you a spy or something?'

Dot chuckled. 'Don't be silly, you've been watching too many movies. I was only a faceless civil servant behind a desk, but I do *know* people, some of whom owe me favours.'

'And you're seriously suggesting I should try to find this reporter and offer him a better deal than investigating boring old me?'

'Something along those lines, yes. Instead of hiding and living in fear of exposure, confront trouble head on and see if you can change the narrative. It's not as if "ex-con becomes cleaner" is much of a story.'

'Dot, I'm not as brave as you,' I told her. 'What if it all went tits up and I got splashed across the tabloids?'

Her steady gaze met mine. 'I've told you before, bravery has nothing to do with not being scared. The worst-case scenario is you'd be a minor story for a day or two until some other poor sod slips up and takes your place as the latest headline. Better to take the risk and brazen it out than to live on the margins, always looking over your shoulder.'

Such an existence sounded awful. There and then I decided Frankie Douglas would *not* allow herself to be intimidated. I'd done my absolute best to let anger and bitterness go, but that was before Henry's threats. If he wanted to play nasty then, fair enough, so could I.

Dot's eyes sparkled as she saw my body language change, and I sat up straight.

'Good girl. We'll track down the reporter's email and offer him a meeting, but in the meantime there's a food bank needing our help.'

SEVEN

We set off across the road to the church hall, where Dot was immediately put on tea-making duty. I'd sort of expected the food bank to be something resembling a London soup kitchen, with a queue of down-and-outs, so I'd put a scarf over my hair in case of nits. Within a few minutes of arrival, I was flushed with shame at my ignorance. For a start, the volunteers were indistinguishable from customers, except some wore tabards saying "Laneways Trust Food Bank". I'd heard of it as a national charity which also advocated for people in need and lobbied to raise awareness, but this constituted the limit of my knowledge.

'Hi, you must be Frankie, thank you for coming,' said a rotund man with a bushy red beard and a clipboard. 'I'm Steven, in charge of the operation here.' He waved towards a row of trestle tables at the back of the hall. 'Pre-packed carrier bags of food over there, the contents are designed to last one person three days. For a bigger household, we give out more bags.'

The central space had been set out in much the same way as for the coffee morning I'd rudely interrupted, with small tables and chairs where people could sit and have a hot drink.

'This is the emergency operation,' said Steven, 'separate from our regular weekly sessions. Fresh stuff over there,' he said, pointing to another table with an assortment of fruit and vegetables. 'As well as donations from the public we can also collect whatever the supermarkets have left, which they send to a central warehouse. We even have sandwiches today but it's unpredictable what we'll get – anything from canned goods, or a sack of spuds, to a crate of oranges and so on. Can I leave you at the fresh food station? Brown paper bags there at the end, clients are welcome to take whatever they can use, otherwise it only goes to waste.'

He was prepared to let me get on with it but must have clocked a doubtful expression on my face. 'Ah, you haven't done this before. Look, these are *people* who've come here for our help. No judgement, no questions. Gillian on the door sorts out vouchers and so on, but we don't turn anybody away, even without one. If somebody needs to chat, steer them towards Andrew over there. Listening is one of the most important parts of our work.'

Standing behind the vegetable station, the voices of Henry's closest friends and political partners kept intruding into my brain, and memories of a dinner party at which the subject of food banks had come up.

Gus, Henry's immediate superior in the ministry, had expressed his unshakeable opinion.

'Food banks are unnecessary because the government safety net provides all the support needed. End of story.'

He'd had no apparent sense of irony that the mahogany dinner table in front of us was groaning with rich food, and Gus himself sported a generous paunch. His then wife, Cordelia, repeated the mantra I'd heard so many times.

'People who can't manage are just smoking and drinking their benefits away. We all know the type: druggies, single mothers, the feckless and workshy. I've heard that many of them are even fraudsters "on the take" with hundreds of fake claim accounts.'

Life in a smart London suburb had been no preparation for questioning the truth of this, but now I was squirming and looked around the hall with fresh eyes. If it hadn't been for Sal's offer of a rent-free room, and the job Buster had found, I might have been in the same place of need as many of the day's customers.

'How about some grapes?' I asked an elderly man in a mac who wandered past the table. 'They're seedless.'

'Nah, love, they give me the wild shites, but thanks anyway. Mebbe some of them spuds though, I can do chips or mash then, and I'll take a few bananas to put on me cereal.'

I loaded these into his wheeled shopping trolley, but he wandered off before I could suggest anything else. Must try harder. Clients came through the door in a steady stream and the next hour went by in a blur serving people, though the broccoli I tried to give away wasn't popular, nor the lumpy lemons. My role was a simple one, providing a friendly smile and basic assistance, so I muddled through without much further embarrassment. During a lull, Dot brought me a mug of the revolting church-hall instant coffee; once again the powdered kind which smells and tastes like you imagine acorns might.

'Best I can do,' Dot said with real sympathy. 'The tea's probably better but you don't drink it.'

'I'm trying to be grateful,' I said, sipping the dubious brown liquid.

'Let me know how that goes.' Dot waved goodbye and headed back to her tea urn.

A young woman with a sleeping baby strapped to her chest pushed a small pram towards my table.

'Oh, fresh stuff, thank God,' she said. 'I'm feeding this one so it's a worry getting enough vitamins to sustain my milk supply. I haven't seen you here before.'

'I'm new,' I said, noting how bony her wrists were. 'Helping out while someone's on holiday. Can you manage to carry everything as well as the baby?'

'It'll be OK. I put her in the sling and the shopping in the pram. It's not far to walk. I'll have to figure something else out when she gets bigger though. This place has been a total lifesaver since my partner left us. I'm on maternity leave but it's a massive struggle to pay the mortgage on my own without his income coming in.'

I filled the pram body with as much helpful nutrition as I could find but looked up to see silent tears falling down her face.

'Don't cry, it's not your fault,' I said, coming around to the front of the table. She wept even more, and I mentally kicked myself for such trite platitudes. There were only a few people around by then and no sign of Andrew, so I steered her across to a table.

'I don't recommend the coffee but let me get you a cup of tea. What's your name?'

'I'm Emma. Sorry… I'm a bit down right now. Can't access legal aid to make Nolan pay child support – apparently my maternity pay from school is too much.'

'You're a teacher?' Another stupid remark. Why should I be surprised? Professional people weren't immune from life's difficulties.

'Yes, then this one came along by accident and Nolan was none too pleased about it. He left us because of her crying at night, and me trying to get her nappies dry all over the house. I wanted to be green and use cloth ones and it's a good job I did. Disposables are so expensive now and I daren't put the tumble drier on because of the electric bills. Sorry, it's all… getting me down.'

Andrew reappeared and came over, saying, 'Emma, lovely to see you. Is everything all right?'

I fetched tea for them both, before going back to my table and trying to give away the remaining overripe bananas and knobbly lemons. I covertly watched Andrew with Emma, as he made her smile and organised someone to take the baby while she drank her tea. Despite the steep learning curve of prison, I was painfully aware of having been a privileged middle-class woman with little understanding of the realities of some people's lives. Shame settled in my stomach and made my face hot.

A dark very tall man strode in through the door, greeted by the volunteers with waves and calls of "Hi, Nik!".

'Good, you've managed OK then?' he said to Steven.

'Ellie rounded up some extra hands.'

Tidying up the remaining contents of my table, I spotted Nik heading towards me. He wore a Laneways Trust badge, proclaiming him to be northern regional manager. Up close, he was well over six foot and broad like a rugby player, with olive skin and a beard liberally sprinkled with grey.

'I'm Nikolaos Vassos. Thanks for coming today,' he said abruptly, his attention elsewhere. 'If you're not busy they could use some help out at the back.' His name explained the dark colouring.

Wanting to be useful, I obeyed his instructions and headed off to a large room behind the kitchen. It was immediately obvious that this was the command module of the food bank. Floor-to-ceiling warehouse-style shelving crammed with tins and packets, cereal, boxes of tea bags, pasta and jars of sauce, everything non-perishable. Another set of shelves held a row of the ready-packed brown paper carrier bags I'd seen earlier.

Steven beckoned me over to stack tins on the shelf and called out to Gillian, who'd left her post by the door to wield a clipboard and pen.

'Plenty of baked beans and tinned fruit,' he told her. 'But we're almost out of tampons and sanitary towels, toddler-sized nappies too. Better track some down before next Thursday's session.'

I carried on unpacking tins of meatballs but, prompted by an urgent sense of wanting, *needing* to contribute and make a difference, said to Steven, 'Is that your regular food bank day?'

'Yes, I forgot you were new,' he said, counting boxes of cereal. 'Various local churches take turns through the week, and we do Thursday afternoons. These emergency weekend sessions are done in rotation, so it usually falls to us about once a month. Gillian, we could do with some deodorant as well.'

'Do you need more volunteers?' I asked.

'Plenty of hands, usually; people are so good, but we're in desperate need of someone who understands the benefits system and can give advice.' I saw doubt in his face, and he was right; not my area of expertise and we both recognised it.

Taking a deep breath, I said, 'I can learn, and I want to help. What would I need to do?'

'Try and catch Nik before he leaves then. There's some kind of training involved if you're serious about it – I'll get on and finish this.'

Back in the hall, the regional manager was saying goodbye to someone, and impatient to be gone. I didn't want to let him get away so dived right in.

'Steven says they need a benefits adviser, and there's training for the job. I could do it.'

A pause. 'Why?' he asked bluntly. Given my accent, he must have had me down as a posh do-gooder with little to no experience of the real world. A fair assessment.

'Because I know what it's like to lose everything and have nothing.'

'Do you indeed?' I had his attention now, and this time he studied me properly.

'I went to prison, for arson, got out in February. Would that matter?'

'You're still on licence then? Maybe not, particularly if I could have a chat with your probation officer. Would you give consent for me to do so?'

'Absolutely,' I said, only too aware Nik wasn't 100% convinced. 'I have a degree in linguistics and did some literacy teaching in prison. It means a lot to be able to make a difference, and anyway, it beats the hell out of brooding and plotting a hideous revenge on my lying husband.'

'OK, full disclosure, I had you wrong – shouldn't jump to conclusions.'

'I do it all the time, but am working on breaking the habit,' I told him.

'Come out to the car,' he said, 'I've got a folder of info. Are you working?'

I put my chin up. 'Two shifts a day through the week; cleaning offices and a school.'

'OK so you wouldn't have time for the full benefits advice training; that's an intensive month-long course and it's mostly retired people who can tackle it.'

He led me to a battered Volvo estate with one wing mirror held on with duct tape. Opening the back revealed an organised chaos of cardboard boxes containing various supplies and plastic crates used as file containers. After rummaging through these, he came up with a ring binder.

'Compromise solution which might work,' he said. 'If you did level one of the benefits training, you could help people with filling in forms or writing job applications, yes?'

'It's a variation of what I did in prison.'

'OK then, have a quick skim of this material which is the basics of how the benefits system works and the application processes. Assuming it's not too daunting, get in touch with me if you want to proceed. My contact details are on the first page, along with our website address. Right, must dash.'

Standing in the car park clutching the ring binder, a bubble of excitement rose in my chest at the thought of being able to make a difference. I still desperately wanted my lost London life: theatres, exhibitions and lunches, but it didn't take a genius to realise that it might take years to fulfil this ambition. At least I could give something back in the meantime.

Dot came out of the hall clutching some of the knobbly lemons. 'Ready for home? I've got a plan involving these and a bottle of gin.'

A couple of Dot's stiff predinner gins meant studying the Laneways Trust folder of information had to wait. Sal's fish and chips (decorated with wedges of lemon also courtesy of the food bank leftovers) soaked up some of the alcohol, but I was a bit foggy around the edges.

Over dinner, Sal and Buster wanted to hear all about our afternoon. Too ashamed to admit how wrong my initial assumptions had been, I described the modest part I'd played. Buster's brows went up when she heard about the training module.

'Well, good for you,' she said. 'We need someone to do similar work in the law centre, but there's no funding for such a post right now, and you won't have time for any more volunteering if you take this on.'

Sal encouraged me too, saying, 'You'll be proper good at it, Frankie. You were always so patient with people at Enderton and let them go at their own pace.'

'Which didn't come naturally,' I told her, savouring the

haddock wrapped in wondrously light and crunchy batter. 'I had to work at it, *learn* to take it slow and not patronise anybody, so don't go making me out to be some kind of saint.'

The corners of Dot's mouth twitched at this; she already knew me too well.

*

My lack of saintliness received further confirmation when during the evening another email arrived from Justin. Dad and I appeared to be on a break.

> *Hi, Mum, or should I call you Mrs Mop?*
>
> *Bloody desperate to get a place of my own – it's hideous here. Jerry and Dad are arguing all the time, and now nothing gets done. No food in the fridge or clean sheets. When I ask about it, they both say "do it yourself" so I end up eating beans in my room while they yell at each other downstairs.*
>
> *Wish you were here.*
>
> *J.*

I contemplated the wisdom of sending a response. Some carefully chosen words did appear to be called for, but I didn't want to damage our newly restored relationship with too much tough love. Being full of gin might have tipped the balance.

> *Hi Justin,*
>
> *Lovely to hear from you, but if you're serious about making a life of your own maybe it's time to give up the internship and get a proper job with an actual salary. You had to do the laundry and cooking at university, so*

these are useful life skills for the day you can get your own place, right?

Love Mum X

PS Yes, I clean offices. Somebody cleans yours.

Consulting Spike about the wisdom of giving my son this dose of common sense, he offered no help at all, only rolling over to have his pale gold tummy tickled. I pressed send anyway.

In the morning, I went downstairs for my regular coffee date with Dot.

'No sign of the reporter following you again?' she asked.

'No, but I'm still jumpy whenever I go out. You were so right that I needed to wrest back control of the situation or spend my life on the run from such people.'

'A brave resolution,' observed Dot.

Yeah, except in the small hours of the night when the demons of doubt and fear tormented me all over again.

According to Dot, it had been easy to get the reporter's email address.

'Freelancers are on a register,' she told me while we drank our coffee, a new blend the Lytham deli was offering. 'Kim Williams used to be a staffer at various big-name newspapers and has a string of international credits to his name.'

'So why the hell is he bothering with small fry such as me?' The coffee was delicious, with smoky notes and complex layers of flavour.

'He's Manchester-based now, lives with his boyfriend, which must have made it easy to come up to St Annes once he found out where you were.'

'But, Dot, it's scary that he was able to track me down so easily. Neither the prison nor the probation service would give out personal information. I'm not on any kind of professional editing register, *and* I went back to using my maiden name.'

Auntie Dot snorted and shot me a look that said such blindingly obvious ploys were unworthy of consideration. She munched a slice of the Battenburg cake I'd brought as a contribution; one of her favourites, although such a category would have to include cake in all its forms and infinite variety. How she remained such a skinny little bird mystified me.

'There are any number of ways to track someone down,' she told me. 'Not all of them legal, but such technicalities never stopped anyone determined to find out, and the tabloids have historically been more than willing to break the law. An obvious way is social media, which you don't use, but your National Insurance number will do it every time. That might be how he found you, though it wouldn't explain why he needed to follow you home. Maybe he wanted to make a more personal approach.'

'And scare the shit out of me in the process? So, all the hiding in the church hall and the back of your car was unnecessary?' I said, feeling like a complete fool. 'OK then, we'll do it your way and I'll be proactive and make contact with him.'

After dismissing several drafts of my email to Kim Williams, Dot's advice was to keep it brief and to the point, with just enough to intrigue him. In the end, we came up with a simple message.

Dear Kim,

I know who you are and why you've been following me. If you want to talk, I will be at the Houghton Street coffee shop, Hot Beans, in St Annes at 2.00pm on Wednesday of next week. This is a one-time offer, take it or leave it.

Francesca Douglas nee Wilton

'That should do it,' said Dot with satisfaction. 'If he's interested enough to come searching for you, it's an offer he can't refuse. By the way, did I mention he's transgender and used to be Kimberley? Not relevant or anything, obviously.'

It wasn't but did give me hope my reporter might be a sensitive person. Someone who'd made such a painful and difficult journey must have had experience of feeling excluded or judged, and any big city held its share of bigots and haters. If this was going to work, I needed him to have some sympathy or kindness for my outcast status because the alternative of telling him to "publish and be damned" remained an unattractive option.

EIGHT

I passed the coffee shop where I'd chosen to meet Kim Williams every day, on my way to and from the office cleaning. Its continental vibe had always attracted me but being frugal with my limited earnings, I'd never ventured inside. I only ever drank good coffee as a treat via Auntie Dot or the occasional brew in my little drip machine. For this make-or-break meeting, no expense would be spared since I planned on making the reporter pick up the bill.

I spotted him immediately seated in a booth at the back, and he waved an acknowledgement. My stomach lurched and a cold chill of fear touched my skin. Taking a deep breath, I marched towards the table with all the fake bravado I could muster. A noisy machine made a terrible racket as it set to grinding coffee, the resultant aroma instantly making my mouth water. A glass cabinet displayed an array of cakes and luscious continental pastries.

Sitting down on the faux-leather banquette, I gave him a hard stare. The effect was somewhat wasted because the machine was still going, but when it finally stopped, I said, 'I'll have a large Americano, Java roast if they have it.'

I studied him as he joined the queue at the counter. Tall

and boyish-looking, but older than I'd expected, going by the lines around his eyes. Probably late thirties, with floppy blond hair slicked back from his forehead in a stylish quiff. The chunky tortoiseshell glasses and tan brogues were part of a metropolitan style only seen in big cities, and occasionally in upmarket Lytham down the road.

He fetched the coffee and brought chocolate caramel brownies too. I'd intended to come across as crisp and efficient rather than hostile, but I was prickling with nervous tension which must have been radiating from me like heat. Dot's voice in my head kept reminding me I'd *asked* for this meeting and remained in charge of how it went.

Before my veneer of confidence could fail, I said, 'So I'm guessing you were planning some kind of "fall from grace" story? Cabinet minister's wife reduced to wielding a mop?'

Kim flushed; not quite the hard-bitten reporter I'd been expecting then.

'Perhaps something a *little* less obvious,' he said, stirring brown sugar into his coffee. 'More about the emotional cost of going to prison, and what it takes to rebuild yourself afterwards. My track record isn't in tabloid journalism, it's more political, or was.'

'Because?' I asked.

'Since going freelance it's not always possible to pick and choose projects the way a London staff reporter can, which is what I used to be.'

Against logic all my instincts told me I could trust this guy; plain crazy given my track record of being judgemental. I'd been wrong about enough people in the past to be wary in the extreme of this one.

'Did you go freelance because of your gender reassignment?'

I hadn't intended this to be an attack, only a question, but it came out as one.

He met my eyes without reserve. 'You did your homework. And yes. I'm based in Manchester now – my partner and I have a flat in Salford Quays. We chose to start all over again somewhere else; guess you did too.'

'Hardly the same!' I was indignant. 'Prison wasn't exactly a choice and the only reason I'm in St Annes is down to the kindness of a friend who happened to live here. Plus, my home is a rented bedsit while yours is probably an upmarket apartment.'

Kim paused for a draught of coffee; he had nice hands and took care of his fingernails.

'The sale of our two London properties bought us a very nice place up north, yes. Mrs Wilton, I'm not out to get you and a lurid exposé piece isn't who I am. Can you please believe that?'

'It's Frankie Douglas now. Look, give me one reason why I should trust you. If you write about me then the life I've begun to build here will fall apart, and the resulting notoriety could force me to move. If you were offering me megabucks for a juicy tell-all story it might at least provide the money to start over somewhere else. Otherwise, I'll be honest and say my preference is for you to piss off and leave me alone.'

Kim leant forward, hands cradling the circular bowl of his white coffee cup.

'Full disclosure then. No megabucks, though maybe a small fee. I wanted to write about what happened to you because it intrigued me – I imagined something thought-provoking with a serious point. It would deal with your experiences of prison, then being released and trying to build a new life on the margins when you aren't used to it. A genuine human-interest piece with some depth, maybe for the weekend magazine supplements? You look different now, and we could stick to using your married name and photos from earlier if you choose. I'm talking quality newspapers, not the trashy ones. It would give you a voice.'

I went hot all over with a molten rage born of years of simmering fury at the injustice I'd suffered. Now it overflowed like lava, and I slapped my hand down on the table hard enough to make the liquid in our cups jump. The other patrons in the coffee shop shot us curious glances, probably assuming some kind of relationship disharmony. My hand hurt.

'What kind of knobhead would I have to be to help you with this?' I hissed across the table. 'There is absolutely nothing in it for me except the destruction of the very small foothold gained in the short time I've been here, and the few friendships I've managed to make.'

Dot's voice came back into my head, telling me not to lie down under the almost inevitable, but fight back with everything I'd got.

I took some deep breaths and forced myself to calm down and speak clearly.

'Allow me to offer a suggestion,' I said, leaning back. 'Something which might be a better story, even if it is more in the realms of the lurid expose you said you weren't interested in. But the price for this information is that the source must remain anonymous, and you leave my personal life alone.'

Kim took off the tortoiseshell glasses. He looked younger without them; perhaps they'd been chosen to add gravitas.

'Try me,' he invited. 'I'm listening.'

'You're a political journalist at heart, so how about a story from inside Westminster? It's sleazy stuff, the tabloids would be interested as well as the serious papers, and it has the potential to cause damage to the government.'

'I'm no fan of the current regime. This is something to do with Henry?'

I nodded. 'But here's my problem. What's to stop you

simply taking my information about him, and writing *both* stories? Then I'd be even worse off.'

Kim fiddled with his empty coffee cup. 'How can I demonstrate my good faith here – a refill?'

He went back to the counter while I picked up my brownie with trembling hands, all too conscious that whatever Dot said, I *was* powerless in this situation. My only option was to take a risk and trust this man, which might turn out to be a self-destructive act. Whether I cooperated on the story or not, he could snap sneaky pictures of me in my cleaning tabard and then make out of it the sort of tabloid piece I most feared. There didn't appear to be any safe way forward and when he brought the coffee, I was leaning more towards the option of running away than working out a deal.

'I have no idea what to do,' I told him truthfully. 'There's no reason to trust you, but then again what choice do I have?'

'You *can* trust me,' said Kim, 'but I can't see a way to prove it to you. Would money help?'

Even worse, cheapening and degrading to the point where it was my turn to blush. But then how did I expect to feel, selling Henry's nasty little secrets for thirty pieces of silver? When I'd imagined horrible consequences for him it hadn't been like this.

'There's no need for you to be embarrassed,' Kim told me. 'This would be a simple transaction in which I pay you for information, cash, off the record. No offence, but I'm guessing you could do with the extra?'

'I'm not ashamed to admit that I need money,' I said through gritted teeth. 'But I don't have to feel comfortable accepting it. You probably think this is all about revenge.'

'Is it?'

'If I'm honest, yes. Henry *lied*, Kim, not only in the court case but about everything over twenty years. Our whole marriage turned out to be a sham – he didn't care about me or truly want our little boy. We were window-dressing to provide a respectable cover for his secret life. Like a fool, I kept believing for a long time he loved me, us. It took years to understand and accept what might be going on, and when I did… well, devastated would hardly cover it.'

At the time, I'd thought I could never get over it, regularly crying myself to sleep, appalled at my naivete. I even slept in Justin's bottom bunk for a time, claiming he was having nightmares that might disturb Henry.

Kim's face softened and his eyes were kind. 'Even twenty years ago, Henry couldn't have been out and proud if he wanted a political career. Now things are different and he has it all: his agent and live-in lover – fiancé now, I believe – and even public sympathy as a wronged man because you tried to take revenge and burn down the house with him in it. No surprise if you feel bitter.'

'Yeah, well two years in jail will do that to you. I do try not to be because I know very well that hate is corrosive but…'

Kim's response was brutal but honest. 'If he lied about the fire then he betrayed you in the worst possible way, at every level. Could you see our arrangement as justice rather than revenge? I'm guessing the information you are offering is nothing to do with Henry's relationship with his agent?'

I still hadn't decided whether to risk trusting Kim. 'Why would anyone care about such things now? But if I said it involves rent boys and a private club for sadists, many of whose members are high-up government officials and civil servants, would I have your attention?'

Kim frowned, pausing to consider his response. 'People can brazen such things out these days. There'd be plenty of voices to say a person's private sexual proclivities have nothing to do with their professional competence. It's not entirely true in practice, as I found out, but…'

The message on my phone had said "keep your mouth shut", but why should I?

'I found some photographs on Henry's laptop – one picture involved whipping and a young victim with his back streaming with blood. They were revolting, made me feel sick, and I've done my absolute best to forget them but can't.'

Kim's expression changed. 'Awful stuff and possibly illegal. There's a question of consent.'

'Some of the boys looked Filipino, Asian certainly, and could have been trafficked and most of them looked quite young, though I suppose they *might* have been over sixteen.'

'You've got my attention. Powerful men abusing their wealth and position is as old as the hills, but hurting underage kids is always plain fucking wrong. Can you prove it?'

'No, but I can provide information which might lead you to the evidence. Someone somewhere is bound to talk. The photographs were horrible, torture scenes; those images burnt into my brain… the faces. I'll never forget seeing them. Henry had a password for his laptop, but I guessed it easily. Those pictures won't be accessible now, he'll have covered his tracks.'

'I can think of at least one editor who would go for this.' Kim's eyes went far away as he came suddenly alert to the possibilities. 'He might even be willing to stump up serious money if we can pin the story down.'

Nauseated by the whole sordid business, bile rose in my throat.

'I have to go to work now, but I'll find a way to send you the information in an email no one can trace back to its origins. A friend of mine has the necessary expertise. An assurance you won't be pursuing the story about me is something I'll have to take on trust.'

As I got to my feet, Kim also stood up and put out a hand to shake mine. 'I won't let you down, Frankie, and you're doing the right thing. If any of the boys in those pictures were as young as you fear, then what Henry is involved in constitutes child abuse and possibly human trafficking. At a minimum, they're exploiting vulnerable young adults, and none of them should be allowed to get away with it.'

I managed to mutter agreement, before fleeing out of the door and heading towards my school shift on a caffeinated rush. Kim had spoken the truth; Henry and his cohort had to be stopped, so why did *I* feel like the bad person, dishing the dirt on the man I'd once genuinely loved? Maybe because two wrongs don't make a right or some such adage?

*

Unpacking our cleaning equipment from the cupboard, the school, as ever, smelled of sweat and unwashed PE kit. Doreen and Shannon kept asking me questions.

'You look bloody shattered, kid; been out on the razzle?'

In other circumstances this might even have been funny.

'I wish. Didn't sleep well, stuff on my mind,' I told them.

This wasn't fooling either of them. 'If you need to rest, we've got this,' said Doreen.

That would mean both women working extra unpaid time to get done, and I couldn't allow them to do it.

'It'll be fine, maybe I can even work off some of what I'm feeling,' I said. 'But thanks for the offer – you guys are the best.'

They were too. As a cleaning crew, we were pretty much invisible to most of the population, who never gave a moment's thought to the anonymous people who picked up their crap. Not only were we unseen, underpaid and unappreciated, but Doreen and Shannon were and are some of the best, bravest women it has ever been my privilege to meet.

Back at Sea View, I couldn't face food, not even Sal's shepherd's pie – a touch of curry powder was her magic ingredient. I claimed not to be hungry, maybe coming down with a bug, which didn't fool anybody.

'Someone came asking for you earlier,' Buster called after me as I headed towards the stairs. 'Big muscle-bound type in a leather jacket. I said no one called Francesca Wilton lived here, perfectly true since you use your maiden name now. Doubt he believed a word of it. Oh, and there's an envelope on the hall table addressed to you as well. Hand-delivered, not sure when, or even if it was the same bloke.'

I grabbed it before heading upstairs, where I opened the window to let some of the mild April air in and rid myself of the stench of corruption. I couldn't shake the feeling I'd done something wrong, and it didn't help when the manila envelope contained £200 in crisp new notes straight out of the ATM and a message from Kim.

A gesture of good faith. K

So, Dot had been right, and he'd known my address all along. At first, I felt even more contaminated, but without a newspaper backing the story, it had to be his own money. He'd offered it in trust that my information would be good; nobody would pay a freelance for a piece until after delivery. A long soak in the bath with sandalwood-scented bubbles (one of Dot's little gifts) soothed my bruised spirit and, to a small degree, my conscience.

Tucked under my quilt with the laptop, I began drafting an outline of everything I could recall for Kim, naming the people where I could and bringing to the surface things I didn't much want to remember. When I was done, it left me feeling sick and angry, but I was defending my little life with everything I had. Henry *deserved* to get pushed under a bus.

I slipped a note under Angus's door, enquiring how to

email information without it being traceable back to me and offering to pay for his help. The money would come from Kim's down payment.

Back from the next day's morning shift, he'd left me a reply.

No charge for helping friends. You clean the bathroom, so Sal doesn't give me grief for not doing it. I notice stuff like that. You're a mate. A.

When I'd first arrived, Sal had a conversation with Angus on the landing which I couldn't help but overhear.

'Angus you have to share the bathroom now, so you need to keep it tidy and not leave wet towels about or skid marks in the toilet pan.'

Angus had muttered agreement, but I figured he had enough challenges managing his daily life already and took it upon myself to clean the bathroom and wash his towels with my own. I was surprised and pleased that he'd noticed.

This reminded me that I had a bag of dirty clothes needing attention, so I set off towards the laundrette with a book tucked into my rucksack. The machines took ages, but it was cheaper to do it myself than pay for a service wash. The place smelled distinctively of hot lint and stale cigarettes but nobody was around, and I could read in peace.

On the way back, lugging the awkward bag of clean laundry, I took my usual shortcut and turned into an alleyway between shops. Out of nowhere, a man cannoned into me, punching the breath from my body, and slamming my head against the brick wall. A meaty hand came over my mouth and his unshaven, stubbly face pressed up close against mine.

'Don't say a fucking word,' he hissed. 'Listen good.'

My ears were ringing, and I didn't have enough breath left to speak anyway, struggling for air, my mouth and nose all but blocked.

'Message from your ex. Don't go talking to *anybody*. You got it, bitch?'

I tried desperately to suck air into my lungs around the thick fingers clamped against my face.

'This is a reminder that he can get you sent back to prison if you step out of line, so if the papers come calling, you have nothing to say. Right?'

He relaxed his grip briefly, then leaned forward and headbutted me. The force behind it whipped my body back against the wall. Rebounding off the brick sent me sprawling onto the pavement alongside the washing. The zip on the cheap striped laundry bag broke, and some of my clean clothes spilt out. In a daze with my ears ringing, I tried to pick up whatever I could reach before they got dirty all over again. My assailant had already disappeared around the corner when a girl bent down beside me to help.

'You all right, love? Bastard mugger. Did he get your phone?'

I shook my head. It hurt.

'Everything happened so fast...' I managed.

'Me and Daniel came around the corner as he headbutted you, but now he's legged it. No, don't get up yet. I'm Shelley, only a student nurse, but even I can diagnose that your brow and cheekbone are gonna be massively bruised, maybe even a black eye. You'll be dizzy, so take your time before you try to stand up.'

A male voice above me said, 'I got his picture, snapped him on my phone. It's not great but...'

'Well done, Dan,' said Shelley, taking his phone to show me the image. 'Do you recognise him, love?'

I shook my head again; more pain, must stop doing that. The impact had apparently knocked all my teeth loose.

'No, total stranger. Not a mugger – delivering a message,' I told them.

Something warm trickled down my face and when I put my hand up it came away smeared with blood.

'There's a cut above your eyebrow, but it's not deep. Shouldn't need stitches,' said the girl.

Using the wall for support, I struggled to get to my feet. The young man had to hold me up since my legs had become unaccountably boneless. Lurching sideways, without his support I'd have fallen again. The back of my head also hurt where it had been slammed back. I blinked, my vision blurring in and out, fighting nausea.

'Steady on,' he said. 'Do you live local?'

'Over the bridge – I can walk from here.'

'No way,' said the girl. 'By rights, we should be calling an ambulance, but they'll only take hours to come. Dan, get the laundry bag, there's a love. Now lean on me, sweetheart, and we'll soon have you home.'

'It's so good of you to help…'

'Not gonna run off and leave you in this state, are we?' said Dan.

With the two of them in support on either side, I tottered the short distance home to Sea View. It began to feel like miles, and my legs didn't want to carry me. If the two youngsters hadn't been there, I might not have made it, but my head had cleared a little by the time we arrived. By then, I possessed sufficient lucidity to say to Dan, 'The picture – can you share it with me?'

'Good idea', he said. 'Show it to the police.'

Sitting on the low wall outside Sea View, we managed to transfer the image from his phone. I thanked them both profusely, but they insisted on seeing me safely down the area steps to the basement flat before striding off with a cheery wave.

Sal answered the door wearing an apron and with a ladle in

her hand. Her expression changed to one of horror as I all but fell inside before the strong arms caught me.

'Frankie, what the hell happened to you?'

NINE

Shock and relief at getting home had turned my legs to jelly again. Sal's strong body provided support as she steered me across the room until I collapsed onto the sofa. The blood from the cut had trickled into my eye, and I could hardly see. She looked at me with doubt and worry in her eyes, then set to mopping up my brow with a tea towel.

'Don't worry, it's a clean one fresh out of the drawer. Stay there and don't bloody *move*, while I get the first-aid stuff,' she commanded.

Even sitting down, I had the weird sensation of everything happening in a kind of slow motion with a buzzing in my ears.

Returning with a Charles and Diana biscuit tin, Sal took one look and said, 'Oh God, don't faint on me, Frankie. You've gone white as Queen Victoria's knickers.'

'I'm OK; bit dizzy for a moment.' Her concerned face came back into focus.

'But who did this? Thank God you made it home, I've only been here a few minutes myself.' Sal pressed me back against the cushions before pouring warm water into a bowl. The tang of antiseptic filled my nose; always such a comforting smell, redolent of childhood and nuns sorting out grazed knees and elbows.

While she gently cleaned off the blood and had a close look at the damage underneath, I managed to provide a brief outline of events in the alley.

'Not a random mugger. Delivering a message from Henry,' I said, flinching as she dabbed at my face with cotton wool.

Sal let rip with some very rude words concerning my estranged husband. I agreed with all of them.

Her extensive vocabulary of profanity finally exhausted, she finished her handiwork and stood back. 'Not quite as bad as I feared,' came the verdict. 'Your face is a mess and you're going to have a proper shiner, but you'll soon mend. There's a big egg of a lump on the back of your head. Keep the damp tea towel on it. Are you hurt anywhere else? Mebbe we should take you to hospital?'

'No, I need to get ready for work – look at the time.'

Sal looked at me in disbelief. 'You daft cow, don't be so bloody stupid. You're in no fit state to go anywhere today, and probably not tomorrow either.'

'But...' I protested before Sal cut me off. 'Frankie, get a grip, girl. Has the bastard shaken your brains loose as well? You might have concussion and won't be fighting your way out of a paper bag, let alone going to work. Doreen and Shannon will understand.'

'Not concussion, didn't pass out,' I managed, feeling nauseous again. 'Only a bang on the head. I can't let the girls down...'

'Total bollocks. I'm gonna get you up to Dot's flat so she can watch you, then I'll walk over to school and explain to the lasses. They'll have to manage for a couple of days. At least tomorrow's Friday, so you'll have the weekend to recover, but if Dot says you need a hospital you're going and no bloody argument.'

'My washing – the bag, I left it outside.'

'Don't talk, you've gone all pale again – not gonna throw up, are you? Hold this bowl and let's get you upstairs.'

Our journey to Dot's provided all the challenges of climbing Everest, involving as it did two flights of stairs, and without Sal's strength I wouldn't have made it. With a keen sense for when something wasn't right, Dot had heard us coming and stood at her front door as we crested the stairs onto the landing. She heard Sal's brief account without comment as the two of them supported me into her living room. Incapable of doing joined-up thinking or talking, I lay down on the sofa, grateful not to need to stay upright any longer. Dot pulled my trainers off and put some cushions behind my head; I worried about bleeding on them, or anything else. I'd mislaid the tea towel on my way up the stairs.

'Right, I'll get on over to the school now,' said Sal. 'Dinner might end up being a bit late, but nobody will worry.'

Dot knelt on the floor beside me and insisted on inspecting me for signs of concussion. 'Pupils equal and reactive,' she said. 'Follow my finger – OK, good. You've probably got a helluva headache coming but you'll live, and a hospital trip won't be necessary.'

She got up and came back with a generous slug of brandy, pressing a glass of golden liquid into my hand.

'Oh, I'm not sure if…'

'Can you sit up a little? Yes, I know, the usual advice is hot sweet tea for shock but it's horrible stuff and in my experience, this is way better. Get it down you. I'll fetch some Steri-Strips to close that cut.'

I dazedly sipped the complex flavours of the best brandy I'd ever had. None of the harsh edge you usually taste, but a smooth rich nectar which slid down easily and warmed me from the inside.

'God, that's good stuff,' I told her, feeling brighter within minutes.

Auntie Dot smirked in satisfaction as she stuck the strips across my forehead.

'XO Reserve, liquid gold. Bloody expensive but you're worth it. No, don't go to sleep, not the best idea. Tell me everything but keep the cold pad on your eye while you do it.'

Fortified by the brandy, I recounted the story again while Dot listened attentively and asked a few questions.

'Interesting,' she observed. 'Your muscle man said *if* the paparazzi come calling, so this attack didn't come as a response to yesterday's meeting with Kim Williams. Henry must not know about it yet.'

I sipped more brandy while struggling to put the pieces together. 'You're right; those were the exact words he used. Should I go to the police with his photograph?'

She frowned. 'Not sure it will do any good at this stage. They don't have time to follow up on minor assaults.'

'It doesn't feel bloody minor.'

'No, I can see that. Share the picture with me and I'll put my contacts onto it.'

*

Everyone at Sea View was kind and concerned to an almost embarrassing degree. Even Angus glanced at my face briefly when he encountered me on the landing. I was using the wall as support on a necessary trip to the bathroom. Later, he pushed a note under my door with a smiley face and the words, *Get well soon, Frankie.*

I didn't feel up to eating proper food, but Sal produced fragrant bowls of soup and Buster dosed me with homoeopathic arnica for the bruising. Even Spike the cat made a gratifying fuss of me, with frequent visits to my room and bumping his nose into my face before settling and purring on my chest. You don't realise how important a cuddle can be until you don't get any.

I spent Friday and most of Saturday lying on the bed swallowing painkillers for my head and sleeping a lot. In my alert intervals, I managed to add a few more details to the information for Kim, including an account of the muscle man's attack and what he'd said. Kim's involvement might put him in danger too, but at least he'd been warned.

I wrote Angus a note thanking him for his good wishes and saying I'd composed the email I wanted to send, and what now? When I bent down to push it under his door it made my head spin, so I returned in haste to bed.

An hour later his reply came under the door.

Password protect the file with a series of random letters and numbers – more difficult to guess – and then I won't see the contents either. Email the file to me and I'll send it on to your man via a circuitous route. Phone him with the password but block your caller ID; then there's only a record of you making the call, but not of the conversation.

A.

It might have been paranoia on my part, but after the text threat from Henry and his violent messenger, I wanted to take every precaution *nothing* could be traced back to me.

Shannon came round on Sunday morning with a plant in a pot and a card signed by her and Doreen. I'd got dressed but was lying on the bed, having been treated to breakfast on a tray by Sal. On arrival, Shannon unashamedly stared around my cosy room but didn't bother telling me I looked fine.

'Shut the front door!' she told me once she got up close. 'Your face is a God-awful mess.'

'Don't dress it up, will you?' I said, wincing as she plonked herself on the bed, jolting my bruised knee.

She gazed around the room again. 'Not bad for a bedsit. I've seen much worse, and you've got it nice.'

'Listen, I am so sorry about letting you down; I feel terrible about it.'

'Don't be so daft.' She studied my face again. 'Bloody hell, Frankie, what a rotten thing to happen.'

'One of those things,' I said, but Shannon wasn't having it.

'Duh. Nothing to do with your ex-husband then?'

I couldn't lie to her face. 'A mugger is the story for public consumption,' I told her. 'But yes.'

'Whatever; you don't have to tell me unless you want to. Doreen sends her love and says try to duck if there's a next time.'

'There'd better not be,' I said. My brain kept replaying the words "keep your mouth shut". Lying on the bed, I'd decided not to obey this instruction. My missive to Kim would spill every bean I could track down from the recesses of my memory – it was time to fight back, and Henry had it coming.

Shannon frowned at me. 'You look kinda rough so mebbe have a kip. I'm gonna hit the supermarket now but take care of yourself.'

'Thanks, Shannon. I'll see you in the morning.'

'Don't come unless you're OK. Listen to your team leader; I'm responsible for your health and safety.' Then she left and I could hear her stumping back down the stairs.

Thanks to the various ministrations of my friends, I made it back to work after the weekend, meeting Jim and the others in the car park at 6.00am as usual. Doreen and Shannon must have filled him in on what had happened because he registered no surprise at my now-spectacular purple shiner.

'Sure you're fit to work?' he asked.

'Looks worse than it feels,' I said, perfectly true thanks to the arnica and some heavy-duty painkillers supplied by Auntie Dot. I didn't care when she was vague about where they came from, because they were pharmaceutical magic.

Jim gave me a dubious look but let it go, saying only, 'Right then, tell your crew first-aider if you feel crap and need a break.'

My colleagues pounced on me as soon as the lift doors closed. I'd already admitted to Shannon it hadn't been a mugger, so provided a short explanation of the "message" from Henry.

'You poor kid,' Doreen commented, full of rough kindness. 'Take it steady today and see how you go.'

Not gonna lie, those first few shifts back at work were tough, and I had to take naps again, often. But the arnica worked its magic and by the end of the week things were much better. My left eye was open again and the swelling had almost gone, the bruising turning green from the original livid purple.

Kim had acknowledged receipt of my email and promised to "get the sniffer dogs onto it". For my part, once my body stopped hurting all over, I did my best to put the whole sorry mess behind me and get on with life again, albeit somewhat more cautiously than before. It took some time before I stopped looking over my shoulder or avoiding men in leather jackets.

*

I made the most of some sunny weather as May turned into June. Walks on the beach had to be early mornings by then, to avoid the day trippers, but being used to getting up for work it was no great hardship to carry on doing so at weekends, or early evenings after dinner. The shore had become my special place, the big sea and sky putting my small troubles into perspective. Sal even assured me that the seagull squirting crap onto my shoulder augured good luck. Yeah right.

Continuing my volunteering efforts at the Thursday afternoon food bank, I was more than ever aware of the extent of my pathetic ignorance. Nik popped into the food bank every couple of weeks, not always staying long, and smiled when I told him I'd been working hard to master the contents of the training file.

'Well done, Frankie, you're obviously getting on OK if you're already helping people.'

I grimaced. 'It's such a good feeling when I *can* make a difference, but massively frustrating to appreciate how the system is weighted against the very people it's supposed to help. For some, life is just impossibly hard, even when they're in work.'

He smiled at me in sympathy, his teeth very white against the dark skin and hair.

'There is a *lot* to learn, not only about the benefits system itself but so many related areas of stress for people. Complicated doesn't cut it.'

'I've learnt not to be afraid of saying that I'll have to find out and get back to them,' I told him.

'Keep it up, Frankie, you're doing good,' said Nik. 'The trust has a test you can take to be fully accredited if you want to go for it. You also need to clock up some hours of working with clients too, so write those down and get them signed off by Andrew or Steven. Can't stay, my daughter is being picked up from school by her *yaya* – that's Greek for grandmother – but she'll fill her full of sugar if I don't get there on time, and then Maddie will be hyperactive and bouncing off the walls.'

Pride in the child lit up his face. 'I didn't know you had a family,' I said.

'It's only me and Maddie – my wife died. Sorry, gotta dash.'

A brief lull followed his departure, so I went back to mugging up on sickness benefits. The volume of information I needed to study had proved a challenge, so I'd taken down my website. There'd only ever been a handful of editing jobs from it, and now I was heading off in a whole new (if unpaid) direction, impelled by an urgent sense of wanting and needing to give something back.

Andrew brought me some coffee as a young man came in the main doors. Dressed only in T-shirt, jeans and flip-flop sandals, even on a distinctly cool day, having got inside he stood there, unsure what to do next. Tears ran silently down his face, and I understood without any words that he'd reached a point where he couldn't take any more.

'It's all right,' I said, moving towards him. 'Come and sit down. Whatever it is, we'll do our best to help. My name is Frankie.'

'Mick,' he said, moving slowly as if in a daze. As he sat down, I covertly checked out his pupils – nothing to suggest drug use or drink on his breath. We didn't judge but needed to know. Andrew brought some more coffee over, raising his brows at me.

'You got this? Call me if I can help.'

Mick struggled to stop crying, tears falling without him seeming aware of it, and he sat there, head bowed, defeated.

I fed him bourbon biscuits with his hot drink and waited.

'There's no food in the house, not even a packet of cereal,' he said at last. 'The kids have had no breakfast or lunch, and my little girl is wearing her last nappy. The cash machine spat out my card, and when I went into the bank they said my benefit payment hasn't gone into the account. What am I supposed to do?' he said.

'Is someone with the children?' I asked.

'My neighbour. She's very good, but an old lady can't be dealing with a three-year-old and a toddler for long. There's nowhere else to go and I need a voucher or something, right?'

'Normally, yes, but don't worry about such things today. We understand about late payments and how it messes things up.'

'My missus is working,' he said, reaching for another biscuit and devouring it, making me wonder when he'd last eaten. 'She's a hairdresser but only part-time because of the kids, and I'm on sickness benefit for depression. Used to be on the building sites, plastering, but the work dried up and then I couldn't... the doctor put me on tablets a few months back, but the job centre treat me as if I'm faking it.' He slumped, despair written in every line of his face and body.

'It's OK, Mick, none of this is your fault, and you're *ill* not lazy.'

In prison, I'd seen depression overtake people, to the point where they could barely get out of bed or bother to wash themselves. Self-harm had been frighteningly common. In the early weeks on the wings at Enderton, I'd gone to some dark places myself and understood all about turning your face to the wall, hoping for nothing more than to cease to exist.

'Could you maybe manage a box of cereal or something?' he said. 'At least the kids could eat it and then the payment should be in tomorrow. Sometimes Lucy gets cash tips, but we can't ever count on it. I feel bad for asking.'

'Needing help is nothing you should *ever* be ashamed of; I've been there myself. Anyway, payments aren't generally more than a couple of days late,' I added, intending to be helpful, but his expression changed to one of total panic.

'It could be another day? I can't tell my kids that, I *can't*.'

Mentally cursing my ineptitude, I told him, 'No, you won't have to, because we're going to fix you up with enough stuff for the next three days.' I waved Andrew across and the two of us sat down with Mick to write a list of what he needed, including nappies. We even managed a few chocolate biscuits for the children.

Mick transformed from a man at rock bottom to one incredulous with joy at the help we were able to provide. He kept saying, 'I'll never forget this, *never*. You people are the best.' I felt privileged to see the difference between hope and despair, and it left me humbled and proud both at the same time to have been part of it. Andrew took Mick home with his shopping bags, and as I waved him off from the car park a moment of clarity came to me, the way rays of sunlight come shafting in through the clouds. I'd discovered what I wanted to do with the rest of my life.

Ellie the vicar, also in the car park, spotted the tears standing in my eyes. 'It's a brilliant feeling when you can make a difference for someone, isn't it?' she said.

'Isn't there something in the Bible about it being more blessed to give than receive?' I asked. 'I've just understood it properly for the first time. Ellie, I want to do more of this kind of work, but I've been in prison…'

Ellie didn't even blink, her response straightforward and down to earth. 'God doesn't care about your record, and neither will Laneways Trust.'

'But will people trust me, after…?'

'The Bible says, "All have sinned and fall short of the glory of God". If faith isn't all about forgiveness and healing, then I'm in the wrong job. There's a blessing we use in church services, and it's what I try to live by, listen…

'Go forth into the world in peace
'Be of good courage
'Hold fast to that which is good
'Render to no one evil for evil
'Strengthen the fainthearted
'Support the weak
'Help the afflicted
'Honour all people.'

The words dropped into my mind as a healing balm. 'That's beautiful,' I said. 'Especially the part about honouring all people. Would you email it to me? I'm not exactly a believer but did go to a convent school. It kind of… stays with you.'

'Doesn't it? That blessing is special to me because it contains nice simple instructions which keep me going on the tough days,' said Ellie. 'Why not have a chat with Nik if you want to get more involved with the work of the trust.'

'Already made a start on that,' I said, showing her the file I'd been studying. 'But I'm so often embarrassed by the things I didn't understand before. My life was so privileged, it shames me to admit how I didn't see the beggars on London streets as *people*, with real lives and stories to tell. I believed it was enough to drop money into a tin.' Heat rose in my neck and face as I flushed with shame.

Ellie nodded. 'Not a comfortable revelation – but at least you get it now. Anyway, what about you, is the prison experience something you need to talk about?'

A tempting offer but after a pause, I said, 'No, not anymore. It's time to move on, I *need* to let go of anger and bitterness, and all the resentment at losing the life I once had. What's done is done, and I can never get back the years I lost, so it makes more sense to begin again from where I am.'

A nudge from my conscience reminded me how I'd recently sold Henry for thirty pieces of silver. Not even for the money, but to save my own life and reputation. Had Kim been right about simple justice, or was I guilty of a malevolent hope for revenge?

I told Ellie the truth. 'I'm trying to be grateful for what I have, to understand how lucky I am, but most of all I want to stop wallowing in self-pity or playing the victim and find a way to be at peace with myself.'

'Ah,' said Ellie. 'That peace which the world cannot give? A lot of us are searching for the same thing so let me know if you find it. In my experience, it comes fleetingly and rarely, but such moments are precious.'

Standing in the car park I thought maybe I *had* found it, along with a new sense of purpose and direction in my life.

Then my phone buzzed with a message from the probation officer.

Very disturbed by reports about you. Come and see me ASAP.

TEN

The air up in my eyrie under the roof was close and stuffy, even with the windows open. My quilt ended up on the floor as even a sheet was too much bedding. Half the night was spent tossing and turning with my imagination supplying images of being sent back to prison, as I tried to understand why probation had sent for me and what the hell I might have done wrong. Even after a cold shower to give me a much-needed kick in the proverbials, it was hard to get started at work the next morning. My mood was as bleak as the thunderclouds gathering over the sea on my bus trip into Blackpool; at least a storm would clear the air.

I was sick with anxiety on arrival at the probation office, where I found Tony scowling at some papers and clearly not having a good day. At the sight of me, his face darkened further; a big change from my last visit when he'd been supportive and encouraging, full of praise for my volunteering efforts.

He waved me to the chair and without preamble said, 'I'm very disappointed in you, Frankie – thought you were going to be a success story, and now this.' He waved the pieces of paper at me.

'Have I done something wrong?'

'Come on, don't waste my time pretending you don't know.'

'Honestly.' My voice came out squeaky. 'I have no idea what the problem is.'

He handed the pages across the desk but then his phone rang, and he had to step outside the glass-panelled office to answer it. I could see him gesticulating, pacing up and down. Presumably some other poor miscreant getting a telling-off.

The shock of reading the typed letter had the same effect on me as that ice-bucket challenge which used to be a thing.

Dear Mr Norton,

Re: Your Client Francesca Wilton nee Douglas

I thought it proper to inform you that the above-named has been seen frequenting the Rushford Arms, a haunt of drug dealers and a very rough establishment well-known to the police.

In addition, she has been consorting with and purchasing drugs from Doreen Turner, who has a record of such transactions. See the photographs attached. All of this would appear to be in direct contravention of the conditions of Ms Wilton's release on licence.

Yours,

James P Browne

32 Rochdale Avenue, St Annes on Sea, Lancs

The pictures attached to the letter were black and white, grainy but clear enough. The first showed me outside the Rushford Arms in my winter coat, taken in semi-darkness but illuminated by the pub lights. With my head down against the weather, I did look furtive but must have been walking past on my way home. The second photo of Doreen and I showed us standing together against what might be the brick wall of the school, probably waiting for Shannon to arrive. The angle of the photo suggested something was being handed over, but this hardly constituted any kind of evidence.

It was a good ten minutes later when Tony's phone call ended. Back behind the desk he glared at me again and barked, 'So, what do you have to say for yourself?'

My heartbeat sounded unnaturally loud inside my head. Taking a deep breath, I tried to be calm. Not going back to prison depended on it.

'This is utter nonsense,' I told him crisply, slapping the letter down on the desk. 'Are you *seriously* accusing me of something on the basis of such blatant mischief-making and lies? While you were out there, I took the opportunity to do some checking on my phone – which due diligence suggests you could and should have done for yourself – and there is no such place as Rochdale Avenue. If you can be bothered to take a look at the electoral register, I very much doubt James P Browne exists either.'

Tony stared at me, mouth open, but I was on a roll, full of adrenalin and fighting back with everything I'd got.

'Before you start accusing me of anything, let's have full disclosure here; you didn't do your homework before hauling me in, did you? For your information, Doreen is currently my colleague at Morley's Contract Cleaning. I believe she did receive a fine for possession of a small amount of marijuana in 2015, clearly for personal use only, and in most major cities she wouldn't even have been charged and got off with a warning.'

She'd talked about it often enough as yet another injustice in her difficult life. The weed had belonged to her ex, but he'd let her take the blame.

'Frankie, I…'

'Furthermore, these photos are clearly opportunistic and could have been taken at any time. I do pass the Rushford

124

Arms on my way home from cleaning the school every day, but I have never been inside it or any other public house since the day of my release.'

Sadly, this was an accurate assessment of my humdrum life; apart from occasional lunches out with Dot, you could safely describe my social life as non-existent.

Tony's face reddened and he wouldn't meet my stern and (I hoped) flinty gaze, shuffling papers on his desk. Then he held his hand up in a gesture of surrender.

'OK, I may have been a little hasty…'

'You jumped to conclusions without checking the facts, or even the identity of the letter writer. I could make a formal complaint.'

'Shit, there's no need for that.'

'There is from where I'm standing! This kind of malicious slander could get me sent back to prison.' I couldn't let him off the hook when my liberty might be at stake. My very ordinary life now appeared positively entrancing compared to the possibility of more incarceration.

'OK,' he said slowly, 'I may have messed up. Yesterday this toothache had me going insane so when the letter and pictures hit my desk…'

'You panicked and shot off a text demanding to see me,' I told him, holding onto my temper with difficulty. 'Then you completely failed to check the accuracy of this bullshit.'

Tony's expression became panicky. 'Yeah, OK, fair enough,' he admitted. 'I've got to go and have a root canal this afternoon, and I'm a big baby about dentists.'

'Absolutely no excuse, as you are well aware. Here's the deal – I will hold off on the formal written complaint *if* you promise to investigate this properly, and then write into my file that you have done so and find no merit in these allegations. You should provide me with copies of both your response and the original letter. I'm not in a position where I can afford to take chances when someone is clearly out to make trouble for me. Now, you should also record the following incidents in your case notes. Got a pen?'

I recounted the story of the threats I'd received and showed him the picture on my phone (taken by Auntie Dot) of my bruised face at its worst.

'Frankie, this is serious.' I had all Tony's concerned attention now. 'Somebody is out to discredit you any way they can.'

As if I didn't know that.

'There's a very strong likelihood this all goes back to my estranged husband, but I can't prove anything. The attacker said the message came from Henry. I'll email you the photo of my injuries for your records.'

'Have you been to the police?' asked Tony, struggling to write everything down as I fired information at him like bullets.

'You think I'd have got anywhere? I'm not only an ex-con and therefore a discredited witness, but as far as they're concerned it would have been yet another street mugging, and nothing was even stolen. Also, in the immediate aftermath, I felt too crap to get out of bed and make a formal report.'

Tony didn't argue – both of us understood the police wouldn't have done anything.

I hadn't finished with him yet. 'Right, if you've made a note of everything, for God's sake sign yourself out as sick and get to the bloody dentist before you do any more damage.'

The top deck of the bus home was hot and airless. I stared unseeing out of the window at the Blackpool suburbs. The reality of the near-miss I'd navigated was shocking – even *contemplating* the prospect of being sent back to prison left me feeling like I could throw up. A breach of my licence conditions would mean being back on the wings at HMP Enderton. I'd be locked up much of the time, not out in the more relaxed regime of the houses where I'd been with Sal, *and* without her protection from the inevitable bullying.

But the thing consuming my overwhelmed brain was why would Henry hate me this much and be so afraid of what I might say. He didn't even know I'd found those nasty pictures on his computer years back because I'd chickened out of confronting him or admitting to snooping in his personal files. Yet he was now scared enough about something to threaten me to silence. He didn't even know yet that I'd told Kim everything I remembered about his strange sexual preferences.

Back at Sea View, the storm clouds were gathering, literally and metaphorically. Still feeling shaky in the aftermath of my adrenalin rush, I went straight to Dot and told her what had happened. She had on a purple turban with heavy silver earrings and fed me strong coffee served with some Florentine biscuits from the Lytham deli.

As she munched reflectively, the gears in Dot's sharp brain were whirring.

'Assuming you're right, and Henry is behind this and everything else, a fundamental question remains about his motivation. Once we understand why, we've got the key to the puzzle,' she said.

'And there's another question,' I said, sitting up straight as it occurred to me. 'What would be the point of trying to get me locked up again? Even in prison, I could still tell a lawyer whatever he thinks I know, or even get them to carry a letter to Kim for me. If this is about ensuring my silence, then from his point of view getting me sent back to Enderton wouldn't achieve a damn thing.'

'True, so then all of this must be an attempt to frighten you so much that you won't say anything to anyone. Frankie, there must be something which is scaring *him*; nothing else makes sense. My best guess is that it's to do with the sadomasochistic group you told me about. I'm sure the photos you found are long gone – he would have been careful to delete those or hide them more effectively. No word from Kim yet?'

'I've had a text to say he's investigating, but not so far coming up with anything concrete he can use,' I said.

Dot gazed unseeing across the room as she wrestled with my problem.

'We could be over-analysing this,' she said. 'Trying to identify an ulterior motive when it might be as simple as Henry being angry and wanting to make you miserable as punishment for leaving him the way you did.'

'Like getting me sent to prison wasn't enough. He has to be 100% certain I didn't set the fire so it's an extraordinary amount of effort to further discredit someone unimportant compared to his weight as a cabinet minister. I mean, who's ever going to believe me over him? The trial judge didn't.'

'Ancient history,' said Dot. 'Never mind, have another biscuit before I eat them all. Listen to that thunder, and the sky is black as hell's best outside.'

Fat, heavy raindrops begin to hit the window and a distant flash briefly lit the sky. It all felt like an appropriate setting for the heavy weight now pressing in on me.

Dot said casually, 'By the way, my sources identified your attacker as a local man, one Wayne Musson, a small-time crook from Blackpool who runs a dodgy gym and deals in illegal steroids. Has a side-line in intimidation as hired muscle, but the police have never been able to get him for anything. Unless, of course, you decide to report the assault.'

'What would that achieve? Henry can easily find someone else to do his dirty work.'

We sat there in silence drinking coffee as the storm briefly pelted the windows with rain before rumbling away inland.

The skies began to brighten again and having Dot to listen to my woes made such a difference. She'd become such a rock to lean on and I went back upstairs fortified by her presence and quantities of caffeine and sugar.

*

After these various alarming incidents, life went back to something like normal. For once, I appreciated the uneventful predictability of it all, silently promising whoever was "up there" never to complain about boredom again. Then one afternoon, Nik rang, his deep voice instantly recognisable even without the caller ID.

'Hey, Frankie, thanks for the update on your progress, but are you sure you want to take on debt counselling as well? It would mean a lot of extra work and study.'

'Experience at the food bank so far is teaching me that the queries I try to deal with are never simple,' I told him. 'The problems often involve debt, with crippling repayments at breathtaking rates of interest, leaving not enough money left over for food and bills. Anyway, it's not as if I'm super busy doing other stuff, is it? Buster got me some leaflets on consolidating your liabilities, but I hate having to send people trailing off to another agency if I could provide the same information. It might be different if I had a social life or a demanding job.'

Nik chuckled. 'I imagine your job is very demanding, but speaking of your social life – I wanted to ask if you'd meet me for dinner this evening, and perhaps we could talk about further training then? I'm at the Catholic church food bank all afternoon, then staying in a local B&B tonight because I'm off to Newcastle first thing tomorrow morning. Maddie is on a sleepover with a school friend.'

The prospect of dinner with pleasant company held strong appeal, but Nik must have taken my thinking time as hesitation because he said, 'Please, Frankie, you'd be doing me a favour. I hate nights away from home with no one to talk to except the TV.'

I didn't even have a TV, preferring to read or use my laptop when I wasn't studying.

'I'd love to come, but not anywhere posh because I don't have the right kind of clothes these days.'

'There's a great Indian restaurant on Standish Street, I've been there before. You're OK with spicy food?'

'Am I ever. My soul craves those flavours.'

With a time arranged, I went through my limited stock of outfits to see what I could come up with. Even smart casual was going to be a stretch.

I walked into the Spice King Restaurant later dressed in the black slacks I'd bought for job interviews, teamed with sandals and a crisp white top. This simple outfit was jazzed up by the addition of a bargain pair of dangly earrings found in a charity shop.

Nik beamed when he saw me, a pale blue shirt setting off his dark olive skin.

'Frankie, you came. It's good to see you, and so we're straight this is my treat, I insist. You're saving me from a lonely evening, and we have a lot to talk about.'

We started with papdi chaat, a dish I'd never had before but which the menu described as "crispy fried dough topped with chickpeas, potatoes, yoghurt, chutneys and spices". Nik assured me I'd love it, and I did. Then came the best lamb rogan josh I'd ever eaten; Indian food this good hadn't come my way since the London days, a lifetime ago.

We'd agreed to leave talk about work until later, so during the meal exchanged summary life stories.

'I grew up in north Manchester,' Nik told me. 'I'm the third-generation son of Greek immigrants and part of a large family which extends across the country. There's only Mum living in Salford now – Dad left when I was a teenager, and we haven't seen him since. She has cousins all over, including Scotland. Since retiring last year, she'd like to move out and get a smaller place, but I need help with Maddie. Since I lost my wife to breast cancer, Mum has held us both together. We couldn't make it work without *Yaya*.'

'My mother had breast cancer too and died when I was eleven. They were older when they had me, and the grandparents were long gone, so then Dad sent me away to a convent boarding school.'

'A tough experience?'

'Counter to the usual narrative, I had a great time; better than being at home if I'm honest. The nuns were brilliant, strong advocates for girls and told us we could do anything if we put our minds to it. I even enjoyed the food – Dad only ever managed simple stuff such as grilling chops and opening tins.'

'And you married Henry straight out of university?'

With a deep pang of regret, I pictured that long-ago wedding day, and saw again the dazzlingly handsome man who'd swept me off my feet during my final year.

'At the time I felt so special and lucky, madly in love with this gorgeous bloke who treated me as his princess. Much later I came to understand how he'd scouted me out as a "suitable" wife for an up-and-coming political man. He's ten years older than me and I was young and seriously green, what with a Home Counties upbringing and convent school. Impeccable credentials back then, but now I'm forever stuck with the label "arsonist" and a prison record.'

'But you *didn't* do it – the fire, I mean?'

'I'm well aware that all convicted criminals say this, but no. If I'd wanted revenge, I'd have done a much better job. Let's not talk about it; leave my husband and ill-fated marriage firmly in the past.'

'Except it's not that simple, is it? My marriage couldn't be described as a happy one either, but I stayed for our daughter's sake, and then when Sophie had cancer I couldn't leave. It was stage three when diagnosed and, despite all the treatment, she didn't make it. The best thing you can say is it gave Maddie a space of time in which to adjust to the idea that her mum wouldn't always be there.'

'I had a similar experience – we sort of lost Mum long before she died.'

Nik was warm, funny and easy to talk to – though he freely admitted to not suffering fools gladly and having a short fuse at times. I told him a little about the harassment I'd experienced in recent weeks (though I played down the violence), and he was seriously indignant on my behalf.

Pursuing a safer option, we switched to talking about some of the cases I'd worked on, and by the time I came to a halt we were nibbling on a selection of Indian sweets.

'Believe me, I share your anger about the things people have to go through,' he told me. 'My time is spent running around trying to get food distributed to those who need it when the official so-called support system is fundamentally flawed and needs reform.'

'I'm beginning to appreciate the truth of that and the more I study how things work, the more obvious it becomes. As vital as the work of the food bank is, I want to do more than provide short-term support and make a difference in the longer term. Maybe even get involved in campaigning for the kind of restructuring of the system you're talking about?'

'A fellow crusader,' said Nik, waving a green cube of

pistachio sweet around in his enthusiasm. 'Sometimes it takes the fuel of anger to keep us going in this line of work. The alternative is to sink into depression at the futility of trying to move a mountain by digging it out with a teaspoon. But, Frankie, are you *sure* this is what you want? It won't be easy doing the study when you're working as well, though it would give you widely recognised accreditation.'

'And will such a qualification offset the disadvantage of a conviction for arson?' I asked, picking up an almond-scented cube.

'In the voluntary sector a criminal record isn't always a problem,' he said, looking at me earnestly. 'For example, former addicts can be the very best people to support those in recovery from drink or drug problems. A lot of volunteers with time and energy to give to this work are retired, middle-class professionals who mean well but don't understand how it feels to hit rock bottom. You do, and it's an advantage not a negative, not least because you'll respect people's pride and dignity. Some of our senior staff started by helping at a food bank but moved on into paid roles.'

'For now, it only matters to me if I can make a difference. Without Sal's help I wouldn't have survived, so it's kind of paying it forward if you see what I mean?'

'OK, well I'll talk to the people at our Manchester office about getting you signed off on the benefits module, get that box ticked before you start on the next. Andrew will continue to be your immediate boss, but to gain certification you'd have to take an online exam to test your knowledge, which must be supervised by someone else. I could do it here in St Annes if that works better for you. I'm assuming travelling to Manchester wouldn't be an option?'

'It's awkward with me working split shifts during the week. Dot might provide transport, if necessary, though I don't like to ask. So, yes please to doing the test locally.'

Nik leaned forward to say. 'Frankie I've had the best time; I don't remember when I've enjoyed an evening so much.'

'Me too,' I said. 'But the waiter wants to go home and if I drink any more coffee, I'll be awake half the night.'

'God, I'm so sorry – you have to be up for an early start.' He waved for the bill, which was delivered promptly with evident relief. 'What am I doing, keeping you out late? Let me walk you home.'

I had to smile at a gallant gesture which hadn't come my way in a long time.

'It's fine, I'm used to doing things by myself.'

'And what if your muscle man is lurking somewhere? It's my duty to protect you from potential assailants.' He meant this as a joke, but it managed not to be funny.

Walking companionably through the summer night and over the bridge to Sea View, I briefly wished this had been a date, rather than a business meeting. I imagined him holding my hand, and it would have been so nice if someone wanted to kiss me, but this relationship should probably remain strictly professional.

ELEVEN

For a southerner like me the month of June was a disappointment; my dreams of golden days walking the tideline hadn't materialised very often. When I mentioned my hopes for warmer temperatures in July, everyone at Sea View assured me that the summer months were always fickle weather-wise.

'This is the Lancashire coast; very different from what you're used to. Perhaps the best description would be "unpredictable",' suggested Buster.

'June isn't always "flaming" around here,' added Dot. 'You just have to take what you get, and that's before you start on the effects of climate change.'

'Never mind global warming,' said Sal. 'It makes a difference locally if the tide is in or out, and even in summer you can get a mist rolling in over the water.'

I couldn't complain, having managed to miss some lovely sunshine by spending far too much of my free time locked away indoors in preparation for the upcoming test. Buster and Sal were incredibly supportive of my studies and encouraged me to work outside in the tiny garden, but I found it either too distracting or ended up falling asleep.

The test questions would cover a wide range of complex sample case studies. Then, assuming I passed, it would be onto the debt module. I'd already got the file but hadn't dared to open it for fear of further scrambling my already over-taxed brain.

'Proud of you, Frankie,' Sal told me one evening over a dinner of sausage and mash with rich onion gravy. 'Buster says the Laneways Trust courses are good, they do things proper.'

Buster nodded in agreement. 'If this is the kind of career path you want, then you're going the right way about it. Once your skills are up to speed, I might even want to poach you for the law centre, except I don't have any funding for paid help right now. I'll get on with submitting a few applications.'

'The last thing Frankie needs is another volunteer job,' said Dot. 'She's got to earn a living, right?'

With the addition of housing benefit, my wages from the cleaning job had so far been enough to pay my way at Sea View, with a bit left over for occasional treats and charity-shop purchases. At Morley's Contract Cleaning, we were all on a zero-hours contract and Jim hadn't yet mentioned any alternative work once the school closed for the summer. I was losing sleep over it and watched out for signs in shops and the local free newspaper, hoping perhaps there might be something seasonal like waitressing or a bar job available.

*

The exam took place on a Friday, arranged for 11.00am to fit in between my shifts. Nik turned up on the doorstep of Sea View on time, but in a state of total panic and had his daughter with him.

'Frankie, I'm so sorry to do this to you, but Maddie has a school inset day and her *yaya* had a phone call offering a last-minute hospital appointment. She's waited so long to be seen I told her we'd manage, and she should go for it but, of course, it means I had to bring Maddie with me.'

Maddie (short for Madison), aged nine, had softly olive skin and her father's dark, unruly curls.

'Hello, Frankie, nice to meet you,' she said, clearly coached to be polite. 'I'm a big girl and I don't *need* looking after. I've brought my book and after you've done your test, Dad has promised me ice cream on the pier.'

She showed me the volume as we all climbed the stairs – the latest in a popular young people's fantasy series.

'Those are super, aren't they?' I said. 'I've read the first three but not the more recent ones.'

'This is the fifth and it's *so* cool,' she said, her face lit with enthusiasm. 'Wait till you find out what happens with the magic sword.'

'Don't tell me,' I begged. 'I'm hoping to find book four in the charity shops, but nobody's giving it away yet.'

'I could lend you mine,' she said doubtfully, 'but *Yaya* always says, "neither a borrower nor a lender be" or something.'

'*Yaya* is right,' I told her, opening the door into my attic eyrie. Father and daughter inspected the light-filled space with its touches of blue, and Maddie went immediately to the window seat, now softened with my handmade cushions.

'This is cool, I can read my book here,' she said. 'Oh, you've got a cat.' Spike had made himself at home on my bed but tolerated Maddie tickling him under the chin, even rolling on his back and offering up a pale gold underbelly to be rubbed.

'Daddy, doesn't Frankie have a lovely room – can we do mine this way? I'm too big for fairies now. And we could get a kitten.'

Nik sighed. 'Now come on, we've talked about this before; you know I'm not a cat lover, but it *is* time we redecorated.

Trouble is there are never enough hours in the weekend to get around to it.'

'You always make excuses,' complained Maddie, but she settled herself comfortably by the window and produced Harry Potter-style glasses to read.

'She's the same as her mum,' Nik told me. 'Short-sighted from an early age. I used to tease my wife that I only looked good to her because she always saw me in soft focus.'

Nik was big and craggy rather than handsome, but I liked the way his hair curled on his neck, or a sudden smile would light up his face.

'It's so fresh and welcoming in here,' he said. 'All your own work?'

'Sal and Buster painted it before I moved in. It was a bit bare at first, but I hope all my charity shop finds have added personality.' I'd acquired another plastic plant and lit a sandalwood candle which had been a gift from Auntie Dot. 'It's all been done on a shoestring but has grown to feel like home.'

'That must have been very important to you, after…'

'My previous accommodation? Yes. Right, let me make us some coffee, and then we can get going. I'm suffering from exam stress and will be very glad once it's over!'

This was a colossal understatement – I hadn't sat any kind of test since university – but was trying not to let my nerves show.

The Manchester office had already sent me a link to the exam website, and Nik signed in with his ID before recording the start time. I did some deep breathing and once he told me to start, sat at my makeshift desk and scanned the questions. Having first decided which would be relatively easy to answer and what needed more time, once I dived in all the nervous anticipation vanished. Now and again, Nik would come and check over my shoulder, but for the most part he worked on his laptop from the comfort of the refurbished rocking chair. The allocated hour went incredibly fast, but I managed to finish within the time and even had a few minutes to check through my answers.

'Right,' said Nik. 'Step away from the keyboard and I'll record the time and press submit. OK, job done. Great work.' He gave me a brief, impulsive hug. I liked it.

'We can have ice cream now,' announced Maddie, closing her book, and reluctantly leaving Spike who'd been curled up on her lap. 'Frankie, are you coming too?'

It was so nice that Maddie wanted me, but I hesitated to invade special time between the two of them.

Nik added his voice to hers. 'You're not at work until 4.00pm, are you? Plenty of time, and we can hit the slot machines too.'

'Well, when you put it that way...' I said.

'Come on,' urged Maddie. 'It'll be *epic*.'

She was right. I hadn't had so much fun in far too long. We did silly touristy things: eating silky whipped ice cream with a chocolate flake and playing the one-armed bandits with change supplied by Nik. When Maddie won a small jackpot, she jumped up and down in joyful exuberance, but I could never get my fruit to line up. Story of my life.

We laughed a lot and even though the wind off the sea was "fresh", ended up walking barefoot out to the receding tide for the traditional paddling where the slightly warmer margins of water could be enjoyed. Nik swept Maddie off her feet, pretending to throw her in the water, producing shrieks of delighted mock terror. It brought back memories of beach holidays in Portugal with a small Justin: buckets and spades, sand in inconvenient places, the coconut smell of sun block and freckled noses. Henry had been perpetually glued to his phone.

I left Maddie and Nik with reluctance when it was time to go to work, but school cleaning beckoned and Maddie had talked her dad into playing crazy golf. Walking away, I reflected how blessedly normal it had all been; most people watching would have assumed we were a family. Except for the early years when I'd continued to believe in our marriage, life with Henry had never been so simple and uncomplicated; always too much duty and never enough *off*-duty.

*

Arriving home sweaty from work, trouser pockets still full of sand and shells, I thought for a minute I'd lost the plot. Powerful memories of time with my son had been stirred up during the afternoon. Now, by some arcane magic, he sat on the top step of Sea View next to a smart leather holdall I recognised as belonging to Henry.

My heart was in my mouth. Was Justin bringing yet another message from his father?

'Hello, Mum. I rang the bell but the old bat in the scarf wouldn't let me in. She asked to see a photo driving licence, but I don't have one, so I got told I'd have to wait until you came home. She told me when.'

Good for Dot, being security-conscious on my behalf.

'Well, hello to you too,' I said. 'But what on earth are you doing here?'

Justin is tall, and physically resembles his father more and more with every year – even down to his taste in clothes: olive-green shorts and a grey T-shirt. He wrapped me in a quick, awkward hug.

'Can't I visit my mum if I want to? You've cut your hair. God, you really are a cleaner then?' He studied the logo on my nylon tabard.'

'We haven't seen each other in more than two years,' I protested, 'and you turn up without warning? A text message might have been nice.'

'I caught the train up here as a surprise – expected this town would be a dump but it's OK, I've seen worse, had a quick wander while I was waiting for you. Aren't you glad to see me then?'

'Of course, and it's lovely you're here,' I said. 'But where are you going to stay?'

'Well… with you, of course. There must be a sofa I can sleep on. I needed to get out of London for a while, or the weekend at least.'

We got it all sorted out eventually. Sal generously made the chicken salad stretch to include him by frying a batch of chips and said he could kip on the settee in the residents' living/dining space.

'I wouldn't say he takes after you, Frankie?' said Auntie Dot, giving him the unabashed once-over and studying my greying dark hair in contrast to the blue-eyed blond Justin.

'People always comment on how much I resemble my dad – can't see it myself,' he said stiffly. His eyes were on Angus, who was silently fidgeting at one end of the table, always uncomfortable around strangers. I'd warned Justin not to engage him in conversation, but my son kept shooting him covert glances and appeared to regard him as some kind of weird zoo specimen.

In contrast, Justin turned on the charm for Buster and Sal, praising the chicken and gushing his gratitude for welcoming him without notice. Part of me was desperate that the people around the dinner table should like him, but none of them were impressed, and it left me feeling ashamed of his behaviour. I'd heard it said you didn't have to be blind to your offspring's faults, only love them unconditionally. Both were

141

proving to be a challenge, but I took him up to my room so we could talk.

'Not much space,' he said, gazing around and dropping his holdall on my bed and disturbing an indignant Spike, who hissed at him. 'And no en suite?'

'You'd get even less room if you lived in a shared London house.'

'God, Mum, don't start. I *have* been trying to find a place, but now work has let me go and Dad is bloody livid, so there's no chance unless he's willing to pay to get rid of me.'

'You've lost your job?' I'd suggested leaving but hadn't meant getting sacked.

'It was only an internship, work experience. They said I wasn't a good fit for their organisation.'

'What are you going to do now? Are things still difficult with Jerry?'

Justin's shoulders slumped. 'Are they ever; he hates me. I'm not even sure he and Dad are going to stay together because they have the most awful rows and the atmosphere is so tense – they're always yelling at each other, or me. I had to get away.'

Jerry, the constituency agent, had been a comprehensive school kid who'd made it to Cambridge and worked several jobs to stay there while he studied politics and economics. I could well imagine how unimpressed he'd be by Justin's lack of drive or indeed effort. Henry and I should probably have made him get a job in the school holidays or something.

Justin sank into my rocking chair, looking unexpectedly young and vulnerable.

'The thing is, Mum, I've been hoping you might help me, but I didn't think you lived like… this.'

'I did *tell* you my work was cleaning offices and I'd got a rented room in a friend's house. So, what were you expecting? Blackpool Tower Ballroom?'

'You might have been exaggerating for a joke, making things out to be worse than they are...' I frowned and he hastily backtracked. 'I guess it's not so bad here, and you've made friends.' I could guess his real opinion of the company I kept.

'Is your father aware you've come up here?'

'Er no, I told him I'd been invited for the weekend by a friend, so he'd cough up for the train ticket. I'm not allowed to talk about you, but it doesn't stop *him* from banging on. Dad says you're out to get him...' Justin's voice trailed off at the expression on my face.

I'd been putting the little coffee machine on, but turned at this, incredulous.

'Henry said *what*? Let me assure you, it's entirely the other way around. There's been a campaign of intimidation and harassment against me, and I have good reasons to believe he's behind it. Justin, I'm too busy surviving and trying to build a new life to be planning my revenge on him right now. I'm also more than grateful to have this place and such good people around me. How the hell do you imagine someone who is released from prison on licence with virtually no money manages to survive? Do you even know that it takes up to seven weeks for benefits to come through? I was incredibly lucky to get a job within a week.'

He had the grace to blush. 'Sorry, I didn't...'

'Think!' I finished for him, getting up to pace around the room while the coffee machine chuffed and gurgled on my desk. 'You have no idea about real lives, or how it feels to struggle. Try starting from nothing, the way I did a few months ago because at least you've got the advantage of a free roof over your head and no negative label around your neck to hold you back. Take whatever job you can get and work *hard*. Be proud of making it on your own.'

'Now you're channelling Jerry, he's always telling me to grow up and sort myself out, how nobody owes me a career or a living. I hoped you'd help.'

'I *am* helping. There's no financial support on offer, but you're getting the best advice I can give. With your law degree, it's time to get out there and pay back your expensive education by doing something for other people.'

'I didn't expect you to be this way.' Justin's sulky expression reminded me all too strongly of the teenager he'd been.

I poured us coffee while deciding how to respond. He got the chipped mug.

'Justin, you're an adult now; you had a happy childhood, a first-class education and went through university without debt. Nobody is going to gallop to your rescue on a white horse, the rest will have to be all your own work.'

The reference probably meant nothing to a kid who'd grown up on *Star Wars* rather than cowboys. His face took on a slightly lost expression which brought out all my dormant motherly instincts. Had I been too harsh, or pushed him away?

'Darling, I will *always* love you and want to hear how your life is going,' I said, wrapping him in a hug. 'But you have to understand it's enough of a struggle keeping myself together right now. I've got nothing to give you beyond some hard-won life lessons.'

We managed to spend the evening together without falling out. Dot asked me about it at breakfast the next day, while Justin hogged the upstairs bathroom. When Sal passed through the dining room to replenish the cereals, I had to apologise for his attitude.

'I'm sorry about my son. He came out of the education system with decent exam results but in some ways boarding school did him no favours. Thanks for feeding him, Sal, especially at short notice – I'll pay you back.'

'It's fine, whatever, I guess we must have been the same at his age, convinced we knew it all?'

'Hell, I hope not. Were we ever quite so patronising?'

Sal snorted her sympathy, and I took Justin to Lytham on the bus to distract him from the modest existence he found so disappointing. We walked on the promenade with gulls calling overhead, and then window-shopped around the high-end stores, stopping for a deli sandwich lunch in the sunshine of the pedestrianised square. I meanly forced him to pay for his food as part of his ongoing education.

As we sat basking in the warmth and watching people come and go, he said, 'It's OK, this place, kind of like a London village but with the sea a few metres away.'

'It's great, but a lot of other people think so too. Property here is expensive.'

'Bet it's dead in the winter, right?'

'Not necessarily, though it doesn't have quite the same cosmopolitan atmosphere when the summer visitors go home. I enjoy living on the coast though, it's fascinating in all weathers. The sea air always makes me hungry. How's your baguette?'

He licked his fingers before answering. 'This pastrami is fantastic. You know what, you've changed, Mum,' he said. 'You're kind of… less brittle and sharp-edged.'

This might have been the most astute observation I'd ever heard from my son.

'Those edges had a lot to do with your father. Our relationship became very strained, especially once it became clear he wasn't faithful.'

How much did Justin even understand about Henry's sexual tastes, beyond the fact he'd finally come out as gay?

'Yeah, but you didn't need to torch the house to get back at him.'

I swallowed, hard. 'You believe I did that?'

He went scarlet and wouldn't meet my searching look. 'All the papers said so. Dad told me not to come to the trial, but I heard you entered a not-guilty plea.' Doubt crossed his face, probably a new sensation. 'So, *did* you do it?'

'Nice of you to ask, but actually no.' My brittle edges were back. 'I couldn't prove it and your father's evidence clinched the guilty verdict. He lied on oath.'

I shouldn't have said that, not wanting Justin to be pulled between warring parents. He hastily changed the subject, and we didn't mention it again, but maybe I'd given him something to reflect on. We walked back along the seafront, and it felt good to just talk and catch up. At dinner, he ate Sal's fish and chips with real enthusiasm and generally behaved much more like a proper human being. Perhaps he'd been nervous the night before. In the evening, the two of us played cards upstairs and he told me about his hopes for the future. These were possibly over-ambitious involving as they did a flash car, a flat somewhere upmarket and an expensive lifestyle. My own life didn't even have a "style".

On Sunday morning, I walked him over the bridge to catch the noon train and, as it pulled in, he turned and hugged me impulsively. 'It's been good to see you, Mum, and thanks... for the pep talk and giving me a break from the atmosphere at home. Maybe I see things a bit more clearly now.'

Having waved him off, I walked slowly back to Sea View with regrets for what might have been whirling around my brain. I still struggled to shake the feeling of being followed and kept looking over my shoulder until I made it to the safety of Sea View. Dot pounced as she heard me go past her door.

'Come on in,' she said, 'I want to hear all about it. Your boy might turn out all right when he grows up a bit. There's bound to be traces of your steel in him somewhere, at least I bloody hope so for your sake. Stiff gin and one of Sal's sandwiches?'

Dot always managed to make things better. 'A regretful no to the gin – especially if it's the raspberry one – because I'm on duty at the emergency food bank this afternoon. Then I've got a date with the debt-counselling file. I couldn't do any work on it with Justin here.'

'I'm bored today,' she said, 'so I might come over and help at the food bank. I need a change, life's been a bit too quiet lately.'

TWELVE

The copy report from my probation officer arrived, and after reading the contents I punched the air with delight. Tony had written an unequivocal statement to the effect that he found the anonymous claims to be utterly spurious, intended only to make mischief for a model client and a rehabilitation success story. Nice that someone believed in me, even if I'd had to come on strong to force him into it.

On the negative side, I'd shortly be losing the school hours when term ended, and so far had no idea how to make up the shortfall in my wages. Time spent worrying about this turned out to be wasted energy, because when I turned up for work on Friday Jim stood there waiting for me, his face grim.

'Shannon and Doreen, you go on up – you'll be short-handed today because I'm letting Frankie go.'

'Hang on, you can't,' protested Shannon, but Jim cut her off.

'Oh, but I can. I'm not having druggies working for me. Going to deny it, Frankie?'

I stiffened and a cold chill passed over me. 'I've never used drugs, not now or in the past. What makes you believe I do?'

Jim waved at Doreen and Shannon to get on upstairs, then

sneered at me. 'Got a tip-off, and a good job too. I thought better of you.'

'Did you by any chance receive an anonymous letter?'

'So what? Someone did me a favour for sure.'

'My probation officer was sent something similar, but he believed me when I told him the claims were malicious lies. Why not ask him if you won't take my word for it? Or get a drugs test, I'm happy to comply, but you can't sack me without evidence.'

'I can, as a matter of fact; there's plenty more casual labour about. We're done here.'

'Jim, this isn't even legal…'

'So take me to court.' He got in the van and drove away, well aware I couldn't afford to challenge him with the law. I might qualify for legal aid to help meet the costs, but it would take weeks if not months to sort out.

I went up in the lift to explain what had happened to Doreen and Shannon.

'I'll be trying to fight this because it's not true,' I told them. 'Let me work this last shift with you anyway, it's the least I can do.'

Shannon shook her head, looping the cord on the vacuum cleaner. 'Better not, insurance and so on, but it's good of you to offer. Shit, Frankie, this is bloody awful. Someone's got it in for you, good and proper.'

'Damn right, and I'm not going to take it anymore. Any news about the school hours?'

'Doreen's recommended me for the pub session because she can't do the lunch shift now her kids are at home. She'll do some evenings instead and it should work out. Look, we have to crack on now, but take care of yourself.'

They both hugged me before turning back to the morning's tasks; it would be tough to get finished without my contribution. I trailed slowly home, all too conscious that my supposed misdeeds were affecting them too. Justin's visit had given my spirits an unexpected lift, and now my world suddenly went from colour back to black and white. Feeling sick with anxiety, this was something even a walk on the beach couldn't fix.

Lying on my bed without even Spike's fluffy warmth for comfort, I couldn't see what the hell to do next. At least the probation service believed me to be a victim rather than a culprit, but getting sacked would be a black mark on my record. It was clear I should get online and submit a benefits claim as soon as possible, especially given it was already Friday. Except I didn't do it, only lay there on my precious quilt, stroking it with my fingers. Sometimes, when life slaps you down, it leaves you so low an inertia takes over. I'd been to the same place when in prison.

Instead of doing something, anything, proactive, I lay there sinking into a deep well of self-pity. Losing my job forced me to recognise the fragility of everything I'd built, and how easily it had all come crashing down. Henry had succeeded in ruining my life – again – and finally anger propelled me into action.

Jumping up to pace the floor I said aloud, "I'm *not* going to take this anymore! Henry Wilton can so absolutely *fuck off*." These last words were shouted at the ceiling, which felt so good I did it again and stamped a bit for good measure.

I'd forgotten it was only 7.45am and Auntie Dot lived right below me. She came rushing up the stairs in a towelling turban, dressing gown and slippers, flinging open my door without waiting for an answer to her knock.

'Frankie, whatever are you shouting about, and why are you home at this time? Are you OK, sweetheart?'

'Don't be nice to me,' I told her, my body stiff and prickly. 'I want to stay angry and not let this upset me.'

But she put her arms around me anyway and needless to say I sobbed against her shoulder, feeling utterly defeated.

I never used to cry so much, but when life knocks great big lumps off your defences, the soft centre we all keep hidden gets damaged more easily.

It didn't take her long to get the basic facts out of me.

'Jim is a stupid bastard,' said Dot, 'sacking you is probably illegal too. Buster will have something to say on the subject, I'm sure she'll help you challenge what he's done. In the meantime, buck up because there *will* be a way through this. Maybe start by selling your engagement ring? This might be the emergency you've been saving it for.'

'Henry won't ever leave me alone, will he?' I hiccupped. 'As if he hasn't done enough already.'

'Harassment and intimidation are also against the law but, as your journalist friend is aware, the problem is obtaining the evidence to prove who's behind it. Now, enough with the self-pity and start fighting back, because it's time to be planning your next steps.'

I was briefly injured and inclined to be defensive at this accusation, but Dot's determined face and her words provided the spur to action I undoubtedly needed.

'You're right. Maybe I'll start with the benefits claim; the first stage can be done online.'

'Good girl. OK so get on with it right now, while I go and put some proper clothes on. Then you and I are going out for a cheering-up session. I could do with one myself.'

I dried my eyes and put cold water on them, before making a superhuman effort to get my brain in gear and fill in the necessary forms. Once the form was submitted online, I only had to wait for a phone call to verify my identity and I'd then be invited to an appointment at the job centre. This time around I knew it would be a lot more difficult to find work, not to mention the minimum five weeks waiting time for actual benefits money to come through.

'Stop it,' I had to tell myself as my heart sank again. 'It's going to be OK – Auntie Dot says so.'

After a freshen-up, a clean outfit and some of the red lipstick kept for special occasions, I spoke to myself sternly in the mirror from the charity shop.

'You have *got* this, Frankie Douglas. You've survived worse, so get your act together.'

'*Nil desperandum* as they say,' said Dot from the doorway, wearing a short, dark wig I hadn't seen before. 'Let's make a start at the jewellers in Lytham, because having some funds in reserve will help you feel more secure during this temporary employment hiatus. You could have my financial support in a heartbeat, but I imagine you'd turn me down?'

'You'd be right – too damn proud,' I said, in rueful acknowledgement.

'I'm a bit the same myself, but the offer stands if ever you change your mind. Any time. Got it?'

'Why are you so bloody good to me?' I asked.

Dot's bright eyes met mine. 'Let's say you remind me of my younger self, and anyway, I've enjoyed my life so much more since you turned up.'

'We're friends, aren't we? It means a lot to me,' I wrapped my arms around her small body in a big hug.

'It's a two-way street sweetheart. I've become very fond of you too. Right, let's put a bad start to the day behind us and have some fun. Shopping and lunch, right?'

We didn't get further than the front door.

*

A package sat on the top step; a box about the size of a large book, wrapped in brown paper and liberal quantities of parcel tape, with a "fragile" sticker across it.

'Why didn't the postie ring the bell, anybody could have nicked this! Whoever sent it should have packed it more carefully,' I said, picking the box up and turning it over. 'Whatever is in it rattles so I hope it isn't broken. Funny, it's not addressed to anyone here, only the street address.'

Dot took a step forward, studied the parcel in my hands for a moment, and then said, 'Put the box back down on the step, Frankie. Gently does it.'

Her voice sounded odd, but I instinctively obeyed her.

'There's only Angus in the house, right?' she said.

'Yes, it's Friday so Sal and Buster will both be at work by now. But what…?'

'OK then, I want you to go upstairs and ask him to work in the garden for a while. Say we'll bring him a chocolate éclair if he does. Do *not* take no for an answer, emphasise the éclair part, use those exact words. Go out of the back door and join him there.'

'Dot, what *is* it?'

'I have to make a phone call. Please, do as I ask.'

Baffled by these instructions, the steely expression and note of authority in her voice convinced me enough to head upstairs and tap on Angus's door.

'Go away,' said a muffled voice, 'I'm busy.'

'Angus, it's Frankie. Auntie Dot says you need some fresh air. Come out to the garden with me, please. She promised to bring you a chocolate éclair.'

To my amazement, after a short pause he opened the door and studied my feet carefully. Over his shoulder I could see several monitor screens across two desks, and a stack of electronics with winking lights. The curtains were drawn, with the dark room lit only by the screens. I couldn't even see a bed though there had to be one in there somewhere.

'She said those words – chocolate éclair?'

'Yes,' I told him. 'You like those?'

'Not particularly, it's a code my dad made up. It means something important is going on and I have to do as I'm told and not argue. Wait a minute while I get my laptop.'

Whatever this coded message meant made it easy to usher him outside, where we both got settled at the plastic garden table. Angus ignored my presence and worked on, oblivious. Bees hummed and gulls squawked, while I sat there with my brain on overdrive, trying to work out what the hell might be going on.

I'd just about chewed my fingernails off with frustration when almost an hour later Dot wandered around to the back of the house with apparent unconcern.

'All sorted,' she said. 'Thank you so much for cooperating, Angus, your dad will be very proud when I tell him about it. You can go back upstairs now.'

He went off without a word, leaving me staring at Dot.

'You require an explanation, of course,' she said, 'but it may have to wait a while since I don't yet have all the answers. Would you mind sitting here with me a little longer, and then I hope we can still go out to a late lunch?'

Eventually, her phone rang, and she answered it, listening but saying nothing beyond a brief "thank you" at the end.

'We can go out now,' she said, as if the events of the morning had been nothing out of the ordinary. 'A car is coming to take us to a nice pub out in the Fylde countryside.'

'A taxi?' I asked.

'Something of the sort, then we can both have a drink. We deserve one after such an *interesting* morning.' Dot looked so pleased with herself I refrained from pointing out that my getting the sack didn't exactly qualify for such a description.

She went off saying she had to collect something from upstairs and soon reappeared, closing the front door behind us as an unremarkable grey saloon car with tinted rear windows drew up.

'Our carriage awaits,' she announced, her face full of mischief. As the driver opened the door for us, she said, 'Hello, Norton, it's been a while. Family OK?'

'Yes, ma'am, thank you.'

I climbed inside saying only, 'Dot, you're up to something, but I guess you'll tell me in your own sweet time.'

'Correct. Now enjoy the scenery and don't ask any questions.'

*

The Blacksmith Inn is the kind of idyllic country pub you see in films or read about in books, a half-timbered black-and-white Tudor building. The bowed roof line indicated extreme age, and below the gold lettering of the sign a timber-framed front porch boasted any number of plaques testifying to the awards the inn had received. Pretty hanging baskets festooned the frontage, and window troughs displayed bright blooms and trailing greenery, with a garden shaded by trees just visible at the rear.

Inside there were no horse brasses or paintings of hounds, let alone intrusive background music. Oak tables and worn leather armchairs contributed to a rustic but modern interior, with whitewashed walls and a polished oak floor. The lunchtime trade was coming to an end by the time we got there – most of the diners were at the coffee stage.

Dot marched us inside and up to the bar, where an older man greeted her saying, 'Hey, you old bat, long time no see. Saved you a quiet table in the corner, overlooking the garden.'

'Nice to see you too, Martin, and less of the old, if you please. Batty may be accurate – I'm cultivating that,' she said.

Not an adjective I'd have used to describe my friend's acute intelligence. As we sat down, a young waiter who reminded me of Justin brought us menus and a bottle of chilled Chablis. Dot inspected the label, saying, 'Domaine Fevre, Martin understands me very well. This will be perfect with the fish.'

'Are we having fish?'

'Of course; it's a speciality here.'

The dining chairs were upholstered in an elegant cream fabric, the table linen starched and heavy. After Dot's approving sip, the waiter poured the wine, and condensation from the chilled alcohol gleamed on the glass surfaces. It was all balm to my bruised soul, but she wasn't getting away with anything. Explanations were long overdue, Dot's mysterious ability to uncover information or make things happen in particular.

'Yes, I can see you're not going to be put off much longer,' said Dot. 'Let's order first and take it from there. I recommend the salmon mousse, followed by the scallops with bacon. Then you shall have the need-to-know basic information.'

I went with Dot's menu choice and sipped at the glorious wine (no need to stay sober for work later) while the waiter took our order. When he'd gone, I gave Auntie Dot my best attempt at a piercing, interrogative stare.

She sat forward, putting her hands flat on the table. 'OK, everyone working in Whitehall government offices receives training to recognise a suspicious package. The box left at Sea View this morning had all the hallmarks, so I chose not to take any chances. The bomb squad has removed it to a safe place. Since it had been sent through the post, there couldn't have been a trembler switch or anything.'

It was a surreal moment; this had to be happening to someone else. 'Yeah, but it wasn't an actual bomb or anything genuinely dangerous?'

'I'm afraid so, yes,' said Dot, as if this kind of thing was commonplace and sipping her wine with obvious pleasure. 'The squad confirmed it by scanning the contents. Somebody slipped up at the sorting depot because it should have been identified before it got to us. The greasy mark on the brown paper and the smell of almonds were a total giveaway. It's caused by the explosive sweating.'

I gaped at her in disbelief. 'You're having me on, right?'

Her face told me no. 'There were other signs. Excessive packaging, lots of stamps to avoid having it weighed, and a small hole in the brown paper where a wire had been removed.'

'But... I picked it up *and* turned it over.'

'Handling it was unlikely to be an issue since it had travelled by post, but I am a follower of Falstaff's advice to the effect "caution is preferable to rash bravery". Ah, here come our starters – you're going to enjoy this.'

I gazed at the white plate the waiter put in front of me, which bore an exquisitely arranged salad garnish with the salmon mousse as the centrepiece. 'Dot, I'm not sure I can eat anything. This is all... a bit of a shock.'

'Nonsense,' she said briskly. 'After two challenging experiences today, this is exactly what you need to stiffen the sinews. Don't let the toast get cold, Martin's chef bakes fresh bread every day.'

Sampling the delicate flavour of the salmon, I changed my mind about not being hungry. Perhaps adrenaline coursing through your body enhances appetite; it certainly had that effect on me.

'Good girl,' said Dot, as I pushed my empty plate away. 'Wait until the scallops come – they are fantastic. It's not only the saffron; there's something else I can't quite identify, and Martin refuses to tell me the secret ingredient. Let me pour you another glass of wine.'

'Can I get this straight? You're telling me the package was a bomb, the real thing?'

'Only a small one, not even a very sophisticated device, but enough to cause a nasty injury if it had been opened…'

She let this information sit in the silence and then continued blithely chatting about the pub and what a success Martin had made of it. When the waiter arrived with our scallops, we gave them our full attention. At least, Dot did. One part of my brain was engaged in appreciation of the amazing food, while the other half struggled with incredulity.

Once our empty plates were removed, I uttered the immortal words, 'I don't believe it, things like this don't happen to ordinary people.'

'I'm afraid sometimes they do, or at least you can get caught up in them. I'm sorry, Frankie, it's a lot to take in, but you've proved yourself to be a woman of character and remarkably resilient despite a regrettable tendency to panic.'

'Dazed and confused would be more accurate right now,' I told her. 'I can't imagine Henry having any understanding of *how* to do this, and why would he hate me enough to send a bomb?'

'While it is abundantly clear he sees you as some kind of threat, it's unlikely he is behind this. My contacts will find out for certain.'

'Who *are* these contacts you talk about?' I said. 'Dot, you have to be straight with me. What the actual fuck is going on here?'

She went completely still, a frown between her brows.

'We do need to rule Henry out of the equation, obviously, but I believe the bomb was almost certainly meant for *me*.'

THIRTEEN

This bald statement made a weird kind of sense to me, having long suspected Auntie Dot wasn't the sweet, slightly eccentric older lady she purported to be. The woman I'd come to value was a sprightly sixty-seven-year-old possessed of a keen mind, and a network of contacts suggesting her past career had been more than your average government pen pusher.

'You're not who you say you are,' I said.

Dot threaded her fingers together. 'Well, yes and no.'

The waiter returned, offering the dessert menu. We both declined but requested coffee, which came with amaretti biscuits, and goblets of pale gold liquid which turned out to be Dot's favourite brandy. The landlord knew her tastes without needing to enquire; they had to be old acquaintances.

I waited.

'You will understand there is a limit to what I'm at liberty to tell you, but I can trust you with enough to make sense of it.'

'You weren't just a civil servant.'

'Yes, I was, in the sense of being a government employee, but something of a specialist in a senior role. I did Middle Eastern studies at university, and as you are aware both read and speak Arabic. I worked overseas for some years, but then mainly in London until I had to take early retirement. I remain an occasional consultant, which gives me access to particular areas of knowledge.'

'Is Dorothy Harmon even your real name?'

Dot sipped her brandy, savouring each mouthful with appreciative slowness. 'Let's just say it is now but hasn't always been. The public persona I cultivate is, as you have guessed, something of a smokescreen.'

I was putting two and two together and came up with a lot more than four.

'You were some sort of intelligence officer?' It made sense but my disbelief was winning.

'Heavens no! Flattering, but you overestimate me, I'm no bloody James Bond.'

'You seriously expect me to believe that? And anyway, how the heck did you end up in a north-west seaside town?'

'People might well ask you the same question,' she said. 'You could describe it as hiding in plain sight. London was no longer safe for me, and after a time Martin suggested my present location might be a good choice. Being tucked away up in the Highlands bored me witless. Nonetheless, coming here was a major adjustment and an occasionally painful one. I did miss the metropolitan lifestyle but have grown to appreciate and value the way I live now.'

'Which means Sea View is as much a "safe house" for you as it is for me?'

'An astute way of describing the arrangement, Frankie. You're every bit as bright as I gave you credit for.'

'But now it's not so safe anymore?' I asked.

'That is a possibility which has to be taken seriously. There is someone who once worked in my department, and whose employment I terminated. He may continue to hold a grievance, not to mention having sufficient expertise to build a basic explosive package. He was in prison but is out on remand now. He could have discovered my location if not my current name, in which case it need not be a major issue and can be speedily resolved. On the other hand, if the package came from the organisation which has tried to hurt me before, then it becomes an infinitely more serious situation, and another relocation might become necessary. I would regret having to do so.'

The surreal feeling had begun to take over again. Dot's account resembled the plot of a spy movie, except for it interrupting my very ordinary life.

'Is this why you wear wigs all the time? A kind of disguise?'

'Well in a roundabout way, yes. I have experienced some hair loss but choose to turn it into a positive and have a bit of fun out of necessity.' Dot's face came alive with mischief. 'Frankie, I do apologise for your accidental involvement in all this, and for possibly placing you and my friends at Sea View in danger, but hope you can understand the precautions being taken right now?'

It was all rather more excitement than I wanted, and my inner tranquillity had received a thorough shake-up.

'And what do Sal and Buster know? Because it has to be something.'

Dot smiled. 'Ah, I have once again underestimated your intelligence. As my local lawyer, Buster understands me to be part of the Protected Persons Service, formerly known as Witness Protection, which is close enough to the truth. Sal was provided with the minimum necessary information and more than happy to go along with the plan if it meant having a guaranteed tenant. My accommodation at Sea View is arranged by an agency which pays a generous monthly rent for a long-term lease, on the strict and legally binding understanding of total discretion. We also have a code word, in a similar way to

Angus, so they both understand that anyone using it comes from me.'

'And Angus has some kind of connection in all this?' I asked.

Dot hesitated only briefly, then gave a rueful smile. 'Having come this far, I may as well explain the rest too. Martin here at the pub used to be part of my team, and Angus is his son. In his early twenties, like any young man, he wanted to leave home and be more independent. Having Asperger's syndrome means he is not necessarily equipped to live entirely without support. Three years ago, I suggested to his father that Sea View might also work for him. It provides a protected living environment in which Sal, Buster and I keep a friendly watch on him. He is stratospherically gifted with computer coding and gets plenty of contracts on a remote-working consultative basis which more than pay his way. Martin supervises Angus's finances, and they are in frequent online and phone contact, so it works well for everyone.'

'And here was me imagining I'd found a temporary home in a very ordinary boarding house. Now I see that for every one of us it provides a kind of refuge from external forces, including Sal, after her violent partner. Except for Buster…'

'Who has problems of her own,' finished Auntie Dot, a sudden edge to her voice. 'Imagine how it feels to be one of the very few black people on the local streets, let alone a gay woman practising as a lawyer. Haven't you noticed how terribly *white* the area is?'

I swallowed. 'Yes, it's such a marked contrast to the multicultural London I once lived in. Do you think she suffers much overt racism?'

'Only every bloody day,' was Dot's response, leaving me acutely aware of my lack of understanding and white privilege. 'Much of it isn't even intentional, but she feels it all the same. Sal talks to me sometimes, to let off steam about the things which happen; it makes her so angry. Buster says mostly it's not worth getting aggravated about, so she ignores it and gets on with her life.'

Martin beckoned Dot over to the bar and they were deep in conversation before disappearing for a time. I stared out of the window at the garden, feeling as if the world had tilted on its axis. When Dot returned to our table she said, 'Finished with your coffee? Then I believe we can go home.'

'Back to the reality that I don't have a job anymore.' The brandy was inducing a sombre reflective mood. 'Couldn't I just stay here and pretend everything is fine? Anything except contemplate my dismal career prospects.'

'Ah, I didn't realise you were worrying so much. Buster says what the cleaning company did is totally illegal. Because of their agreement with the probation service, they are required to give you a contract with proper hours. She will be taking up the matter on your behalf after the weekend, and Jim may find himself with a fight on his hands.'

'When did you talk to Buster?'

A definite smirk appeared on Dot's face. 'I called our landlady from the pub to let her know we'd be late for dinner. She passed on Buster's thoughts on your situation.'

When the car came to take us home, Dot became visibly edgy and out of sorts, drumming her fingers on the armrest and paying little attention to the scenery outside.

'I probably ought to tell you something,' she said.

'What? You mean there's more?'

'I've been concerned you might believe me to be overreacting to the parcel, but there's a reason why I might be a target.'

'Look, you don't have to tell me anything,' I said. 'Presumably, former spies are supposed to keep it zipped, official secrets and so on, I get it.'

'Let me repeat, I was only a civil servant. However, some years ago, I became the victim of a car bomb, which changed everything for me.'

I gaped at her. 'Seriously? Were you hurt?'

'Quite badly, yes. My husband and I were colleagues, and part of the same department; married late in life so never had any children. We were ready to leave for work one morning, and already in the car when I had to go back inside for the office keys. It was a cold morning, so while waiting for me he switched on the engine to warm up the interior. As I closed the front door, the bomb went off.'

The pain of memory made new lines across Dot's face.

'I woke up in hospital to discover my husband had been killed. If I hadn't gone back inside, it would have been me too. It ended my career, partly because of the injuries I sustained, but mainly because I could no longer be safe in London. While convalescing in Scotland, my hair fell out – the effects of shock and grief – and never grew back properly.'

'Dot, how terrible for you.' It was the best I could do but sounded utterly trite and inadequate.

She leaned back. 'Yes, it was a bad time, but I'm fully recovered and have grown to be happy and content with life in St Annes, and all the more so since your arrival. However, you should understand why the threat is potentially serious enough to require extreme caution. Today's bomb might only have been small but indicates a level of risk we hadn't anticipated. Someone could have been badly hurt, and it might have been any of the Sea View family. I would feel so guilty if anything happened because of me. Anyway, we won't need to discuss this again.'

She gave me a bright, unconvincing smile, so I resisted asking any of the questions which came to mind. She'd probably told me more than enough and I had to respect her wish not to talk about it further.

After a further pause, she added, 'You will also be pleased to hear Henry had nothing to do with the bomb. He has, however, been spoken to and instructed to "cease and desist" in terms of his petty hate campaign against you.'

'Seriously?' I wanted to believe this so much; the relief would be incredible.

'How shall I put this? Your estranged husband has been made fully aware of the possible consequences if he doesn't comply.'

The mental image of Henry being scared off by a couple of burly operatives provided deep satisfaction. If he would just leave me alone in future, I could get on with my life. Then my brain made some more connections, not functioning at its best after the mind-numbing effects of the brandy.

'But, Dot, that must mean the bomb was meant for you?'

'No question about it, but as I suspected it was a gift from my aggrieved former colleague. Sheer chance that he was able to locate me, and since he'll be going back to jail for a very long time, it need not concern us further. Job done, as they say.'

On the outskirts of St Annes, Norton accelerated just as the traffic lights went to amber. Dot's capacious handbag fell off the seat, scattering the contents across the floor. I bent down to help her put everything back, and Dot hastily snatched up a small matte black pistol, no longer than my hand, and tucked it out of sight again.

'Only a precaution,' she said lightly, as if people dropped guns at my feet every day of the week. 'Perfectly legal, I have all the paperwork. Nice piece of kit the Glock 42. Be glad I didn't have to use it though, my marksmanship isn't what it used to be, even if I don't need glasses.'

I was living in some kind of parallel universe, one in which Auntie Dot was armed and dangerous.

FOURTEEN

Being back at Sea View wrapped me in such a safe, warm and comfortable feeling, especially at dinner which was later than usual because of our absence. Sal's sausage and chips were the best kind of comfort food, the chips thick cut and handmade, with fat herby sausages from the local butcher. I hadn't yet learnt to appreciate the northern tradition of mushy peas, even if Sal had introduced me to the joys of HP brown sauce.

Angus was deep in a coding book and munched his dinner in rapid abstraction before taking himself back upstairs, leaving the rest of us savouring the last of the gravy. I'd have licked the plate if the nuns hadn't impressed upon me the impropriety of such conduct.

Buster leant back from the table, hands spread across her stomach in appreciation, and smiled at me.

'When I heard what had happened, I took the liberty of composing a letter to your former employer,' she said. 'I hand-delivered it to his home address on my way home. It points out that you are not, in fact, on a zero-hours contract because of the arrangement with the probation service. I also reminded him that under the provisions of the Employment Act, he acted illegally sacking you as he did without a verbal or written warning and with no actual evidence of drug use beyond a malicious letter.'

Sal beamed with pride at her wife. 'Buster thinks Jim is assuming you'll just lie down and accept it without making a fuss because you don't have the money to take him to court.'

'He's got that part right,' I said.

'But this is what the law centre *does*,' Buster told me firmly, stacking plates to take downstairs. 'We advocate for people in your kind of situation who can't afford legal advice. I further suggested Jim should take the matter up with your probation officer and discuss the accusation of drug use with him. Hopefully, this will produce results. He ought to reinstate you, assuming it's what you want, or we can take him to a tribunal for unfair dismissal instead.'

'I *do* want my job back, not least because I'm very fond of my colleagues and don't want to drop them in it. However, the main reason is because of how well the hours fit around volunteering at the food bank and my studying. The bottom line is that it might be difficult to find something else that works so well.'

'You're not going to try and build up your editing business then?' asked Buster. 'Wasn't that the original plan for supporting yourself?'

'Yes, but the website has never brought in more than a trickle of jobs, so I took it down. Now I've found the thing that really lights my fire, I'm happy to consign the editing work to the past.'

'Good for you,' said Sal. 'I figured you wouldn't stick at the cleaning job, but you've proved me wrong, and I'm sorry for thinking it.'

I grinned back, fully prepared to admit the justice of her original opinion. 'You got me there; I came bloody close to quitting the first week, but then things gradually improved. Buster, could you copy my probation officer in on your letter? I'm hoping he will back me up with Jim.'

'Absolutely. I'll email it to him,' said Buster, heading for the stairs with a tray of crockery. 'And try not to worry too much; Jim doesn't have the law on his side but for once you do. Come by the office in the morning and we can sit down and talk about it.'

Lying on my bed at the end of Dot's "interesting" day, my phone rang, and Nik's deep voice said, 'Hi, Frankie, I hope it's not too late to be calling?'

'Not at all. In fact, you're a welcome distraction after the past few hours.' Talk about an understatement.

'Oh dear, is something wrong?'

'Well, I lost my job this morning and things kind of went downhill from there, except for being treated to a lovely lunch.'

'Perhaps I can add a bit of sunshine then? I'm calling to say you got 92% on the exam module and the pass mark is 75%. Well done, but I'm so sorry to hear about the job.'

'Not as sorry as me, but thanks for the good news, which is something to hold onto. Buster says my dismissal wasn't legal, but right now I can't summon the energy for a fight over it.'

'Hey, I hope you aren't planning to lie down under this. Unfair treatment has to be challenged, otherwise the bad guys win. Wait, you didn't set fire to anything did you?'

Not many people could have got away with making jokes about arson, but Nik had believed without question my assertion of innocence, and his faith in me meant a *lot*. I ended up explaining about the drugs accusation and the poisonous letters as well, though I left out the part about explosive devices.

'Bloody hell, somebody has it in for you… this is nasty stuff. And your ex might be behind it?'

'The muscle man delivering the warning said it came from Henry, and anyway, who else could it be? But I don't understand why; he's rid of me, even if we aren't divorced yet. He got the house and his long-term lover, not to mention the ministerial appointment he always wanted. I'm only surprised he *bothers* to harass me – I never believed him to be this vindictive.'

'It's troubling, though,' said Nik. 'You must represent some kind of threat for him to go this far and risk so much?'

'Auntie Dot says the same, but it doesn't make any sense to me. All I'm doing is trying to build a new life and the old one keeps rudely interrupting my progress.'

'You *are* rebuilding, and in the longer term potentially have a whole new career in front of you. You've been so brave, Frankie, after everything that's happened. Focus on the future and believe in yourself. As of Monday, you're officially registered on the next training module for debt counselling.'

This should have been exciting news but managed not to be.

'Look, Nik, the cleaning hours I've been doing were what made it all possible, including time to study and volunteering on Thursdays. Even if I manage to get another job, it might not fit so well around those activities, and I could lose everything I've worked for.' My voice wobbled, at least in part a reaction to the day's events.

'Hey.' Nik's voice changed, became softer. 'Don't be upset, you have my unfailing support, and your fan club has another member as well. Maddie thought you were great and enjoyed our time together. She keeps pestering me to say when we can do it again. She even asked if you were my new girlfriend.'

I suddenly discovered a need to know what his reply had been. 'And you said?'

'I told her not right now, but asked if she would mind if

you were and her verdict is that you are *cool*. High praise when she's seen off some potential candidates for the job.'

'Oh,' seemed to be the best I could manage. 'So, are you saying you'd welcome an application from me?'

Without even a hint of hesitation, he said, 'Very much. After all, you've already been vetted and approved by senior management in the form of a nine-year-old who calls all the shots. Perhaps we could discuss it over dinner sometime?'

'Job interviews work both ways,' I said.

'Let's set one up – I'll see you on Thursday.'

The difficult day I'd been experiencing had got a whole lot better. Maybe my life wasn't over after all.

*

After a very satisfactory meeting at the law centre where Buster explained all my rights in detail, Dot and I went on into Lytham. There the jeweller made good on his previous offer for my platinum and diamond engagement ring, and I handed it over with only the slightest pang of regret. My heart had leapt for joy when Henry got down on one knee in the beautiful gardens of a historic house, and I'd practically flattened him in my eagerness to say yes. The beautiful ring he'd chosen for me had symbolised so much to the naive twenty-year-old he'd swept off her feet. I wasn't that girl anymore.

I tucked the cash safely into my rucksack with a sense of satisfaction, but although I would have a substantial amount of money in reserve, I didn't want to live on it. There was a time when it might have seemed a very modest sum, but lately my fiscal standards had been subject to extensive revision. Part of me was even glad to be rid of the ring because it also drew a line under my marriage and all the things I'd left behind. Dot and I celebrated with a toasted sandwich; my treat this time. If

Henry wanted a divorce to marry Jerry then he could pay the lawyer's fees, as I had better things to spend my money on.

I filled in the empty, jobless days by starting my new studies and on Thursday arrived at the food bank early to find Nik already there. He beamed an enthusiastic welcome at the sight of me, and Andrew's smirk across the room at us made my face flush hot. I was acting less like a sensible forty-three-year-old adult, and something nearer to a teenager with a crush.

The afternoon session was a busy one, and my newly acquired skills were much called upon. Nik brought me a coffee between clients, asking, 'Are you by any chance free this evening? My mother is available for babysitting duties, and I could drive back to Manchester afterwards.'

'Sounds great,' I said. Then, wanting to be clear, added, 'Would this be an official date?'

Nik's eyes searched my face. 'As long as you're happy with that, then absolutely it is. You have, after all, been approved by the management.'

We went back to "happy hour" at the Spice King, where I toasted our fledgling romance by sampling one of their cocktails. I was oddly shy with Nik at first; even the idea of a new relationship being uncharted territory. He must have read my mind.

'Does this feel a bit strange?' he asked, reaching across the table to hold my hand. 'Because it does for me. I've only been on a handful of dates in the past couple of years, and I never went out with anyone more than twice. No sparks.'

'It's all pretty new to me too,' I told him. There were definitely sparks on my side at least. 'I haven't done this in more than twenty years.'

His large brown fingers wrapped around mine, which I hoped weren't too rough from all the cleaning chemicals. At least good hand cream was a luxury I could now afford. The waiter brought us steaming plates of lamb bhuna served with freshly made chapatis.

'I'd be more anxious if Maddie hadn't given the official seal of approval,' he said with a grin. After swallowing a folded piece of chapati, his face became serious. 'Frankie, I'm not messing about here, I'm really attracted to you, and have been since our first proper conversation. I don't want to rush you into anything until you're ready, but for me this could be something special.'

His words made me glow all over, and it filled my heart to feel wanted after so many years.

'I think we might be special together too, but this is only our first date, so let's not get ahead of ourselves. Let me just say I'm not messing about either; I wouldn't waste your time or mine.'

'I'd pretty much guessed that,' he told me, his eyes lighting up. 'It's part of what I like about you – that you're so open, honest and straightforward. I've never understood how to play those guessing games where you have to work out what's happening when someone blows hot then cold.'

I speared another chunk of lamb before asking the question uppermost in my mind.

'And you genuinely don't care about the prison thing? There is Maddie to consider.'

'Frankie, have you any idea how often people get convicted of things they didn't do?'

'If that's true then it's bloody awful.' I was going hot with indignation. It could have been the spicy food, or perhaps the proximity of Nik producing long-dormant feelings my body had forgotten how to respond to.

'According to a legal friend of mine, it happens all the time, so I've never found it hard to believe in your innocence.'

'Thank you,' I said, with real feeling behind the simple statement. 'Although I should confess upfront given the

172

opportunity to lay hands on my estranged husband, I wouldn't be responsible for my actions.'

A shadow crossed Nik's face. 'After Sophie died, I was bloody *furious* with her for leaving us, and part of me hated myself for feeling that way. We didn't have the best marriage, so I never expected to be so angry, wanting to break things, but there was always Maddie who had to be put first. Without the counselling provided through work, I'd still be nursing a lot of unresolved grief and anger. Anyway, Henry behaved despicably and I sincerely hope he gets his comeuppance one of these days.'

'That would be very satisfying, but I'm not holding my breath.'

After sharing a dessert of rasmalai with pistachio nuts – one bowl, two spoons – we talked about our hopes for the future. My own newly developed dreams of a meaningful career in the charitable sector where I could make a real difference to people, and Nik's plan to move Maddie out of the big city and into the countryside.

'She loves primary school, but the very idea of her in any of the local high schools makes me go cold all over. Unfortunately, what I can afford in a nice rural area is a rabbit hutch. At least our Manchester flat has good-sized rooms – we bought at the right time – and there's a park in easy walking distance.'

'Just so you know, I've never wanted to live in the country,' I confessed. 'Green fields and pretty villages are lovely to visit but I'd miss the coast and walking on the shore. I also need retail experiences and the buzz of people, places to eat, things to do and see.'

'Don't forget charity shops – Mamma is with you on the subject of urban versus rural. She used to go back to Greece to visit family while her dad was still alive, and always complained about the dullness of life in their remote hamlet. But didn't you grow up in the Home Counties – no thoughts about going back there?'

'Amersham isn't exactly rural,' I said, snaffling the last spoonful of pudding. 'It's London commuter belt and very expensive. Anyway, since I went to prison my dad has moved away – he bought a unit in a retirement complex in Leighton Buzzard – so I've no ties to my hometown anymore.'

'You're an only child, like me? I never wanted Maddie to be one, but these days I don't worry about it as long as she's happy and thriving despite losing her mum. Speaking of which, I should set off home, but it's been a lovely evening, and I hope we'll do this again.'

We walked back to Norcross Road hand in hand, and on the doorstep of Sea View he fulfilled my hopes by kissing me, slowly and tenderly, and then traced my lips and cheek as if exploring my face fully for the first time.

'Frankie I... oh, never mind,' he said, clearly uncertain of what he wanted to say to me.

I held him close for a long moment, my head against his chest. 'I've had such a good time, Nik. Send Maddie my love and let's do the ice cream and beach thing again soon – before she goes back to school in September.'

I watched him walk away until he turned back at the corner. His face broke into a huge smile at the sight of me still standing on the doorstep, and he waved and blew kisses before setting off back over the bridge to where he'd parked his car. I went up to my room with a heart full of hope and possibility, but also recognising the perils of getting too far ahead. Wherever this relationship might be going it couldn't be rushed, especially with a child involved.

*

My phone rang at 8.00am the following morning. I was already up, being in the habit of rising early, but not dressed. Who on earth could be calling at that hour – not Justin in some kind of trouble?

'Frankie? It's Jim Morley…' A long and excruciating pause followed, and I didn't immediately help him out with it.

'Hello,' I said carefully, with as much calmness as I could manage. 'How can I help you?'

'I got your lawyer's letter and went to see your probation officer yesterday. It seems an apology may be in order as I did rather jump to conclusions. The thing is, I've had a drug user on my teams before and it didn't end well so I panicked. Now it's different, and I've been assured that the accusation isn't true, so can you come back – start Monday? I've got you some replacement afternoon hours over the school holidays too, at a small hotel on Ashton Road.'

'Well, I might have to think about…'

'It's also been agreed with probation you'll get paid for the time since…' I could almost feel him squirming on the end of the phone, but decided to be nice, what with everything going my way, thanks to Buster and Tony.

'Monday will be fine,' I told him.

'Thank God. Shannon and Doreen have been bending my ear something chronic. See you Monday then.'

Although Jim had admitted to owing me an apology, I'd never got one, but this only occurred to me after he'd rung off. Never mind, things were looking up; I had a job again, and a new purpose in life, not to mention the possibility of romance. I was even starting to believe Dot's assurance that Henry wouldn't trouble me anymore.

*

Over the summer weekends when I wasn't working, Nik, Maddie and I went on all manner of seaside jollifications, even a trip to the famous tower in Blackpool. From the top, the view was incredible: the pier and shore stretched out ahead, the sea and sky so wide and blue that looking beyond it made me dizzy. Later, we hired deckchairs and did the whole bucket-and-spade and stick-of-rock thing.

'Come on, Frankie, this sandcastle isn't going to decorate itself,' said a happily bossy Maddie. She sounded so like her dad that we both collapsed into helpless laughter.

I knelt on the sand in my swimsuit, the scents of ozone and sun cream mingling, and all my senses alert to the moment. Nik in his boxer swimming trunks and sexily hairy chest, and a child who I could easily grow to love. *It doesn't get better than this*, I thought, adding the last of the cockle shells I'd collected to the magnificent edifice father and daughter had constructed.

Maddie so obviously enjoyed herself on these trips, even happy to play the slot machines when the rain came down. It's easy to forget how much pleasure kids get out of simple things such as ice cream and the undivided attention of adults. It all took me back to Justin's early childhood, a pure and uncomplicated time when I still believed we were a happy family and, despite his infidelities, Henry genuinely did care about me.

Thursdays, after the food bank session, became our regular date night, thanks to a combination of sleepovers with friends for Maddie and *Yaya's* willingness to babysit. One regular haunt was the Spice King, although we had also discovered a bistro in Blackpool.

'My spending so much time with you has got Mamma asking lots of questions,' he told me. 'The only pictures I could show her were the ones Maddie took on her phone.'

I groaned. 'Tell me it wasn't the kiss-me-quick hat?'

His eyes danced. 'Yes, but she needs to know everything about the woman who has stolen me away.'

I wanted to think more about this statement but had a serious question that needed an answer. 'You haven't shared the prison part with her yet?'

He understood. 'No, I've only said that you've been through a marriage breakdown and recently become involved with the Laneways Trust. Did I do right?'

'I guess so, but she might have to know eventually.'

Nik had agreed to take things slow and steady in terms of our growing relationship. After the disaster zone of my marriage, I needed to take baby steps before trusting someone with my heart again. All through what seemed like endless golden weekends, I kept telling myself to take it slow. Some of my emotions took absolutely no notice of this sensible advice.

*

Kim kept in touch faithfully by text but had nothing much to report, which left me nursing a whole heap of guilt because he'd given me money for a story which hadn't gone anywhere. I'd passed on the information from Justin about Henry's relationship falling apart, but this didn't provide much of an insight either.

Still digging, and some promising leads but it's taking a long time to pin them down. K.

I feel like I should give your money back. My information hasn't been of much use. F.

Don't be silly, consider it a down payment. K.

I thanked all the deities out there (including Auntie Dot's "sources") when there was no further harassment, and I could relax and stop living on high alert. Henry appeared to have problems of his own, at least according to Justin's regular emails. I guessed that he wrote them in quiet intervals at his new job, trying to appear keen and busy.

> *Hey, Mum,*
>
> *It's OK here at Blades & Rossington – they're way less stuffy than the other lot and we're doing some interesting work on immigration law, representing refugees and such. You wouldn't believe some of the stories I hear – people go through so much – it's been a bit of a steep learning curve. Basic graduate salary for now, but living at home it's OK, and the job might lead to bigger and better things one day. Hope so, because Dad and Jerry are barely speaking, not sure what's going on, but think they could be close to splitting up.*
>
> *There's a girl I really fancy here at the office, and I'm trying to do what you said and be more of a grown-up to convince her I'm not a total knobhead. Wish me luck.*
>
> *Justin x*
>
> *PS hope you're doing OK too.*

The summer idyll had to end when cooler September days meant back to school for both Maddie and me, and I understood exactly what my son meant about steep learning curves. Some days I stared at the debt counselling materials like they were in a foreign language. The module was proving a real challenge and even haunted my dreams. It made me so viscerally angry to discover how necessity forced people to borrow more than they could afford to repay. This trap inevitably led to a downward spiral, as high interest rates then made the debt many times larger than the original loan. The problems seemed insurmountable, and there was no quick fix to resolve them, only helping people take the small incremental steps that led to financial freedom.

Nik carved out from work all the space he could to develop our growing relationship. We'd done a lot of kissing, talking and touching, but even though some of our precious evenings were spent up in my room, we hadn't moved much further. The old house creaked enough anyway, and an active sex life would have to wait until we could do it without Auntie Dot living underneath.

She frequently gave me knowing looks, as did Buster and Sal. They all called Nik my "boyfriend" and treated him with genuine warmth and affection when he joined us for occasional meals. Even Angus laughed at some of his jokes. Nik never knew, but I insisted on paying Sal extra to cover the costs. Best to keep things straight and not take advantage.

Life was looking good, what with gainful employment, friends and a promising relationship. All that changed when early one evening, I was reading on my bed when Kim rang.

'Frankie, something's going on. There are rumours of a major scandal involving a senior cabinet member who's been massively indiscreet while drunk, and Henry is somehow connected. I'm working on it and have made cautious approaches to Jerry – according to the grapevine he's steaming with fury, so might be ready to talk to me. All I know is that he's resigned as constituency agent but nothing more right now. If the shit hits the fan, then brace yourself because you could get dragged into it.'

My hand shook as I disconnected, hearing the first rumblings of a distant avalanche.

FIFTEEN

Kim's information had me panicking and jittery, but I didn't want to introduce a negative note into what had become the nightly ritual of a phone call with Nik. Instead, I turned to Dot for wisdom and advice – she'd told me to call on her "any time" and I took shameless advantage. Since the bomb incident, our friendship had grown, and we'd become even closer; a precious thing for me when I'd grown up without a mother or older female relatives. Buster and Sal were also solid rock for me to stand on, but although they'd be willing to listen if I needed them, I was generally reluctant to invade their private space or time together.

'What if the paparazzi come sniffing around?' I asked Dot, who handed me a stiff gin without asking if one was required. It was. 'Kim says they might, and I've been thinking since he managed to find me, presumably they could too.'

Dot took a large swallow of her drink before offering a calm and practical response.

'Why would they bother? Kim mentioned a senior minister, so they'd go after them first. And even if Henry *is* involved, your break-up would be seen as ancient history so whatever might be going on now, they'd be focused primarily on him and perhaps Jerry.'

I groaned. 'But that means Justin could get dragged into it.'

Dot looked at me like I was being particularly thick. 'Since they all share a house that's inevitable,' she said. 'Look, if they do come after you then we'll deal with it whatever happens, though I can't do much to protect you. I might be able to make a case with my superiors for diverting unwelcome attention around this address, but it would be a stretch. I'm so sorry.'

'No, I'm the one who should apologise,' I told her. 'I'm not expecting you to wave a magic wand and summon up the cavalry again. It isn't your responsibility to take care of me, and you're probably right to say I'm worrying about something which hasn't even happened yet. It's not as if I could tell the press anything new – it's close to three years since I've even *seen* Henry.'

Dot leaned back in her chair, frowning in concentration. 'I've always thought you must have some information which gives you a kind of power over him. Why else has he been so insistent you "keep quiet", when he doesn't even know that you saw those photographs? It might be about something so ordinary and everyday you don't even realise how significant it is. And while I may not be responsible for you, I *do* care.'

'Oh, Dot,' I said, putting down my glass to wrap my friend in a hug, 'this house and the people in it, but most of all *you*, have become so important to me. You've been a family and a life raft to cling to since I got out of prison. But it feels like every time I try and get my life on track, something derails me all over again, and it usually has Henry behind it somewhere. You know very well I only spoke to Kim in an entirely selfish attempt to protect myself and divert his attention to Henry.'

Dot adjusted her headscarf – a striking design with zebras on a teal background.

'Stop right there, Frankie Douglas, and don't be such a wimp because you aren't a victim anymore. You've served time

181

and fought back to make your own way ever since. The woman I see now is very different to the one who first arrived – strong and independent, building a life of her own. Whatever Henry's been up to might not need to involve you in any way.'

'Except we're still married, despite the legal separation.'

'These days politicians can get away with almost anything, but it might well be enough to cause a big stir, provided Kim can come up with solid evidence. Jerry and Henry parting company wouldn't be anyone's idea of a story.'

Thanks to the gin and Dot's wise counsel, I was able to chat with Nik an hour later in a more relaxed state of mind. His call came as I snuggled up in bed with Spike, my head resting on an antique lace-edged pillowcase, one of my latest charity-shop finds. A little bit worn (aren't we all), but still beautiful.

His dark voice came down the phone and if I shut my eyes, I could pretend I had him there next to me.

'You,' he said softly, 'are becoming as necessary to me as breathing. I spend much of every day saving up little stories and snippets to tell you about, and our conversations keep me going in a way nothing else can.'

'I look forward to them too. Chatting to you helps me get to sleep.'

'Are you trying to say I'm boring?' Nik demanded in an indignant voice.

This made me chuckle, causing a stir of protest from Spike who was sitting on my chest at the time.

'Absolutely not, but I can drift off feeling everything will be OK because of you.'

His response left me in no doubt my growing feelings for him were entirely reciprocated.

'Before we say goodnight, Maddie and I...' he began, then hesitated. 'We were wondering if you'd like to spend this weekend in Manchester with us?'

'That would be very special,' I said with genuine enthusiasm. 'So yes please, if you're *both* sure?'

Neither of us tacitly mentioned it, but I accepted in the knowledge the flat had only two bedrooms, so unless Nik intended to sleep on the sofa it meant we'd be taking our relationship to the next level. At least I hoped so; about bloody time, and I felt more than ready for something physical and longed to wake up with him.

Buster lent me a faux-crocodile holdall for my weekend tryst, and from a limited wardrobe, I chose the smarter of my casual clothes, before investing in some new underwear and a short pair of pyjamas. I did have concerns about Maddie being OK with having me in their home, but in another of our evening calls Nik had a message to give me.

'She wanted me to ask if you liked Barbies. She says I am total rubbish in the dolly department and don't play properly.'

I had to laugh. 'Tell her I had gazillions of them at her age and loved them very much. I am more than happy to play as much as she wants.'

'Hey, don't forget to save some of your time for me too,' he protested.

'Once Maddie's gone to bed, I'm all yours,' I told him.

'I'm kind of counting on that,' he said.

*

When Friday came, I'd texted Kim but had no idea if he'd been able to speak to Jerry. Anyhow, other things were occupying my mind, not least the ending of a long period of involuntary celibacy. As I showered and changed after work, I contemplated this prospect with pleasure but some slight anxiety. I was lean and fit, but my body had seen better days, not to mention still bearing the silvery stretch marks collected in pregnancy.

I wanted Nik so much, but would he find me desirable? We'd have to wait and see.

He collected me from Sea View at 6.30pm prompt. 'Your carriage awaits, Cinderella,' he said, handing me into his elderly estate car.

'I'm hoping for more princess than cinders in the ashes.'

'Wait and see,' he told me as we headed for the motorway. 'Tonight, Maddie gets to stay up late and we're going to have a takeaway feast in front of the TV. Her idea and I hope you enjoy pizza because it's all her heart desires.'

'I love it, especially when anchovies are involved.'

'Ah, a woman after my own heart. We get the pizzas on take-out order from the local Italian restaurant, and they are seriously good. Maddie won't touch the supermarket ones since we found those.'

I was assailed by sudden misgivings. 'And who's with Maddie right now?'

'Her *yaya* picked her up from school and is staying with her until we get there, and then says she'll make herself scarce.'

My heart sank: his mother would be inspecting me too?

'Um, right.' Talk about dropped right in it.

He reached out a hand as we stopped at the traffic lights. 'Don't worry, Frankie, my mamma is a darling and she's excited about meeting you. You'll like her, I promise.'

This might be true, but how would Mamma feel about the jailbird her son was bringing home?

Nik's Salford flat was in a modern concrete block, smart and well-kept, in a nice area with trees on the street and a park close by. There were two flats on each floor, with theirs on the third. Going up in the lift, he kissed me with more than a hint of passion, and as his body pressed against mine, I stopped worrying about whether he'd fancy me in bed.

Maddie must have seen the car arrive downstairs because

she was waiting at their front door wearing Barbie pyjamas and squealed with excitement as we stepped out of the lift, both a little flushed.

'*Yaya*, they're here,' she called out, grabbing my hand and all but dragging me inside. At the end of a short hall stood a diminutive figure with Nik's dark colouring. He must have got the height gene from his father because Mamma was petite, no more than 5'2" soaking wet; nothing even close to the large, plump Greek matriarch of my imaginings. She wasn't even dressed all in black but wore a bright shirt with leggings and floral ankle boots.

Maddie drew me into an open-plan living room with the kitchen at one end, a light-filled space painted in simple white, furnished in greys with occasional splashes of red.

Mamma reached up to plant continental-style kisses on each of my cheeks. 'Niko described you to me,' she said. 'But he never told me you were beautiful.'

She shot up in my estimation for this generous if inaccurate assessment.

'The pizzas should be here in twenty minutes, I told them 8.00pm,' said Nik.

'Did you order from the car, Daddy? Me and him always have the same, but what did you pick, Frankie?'

'Tuna and anchovy with extra mozzarella,' I told her. Serious teeth brushing would be necessary for later; maybe even mouthwash, which, of course, I'd packed.

Mamma put her coat on and hugged her granddaughter before turning to me.

'Nice to meet you, Frankie, we will get better acquainted on Sunday.'

'Sunday?' I asked, confused.

Nik reddened. 'Sunday lunch with *Yaya* is a family ritual – didn't I mention it?'

'Niko, you bad boy,' she said with a chuckle. 'You didn't even tell the poor girl? Don't worry, Frankie, as you are the first woman he has ever brought home since... well, I shall be on my very best behaviour.' The wink suggested we were going to get on.

'So, *Yaya*, no bossing her about the way you do me,' Maddie instructed.

'As if,' she said. 'And who is the bossy one around here, little miss? *Kalinikta*, everyone, see you Sunday.' Then, as promised, she left, and I appeared to have passed the first test.

'Come on,' said Maddie, leading me to the sofa. 'Pizza night is for special times, and we always have a film. I've picked some you might want to see.' With expert familiarity, she navigated the remote control to offer me a selection from the streaming service.

'They all sound good to me, so I'm going to let you choose.'

Nik groaned, gathering plates and paper napkins. 'Then we'll be having *Harry Potter and the Goblet of Fire* again, for about the hundredth time.'

'No, Daddy. Frankie will prefer *How to Train Your Dragon*.'

'Sounds perfect,' I told her. 'There's no TV in my room, so I mostly read or catch up with things on my laptop, and I haven't watched a film in ages.'

'This will be fun,' Maddie told me, with the blithe confidence of a child who has no doubt how much she is loved. It made me wish I'd had the same.

The three of us curled up on the big sofa with Maddie between us and when he could, Nik reached around the back of her head and stroked my hair and neck. His touch crackled with a promise of things to come, and all my nerve endings were alert and fizzing with possibility. The pizzas were also every bit as good as promised, and I'd never seen the film which made us all laugh.

Maddie was drowsing by the time the credits rolled, and her hand had crept into mine.

'I've got the books too, and I've read them *all*,' she said, yawning. 'Daddy wouldn't let me watch any of the films until I'd read the books. He said the same with *Harry Potter* – it's the rule in our house.'

'Time to brush your teeth, then bed,' Nik told her.

'Frankie can help me,' she announced.

After I'd supervised the teeth brushing, Maddie gave me a minty kiss on the cheek. 'Daddy thinks you're special, so you must be extra *extra* careful to be nice to him. You will, won't you?'

'I promise,' I told her with due solemnity. 'He's quite special as well. And you are too.'

'Well, of course,' she said, with the devastating smile which mirrored her father's.

Inevitably, Maddie pleaded for a bedtime story, and I discovered father and daughter were deep into *Through the Looking Glass*, having finished *Alice in Wonderland*. As part of the next chapter, it fell to me to read the Jabberwocky aloud, something I did with drama and relish, even while privately admitting to hamming it up and trying to impress.

'I love the bit about the Jabberwocky "whiffling through the tulgey wood, and burbling as it came",' said Maddie at the end. 'Is that a kind of zombie apocalypse?'

It was evident that the sophisticated modern child required a whole other category of scary monsters. When I finally made it back to the living room, Nik had tidied up the detritus of our meal, turned the lights down and put on some background music. The scene was all set for seduction, and I didn't need any persuading...

Nik's bedroom was on the opposite side of the living room from Maddie's, with its own en suite bathroom, so any anxieties

187

I might have had about waking her were needless. Since my university days, I'd only had sex with one long-term partner, and none at all in more recent years. Both of us were more than ready, but also a little shy with each other, so we took our time and let the first exploration of each other's bodies be slow and gentle until we couldn't anymore.

Nik hadn't drawn the bedroom curtains and, accustomed to early starts, the September sunrise had me waking before 7.00am. Nestled into his shoulder, studying his sleeping face and the long dark lashes, I felt so lucky to have met someone to care for. After Henry and then prison, there'd been a time when I'd found it hard to believe anyone would ever want me.

Even in my late teens I'd never been particularly "pretty", though a girlfriend had once described me as handsome and striking, with my dark colouring and long shiny hair. The popular girls tended to the petite and cute, and I was neither, not to mention my nose being over large. Access to the best hairdressers and expensive clothes meant I'd been able to turn out as a stylish woman and become what Henry described as "presentable" for doing the political circuit.

Things had changed: since prison, I'd kept my hair short, worn no more make-up than occasional lipstick and almost all of my clothes were second-hand. I had to remind myself that it was this new persona that Nik had been attracted to and begun to have feelings for.

In the early light, I padded naked to the bathroom, dodging the windows in case of low-flying helicopters or neighbours with binoculars. Coming back, I picked up my pyjamas from the holdall and put them on in case Maddie got up early, the way Justin had done at her age. Back in bed, I traced Nik's lips with my fingers; he stirred, slowly coming to full consciousness and reaching for me.

'You're here,' he said, tightening his arm around me. 'Oh, Frankie, I've wanted this for so long, to wake up with you.'

Things were beginning to get interesting when the door burst open, and Maddie bounced onto the bed.

'Hey, we talked about this,' said Nik. 'Didn't we agree when Frankie came you would knock first?' He'd obviously prepared his daughter for the fact we'd be sharing a bed.

'Sorry, I'm so excited and forgot. Can I join in this cuddle too?'

She inserted herself between us, leaving Nik and me to exchange rueful glances across her head; thank God I'd put my pyjamas on. Blended families could often be problematic, so I felt incredibly lucky Maddie had taken to me so readily. The voice of reality from the inner recesses of my brain reminded me how being a visitor to have fun with was one thing. If the relationship with Nik lasted, then further down the line there might need to be discipline and an insistence on certain rules (such as not bursting into the bedroom), at which point things would undoubtedly be different. Might have been getting a bit ahead of myself there.

Maddie's dark curls tickled the side of my face. I guessed Nik's would be the same if he allowed it to grow. I'd come to love the way his hair curled on the nape of his neck.

'Frankie, you promised to play Barbies,' she said, sitting up.

'And I will, but only when I've had coffee,' I told her.

'Daddy always says the same. And he told me we had to do things today *you* would enjoy as well as the stuff I want.'

'Only fair, right?' Nik pretended to eat her, making chomping noises on her arm, and she squealed with delight. 'You get to play dinosaur golf and then Frankie gets to visit the nice shops and have lunch out.'

'Dinosaur golf?' I asked.

'It's awesome,' Maddie told me. 'Me and Daddy go but he's *rubbish* at it, and I always beat him.'

Nik pulled a face. 'It's kind of crazy golf on steroids, in a huge adventure park. Then we'll go to the Trafford Centre. You girls might enjoy doing some big city shopping?'

Maddie and I played with the dolls while Nik made us breakfast of toast and coffee, which we ate as a carpet picnic in her very pink fairy bedroom. All the Barbies had to be redressed, with suitable accessories as they were going to a party.

My skill at dinosaur golf turned out to be no better than Nik's, and having been beaten soundly by Maddie at every hole, we set off for the shopping centre. It was a marble Temple of Mammon, which brought back echoes of my London life, reminding me how much I'd changed. I'd once enjoyed such places but not anymore, though I did manage to buy myself a pair of ritzy earrings in a sale without breaking the bank. Arriving at the food court, we were assaulted not only by an explosion of food aromas but also by enthusiastic people offering sample tastes of various dishes.

'You choose what we have for lunch,' said Nik.

'Daddy always has Chinese,' Maddie artlessly informed me, and I was happy to agree. We selected our noodle dishes and ate them out of cardboard trays with bamboo chopsticks sitting on hard plastic chairs under the wide atrium. It was noisy and thronged with people, but we had the best fun watching the other customers and making up stories about them.

'The man over there is definitely a spy,' said Maddie in a stage whisper. 'You can tell because of his black leather jacket. They always wear that stuff on the TV. And shades, of course.'

I couldn't quite picture Auntie Dot in black leather, but real life could sometimes be stranger than fantasy, and she did carry a gun in her handbag.

We then visited an enormous toy store where Maddie and I admired the floor-to-ceiling display of Barbie dolls. Nik's expression resembled someone dragged into a vision of hell.

'You're not enjoying this are you?' I whispered.

'As a man who dreams of living in the countryside, I admit to feeling alien at such an altar of rampant consumerism,' he whispered. Then Maddie claimed his attention and he agreed the birthday fairies might bring a Doctor Barbie when the long-anticipated date came around. He'd probably have promised her a dozen to get the hell out of there.

'Are you having fun, Frankie? Do you love shopping?' Maddie asked.

'Not as much as I once did. I used to have lots of money but now I don't, so this isn't the kind of place I usually shop, but it's fun looking in the windows.'

Nik beamed with relief when I suggested we go home. He'd clearly been doing his best to offer us both something we'd enjoy, with more success in the child-friendly offerings. Back at the flat, Maddie watched TV while I helped in the kitchen with preparations for dinner.

'Did I get it wrong about the shopping centre?' he asked. 'I thought you'd like it.'

'Once I would have been all about labels and retail therapy,' I told Nik. 'Now those things feel kind of hollow, even if I could still afford them. These days I surprise myself by being more into walking on the beach and simple pleasures which touch my soul the way only a few things can.'

'You've no idea what a relief that is,' he told me. 'I loathe that big mall and wouldn't care if I never went there again, though Sophie used to enjoy it when she was well enough. We have good enough shops on our local high street, so I can't see the point.'

'The attraction is the big-name brands I guess, and the whole experience of an enormous shopping centre. There must be an entire quarry full of marble in the place. If I'm honest it doesn't do much for me either.'

'You're wonderful,' he told me, and his look promised much for later.

On Sunday morning, after a slow start, we all went to lunch with Nik's mamma.

'Call me Val,' she said, welcoming me with a kiss and genuine warmth. 'It's short for Valentina, which is reserved for formal occasions or old aunties.'

She lived in a modern terraced house and wouldn't let me help in the small kitchen. Of course, she turned out to be an amazing cook, producing, with minimum apparent effort, mouth-watering Greek dishes. No pressure to compete there then.

'This blue bowl is lamb meatballs with feta and tomato, and the other is an aubergine bake. Later we shall have the best baklava you've ever eaten, my granny's recipe.'

At the end of a lovely afternoon, *Yaya* kept Maddie with her so Nik could drive me home, despite my protests about getting on a train. We were so full of food I was almost comatose, lulled by the motion of the car, when my phone jolted me out of a doze. My distended stomach lurched when the caller display told me it was Kim.

'Frankie? I might be onto something. Does the name Cabot Lyle mean anything to you?'

It definitely did, but fogged with food and red wine, I couldn't quite join up the dots. Having struggled and failed, I had to say, 'I'm so sorry, Kim. Maybe it will come to me if I sleep on it? I'll call you if it does.'

Inevitably, I remembered in the middle of the night.

SIXTEEN

The name Cabot Lyle *meant* very little, but I finally recalled where I'd seen it – on our credit card statements while Henry and I had still been married. He didn't always remember to use his separate constituency office credit card, so when Cabot Lyle became a regular item on our bills, I queried it.

'Put it down as a private expense,' Henry said. 'It's a membership association for people in the political and business spheres, and I use their facilities occasionally. Networking, if you want to describe it that way.'

That was the limit to what I could remember. As I walked to work early Monday morning, wrapped up against the late September chill, I left an answerphone message for Kim. What I'd remembered didn't seem likely to contribute much to the investigation.

Doreen and Shannon jumped on me as soon as we got into the lift, insistent on hearing how "everything" had gone. I resisted at first, but they weren't having it.

'Come on then, Frankie,' said Shannon, hauling the big industrial vacuum cleaner out of the cupboard. 'Give us all the juicy bits.'

'As if,' I told them, emptying a bin into a black plastic bag.

'Well at least tell us if he were any good in bed,' called Doreen from across the office.

'My lips are sealed,' I said firmly, but couldn't quite suppress a smile, which told them what they wanted to know. Much ribald teasing followed, but I refused to share any details.

By the time we got towards the end of the shift, they'd heard instead all about Nik's mamma.

'Bloody cheek not to warn you about meeting her,' said Doreen, wiping one of the toilet cubicle doors.

'Nik chickened out of telling you. Too scared you'd decide not to go.'

I'd come to the same conclusion. He'd dropped Maddie on me without notice too, but there'd been genuine reasons on that occasion, even if he could have texted first. Then there'd been the Sunday lunch thing.

'I guess you and Maddie getting on well clears the way, don't it?' Shannon observed, scrubbing at a chrome tap. 'But are you sure he isn't just looking for a mother for his kid?'

This question gave me a sudden jolt, and my silence told them Shannon had shrewdly identified a doubt I hadn't even known was there.

Face reddening, I said, 'OK, maybe at some level the weekend constituted a sort of a test. I mean, he needs to be sure Val and Maddie are comfortable with me. If they're not then the relationship isn't going anywhere, is it?'

'Yeah, but you should have had time to brace yourself for meeting his mum.'

This left me considering Nik's cowardice where his family were concerned. He'd left me to sink or swim twice now, and my elated mood went down just a bit.

Auntie Dot had made me promise I'd tell her all (well, most of) the details of my weekend away, and in return promised me lunch in Lytham. At 12.00pm I knocked on her door, and she emerged in a faux-fur leopard-print jacket, teamed with a black turban with hints of blonde wig showing beneath it. My outfit was less spectacular – the red riding hood coat had come out again because there was a distinct edge on the wind off the sea. She took me to a little bistro in Lytham I hadn't visited before, where they offered tapas dishes from a buffet counter at lunchtime and in the early evening. Such food suited me because I found it hard to work the later shift if weighed down by a heavy lunch.

'You look well,' observed Dot as we carried our plates to a corner table. 'Positively smug, in fact. So may I infer you found everything satisfactory in the romantic department?'

'You could put it like that,' I said carefully, savouring the garlic prawns with chorizo. Better not breathe on the team at school later.

'Don't be coy, Frankie. Such things are important. Physical compatibility is a key ingredient in a good relationship, but I'm guessing you have no complaints?'

'Um, no,' I said. 'But I'm not going to discuss his technique so you can dream on.'

'I wouldn't dream of being so intrusive,' said Dot. 'But I hope, for your sake, Nik has a bit of fire in the bedroom department – Mediterranean men are famous for it.'

'Nik grew up in Salford not Greece,' I said, 'but appears to have learnt a thing or two despite this obvious disadvantage. His mother and I got on well too.'

Dot nearly choked on her olives stuffed with white anchovies. 'Dear God, he introduced you to her as well? Talk about trial by fire – you weren't expecting that, were you?'

'No, but Nik clearly decided we might as well cross all the hurdles in one weekend. Val is great, a woman of character who reminds me of yourself; petite but fierce and strong. She kept calling me *omorfo*, beautiful.'

'I wouldn't go quite that far,' said Dot, 'but you scrub up all right.'

'Don't hold back,' I protested. 'Honestly, Dot, it was such a struggle not to be self-conscious and aware of Val watching as I played with Maddie, but later she admitted to being impressed by how easy and comfortable we were together. I guess it's only fair for her to be concerned – she wouldn't want her precious granddaughter in the hands of some man-eating cougar.'

Dot chuckled. 'Not a description I'd ever apply to you, but what an ordeal. I imagine you'd rather take your driving test again than face a potential mother-in-law?' She speared a cube of feta cheese and chewed on it with relish.

This comment startled me so much that I dropped my fork. 'Whoa, hold on there. Nik and I are in the very early stages of our relationship. Nobody's even talking about love let alone walking down the aisle, and anyway, I'm not divorced from Henry.'

'It might not be on your or Nik's mind yet, but I'd put money on it his mother is ahead of you there. I take it she doesn't know you've been to prison?'

'No, and such information will only be supplied *much* further down the line on a need-to-know basis.'

Dot wiped her mouth and gave me a direct stare. 'You shouldn't be ashamed about your record, Frankie. Even if you *were* guilty of arson, a lot of women wouldn't have blamed you for one second if you'd done it. Think of all those delicious reprisal stories about wine redistribution, or significant parts removed from designer suits. If you now wanted revenge for the way he perjured himself in court, most people would consider it eminently justifiable.'

Munching on a sundried tomato, I considered this. 'If I'm honest, retribution was all I wanted once, but now it doesn't feel as important, especially since he's been told to leave me alone. Those two years in jail are gone, and nothing can ever bring them back. It might sound cheesy, but I learnt a lot in prison – about myself as well as other people – and even if those lessons were often painful, I can't regret them. Henry Wilton isn't getting any more of my precious time and energy unless it's to sign divorce papers. Wanting to clear my name is something else, but it's not going to happen in the foreseeable future, if ever.'

'The likelihood of new evidence emerging being vanishingly small,' said Dot.

After lunch, we wandered along the main street to window shop, and during the short drive back to Sea View my phone buzzed with a message.

'It's Kim again,' I told Dot. 'Listen to this: *Have unearthed some stuff about Cabot Lyle, and there might be an ex-employee prepared to talk to me for money. Editor is keen. Will keep you informed.*'

Dot honked the car horn at a pedestrian wandering across the road in an all-too-careless and unobservant fashion.

'Silly old fool; he'll cause an accident one of these days.' Since the gentleman concerned looked to be around Dot's age, it made me wonder how old she considered herself to be. I wisely decided not to enquire.

'Well, let's hope Kim can turn something up; he deserves a break after all the effort he's put in and I want to understand what's been going on,' I said. 'None of Henry's harassment has ever made logical sense. I mean, why wouldn't he simply arrange a quick divorce and get rid of a wife now surplus to requirements – it's not as if he ever loved me.'

'Want me to float the company name Cabot Lyle around my contacts and see what comes back?'

'Maybe not, but thanks all the same. It might be better if they don't suspect they're being investigated, whoever they are.

Suppose the tabloids were to get there first – I'd feel bad if Kim had laid out his own money on potential witnesses without getting anywhere.'

'It's how freelance investigation works,' observed Dot. 'You have to take risks for the big rewards, and it doesn't always pay off.'

*

The next few days brought no further information, and I could only conclude the political scandal Kim had mentioned had been somehow contained or hushed up. An email from Justin cast no further light.

> *Hey, Mum,*
>
> *I finally asked the girl at work out – we're going to the cinema on Sunday. Her name is Elizabeth, but everyone calls her Betty, and she shares a flat with friends. I've thought about moving out myself – if Dad would fund me for the deposit, I could probably manage the rent if I join a shared house. The atmosphere at home is worse than ever, something's going on, but nobody will talk to me. All I could get out of Jerry was "ask your father". As if.*
>
> *Love,*
>
> *J*

He wasn't the only one with a developing love life. Our regular Thursday evenings had become special for me and Nik, and that week we were in a local pub which did fabulous steak and kidney pie. We'd established a routine to make such meetings possible which involved Val picking Maddie up from school and taking her home for a sleepover, before transporting her back to school in the morning. She and *Yaya* had fabulous evenings together, often making a cake or different kinds of pasta.

We'd scoffed our pie and were sipping drinks when Nik told me what a positive impression I'd made on his mother.

'Mamma doesn't warm to everyone; in fact, she can be quite judgemental and takes against people for no reason at all I can identify.'

'Well thanks for dropping me in that without warning,' I said in mock anger.

He reddened. 'I'm sorry, Frankie. I *should* have mentioned about Sundays, but I didn't want to make you nervous. I so wanted the weekend to go well – and it did, didn't it?'

'I had such a good time,' I told him, taking his hand as a teenage waitress took our plates away.

'So did we, and I for one can't wait to do it all again. It seemed so… right having you there, like we all belonged together. Another beer?'

I agreed to the beer but while he was at the bar, remembered wondering if we genuinely wanted the same things. Apart from sex, obviously.

When he came back, I said, 'Nik, what about your dreams of a rural cottage? Would I still belong in your life then? Full disclosure here: I'm not a country girl and you did say Val isn't either.'

Nik grimaced, though it might have been from the taste of his alcohol-free lager.

'Ah, well, I was going to mention this. Realising my budget priced me out of the nicer locations, Mamma and I have been talking about pooling our resources. If we sold her house as well as my flat, we could afford a larger property to share, and then she would always be there for Maddie. Which would help me a lot.' He studied my face with anxiety in his own – an unspoken question behind his information.

Another major rearrangement of the goalposts and I needed more time to take it in. Much more time.

'Listen, Nik,' I said, choosing my words carefully. 'Such decisions about your future have got nothing to do with me, though I can see how going in together would make perfect sense for the three of you on so many levels. You have to do what's right for your own family.'

Nik's face was eager. 'But my concern is you would be getting not only me and Maddie but my mamma as well. We'd kind of come as a package deal – would you even want all three of us?'

I *definitely* hadn't had enough time to reflect on this and drank some more beer to give myself thinking time before I answered. My brain was whirling. One part of me wanted so much to spend every night in Nik's arms, but another wasn't yet ready to take on a mother-in-law and a child.

'Slow down, Nik, we haven't even talked about moving in together and out of nowhere you've got all four of us sharing a house? It's much too soon to be planning so far ahead, and anyway, aren't we taking our time and seeing how things go?'

'We are,' he said, 'well we were. Last weekend changed a lot for me, and I want to be with you more than ever. Not only occasional weekends or evenings but all the time. God, I'm making an awful mess of this. Frankie, you're so special and I can't imagine a future without you in it. Please tell me you feel the same?'

There seemed no reason not to be honest. 'I do, and if we have a long-term future together it sounds very good to me. But Val and I haven't spent enough time together yet to understand if we could share a home. Taking on a stepdaughter would be a big enough challenge for most people, but I could easily grow to love Maddie.'

'It makes me so happy to hear you say that,' said Nik with a huge smile, taking my hand.

The teenage waitress returned with our sticky toffee pudding. Being so full of pie, we'd agreed to share a portion, but I didn't anticipate finding room for it.

'Nik, let me finish. Please don't rush me into anything, because it's much too soon to be making such important decisions, for everyone's sake.'

Nik's face fell, but he gripped my hand tightly. 'I knew this might be going too fast, but I had to tell you how much I care. You do feel the same?'

'Yes, I do, but too much to want to mess this up. All of us have to be very sure before we take the next step. It's such a big commitment to each other, and a child's happiness is at stake, so it's all the more vital we take time to get to know one another properly, right?'

The pudding smelled so good; maybe I could manage a bit after all.

'Of course. I understand, and I'm sorry,' said Nik, picking up his spoon. 'It's bloody typical of me to make quick decisions, see something I want and go for it in a headlong rush. I proposed to Sophie after three weeks but she being a sensible woman turned me down and said we should wait. And now I'm doing it again, stomping around in my size twelves, making a complete omnishambles of declaring myself, but I don't want to lose you or scare you off.'

'You haven't, but let's take things slowly and be sure. We've only been together a few months, and your mum needs to feel confident she can get along with me too. I might turn out to be a domestic tyrant. And maybe you should also be considering your options carefully before you become the only male in a houseful of women?'

'You can't scare me,' he said with a grin. 'The Greek family community is, and always has been, matriarchal. And probably a good thing too because it ain't broke so why fix it?'

Deliciously full, we walked back to Sea View across the bridge arm in arm, but some distant part of me was unsettled and overwhelmed. A glow of happiness had begun to grow that Nik so obviously cared for me. At the same time, I was anxious about letting Maddie down or messing things up with his mother, who had yet to be informed about my time in prison.

We said a lingering and lovely goodbye on the doorstep, but Nik needed to drive home, and I'd got to get up early for work in the morning.

'We have to come to a better arrangement than this,' Nik groaned into my neck.

'True, but without making any hasty decisions,' I said. 'Selling your two Manchester properties will take time, which should provide us all with months of breathing space, right?'

Lying in bed trying to go to sleep but with everything revolving around in my head, it suddenly dawned on me that Nik hadn't asked me where *I* wanted to live. Not that I knew, but I couldn't have been clearer about my aversion to country living, even if the big city no longer held any attractions.

Walking home from work the next morning, the air smelled fresh after overnight rain, which had cleansed the dusty streets. With one of those unexpected moments of clarity and insight, I saw that everything I needed or wanted was right there in front of me, and that this place had become home. Dot had once talked about learning to be content with what you have, and I'd grown to love the funny little town. If I wanted a future with Nik, would it mean giving up somewhere I'd come to feel safe and happy among friends?

I didn't have to ponder these questions for long because I'd barely got back to my attic and made myself some coffee when Kim rang again.

'Frankie, I hope you're sitting down.'

'I'm lying on my bed. You've found something?'

'Have I ever, and it's a complete shit storm,' he said. 'Let me give you the short version of a long and complicated web of deceit and obfuscation. For starters, Cabot Lyle is a shell company.'

'Aren't those a kind of front for tax evasion?'

'They can be – fundamentally it means there are no assets as such, but it's used only as a vehicle to hold and shift money in financial manoeuvres. It provides an umbrella cover for any number of other companies, subsidiaries if you will. One of these is a London club, very private, by invitation only.'

'When I queried the credit card charge with Henry, he described it as a place for like-minded people to talk and exchange ideas.' Things were starting to fall into place. 'It doesn't take a genius to guess that Henry must be a member. What is it called?'

'It doesn't even *have* a name, and officially the premises are a private house. It's known only by its street address, number fourteen. The senior minister I mentioned has kind of blown the lid off the place by getting very drunk and being indiscreet, showing photographs to some of his friends. I spoke to one of them, which led me to a former waiter – Dakila – currently in jail for dealing cocaine. His story is that the club hosts exclusive sex parties where the members enjoy the company of other people who appreciate various forms of sadomasochism.'

A cold feeling came and settled in my chest. Not only had my husband never loved or wanted me, but the kind of sex he did enjoy was also a million miles from our pedestrian love life.

'And why was this waiter willing to tell you about it?'

'I went to see him in prison, and he talked to me in the presence of his lawyer on the understanding that money will be sent anonymously to his parents in the Philippines. He'd been contributing to the family finances as much as possible but can't now he's in jail, and the extra income made a huge difference to them.'

'Those photographs… I'm afraid to listen to what he told you.'

Kim paused. 'I won't give you unnecessary detail, but according to our waiter, some of what goes on there is kind of extreme, amounting to torture even. The worst part is that you were right – some of the young men who are paid to take part are most definitely only boys. They trafficked Dakila to the UK at age thirteen to serve this purpose.'

'Oh God, it's worse than I imagined,' I told him, trying to banish the images that rose in my mind.

'Sorry, but yes. When the boy got older and more masculine, he was no longer so appealing, becoming a waiter there instead, and living in the attics with a couple of other members of staff. He's been threatened with horrible consequences if he doesn't keep his mouth shut.'

'So why is he risking everything by telling you all this?'

'If he's prepared to sign a witness statement, the newspaper I'm now working with will exchange the information for a substantial payment to his family. He also wants the membership to be punished for the abuse he and others suffered, and because he's in this country illegally it will mean deportation at the end of his sentence. They've ruined his life, but just maybe Dakila can start over.'

I felt sick, flushed hot with shame as if Henry's misdeeds were my own. The photos I'd seen had involved whips and people tying each other up, but I'd assumed it was consensual. It had never occurred to me that Henry could be involved in something so vile as torture, let alone the abuse of young boys even though I'd suspected some of them were young. Then again, any number of previously unimaginable things had happened in the past three years. Had I been incredibly stupid and naïve, or just in denial?

'Kim, this is horrible…' My mind was spiralling down into a vortex of terrible images before Spike brought me back to the present, landing with a thump on my chest.

'Nasty, isn't it?' Kim sounded world-weary. 'Not the kind of story I usually work on, but when I heard how some of the young men involved were children who'd been trafficked, it crossed a line for me. Some of them were physically injured during the sessions and needed medical treatment, which made me very angry.'

'No!' The protest was forced out of me. 'Don't say any more.' I'd wanted to understand, but the truth loomed out of a darkness almost too painful and ugly to contemplate. Spike must have picked up on some of these feelings because he became attentive, as if wanting to reassure, headbutting me in the face and leaving cat fluff in my mouth.

'My next step is to talk to Jerry,' said Kim. 'I suspect he's become aware of at least some of this, and not only has he resigned as constituency agent, but their relationship is undoubtedly over. The word is he's so crazed with anger and grief, he might be willing to bring Henry down and through him the whole lot of them.'

That scared me. 'This must sound selfish, but if the story is published will the gutter press be tracking me, trying to find out what I can tell them?'

Kim sighed. 'It will be published, for sure. We're going to blow the lid off the whole stinking putrid mess. These people are arrogant and think because they're rich the rules don't apply to them, but they do! Look, I can't give you any guarantees, Frankie, and while I'll do my absolute best to keep you out of the investigation, once the story breaks the tabloids will be all over it. I'll keep you up to speed when I can, but things are moving fast. The best news from your point of view is if Henry is exposed for what he is, then down the line there might be grounds for challenging your conviction on the basis his evidence can't be trusted.'

After the call ended, I sat there stunned, holding the furry weight of Spike close for comfort. Tabloid exposure could mean I'd have to leave St Annes; ironic, when I'd just decided how much I wanted to stay. But if my face and name ended up splashed all over the papers, Nik couldn't possibly have me involved with his daughter or mother. Any hopes and distant dreams for a future together would explode in our faces. Worst of all, I'd brought it on myself by dishing the dirt on Henry, and now there wasn't a damn thing I could do about it.

SEVENTEEN

Holding him tight in a desperate hope of reassurance, I almost strangled Spike, who clawed his way out of my arms with a squawk of protest. I gave him some cat treats to show that I was sorry before heading blindly downstairs to Dot, who, to my immense relief, hadn't gone out. Blurting everything out almost before I got through the door, she pointed to a chair, handed me coffee and listened to my garbled narrative with admirable calm.

I drank gratefully. 'Justin will inevitably get caught up in this, and what about Nik and his family? This could hurt them too unless I'm careful to keep them out of it,' I said. 'Henry has already ruined my life once, and now he's going to do it all over again, but this time it's my own stupid fault. It was me who put Kim onto the story to deflect him from the ex-con/fallen socialite idea, and now that decision is coming back to bite me. Why didn't I leave well alone?'

'If you had, Kim could have written the piece about you anyway, with or without your cooperation. Frankie, don't waste a second blaming yourself because it's Henry who's the bad guy here, and it's time to end the suffering he's responsible for; he deserves everything he's going to get,' pronounced Dot. 'At least the members of the club are going to be exposed and none of them will be able to hurt anyone else. What we have to do is keep you out of it as far as possible.'

I took a long, restorative draught of coffee. 'There is a slim chance the paparazzi won't come after me but limit their focus to the main players. The one thing I daren't risk is little Maddie getting dragged into anything by association, or Nik and his mother. It wouldn't be fair to them. Dot, what am I going to do?'

She was straight with me. 'I can't give you any easy answers, sweetheart, but before anything else you have to talk to Nik. You need his support and understanding. If he loves you, then he'll want to help. Now how about you go downstairs and get us some of those chicken salad sandwiches from Sal's fridge, brown bread if there are any? The newspaper exposé isn't even written yet, so you've got some time and space, at the very least over the weekend.'

When Nik called at the end of the evening as usual, I was calmer and able to give him a more straightforward and less emotional account. He heard me out with only the occasional sharp intake of breath.

'Shit, this is awful for you,' he said when I ground to a halt. 'But let's look at things clearly – you could be worrying about nothing, right? I mean, would any of this need to involve you?'

'It might not, and Auntie Dot thinks I'd probably be considered old news by the mainstream media, with no recent insights to contribute. What we can't be sure of is whether the tabloids will see it the same way. If they come after me then the immediate priority is not to drag you and Maddie into any of this.'

'But, Frankie, I want to be there for you in all of this, because I love you.'

He'd never used that word before, and part of me knew I

should have responded in kind but there was too much other stuff in my head. Nik thought my silence meant distress.

'Darling, don't cry; if you're in trouble, how could I not want to stand beside you? We'll get through this together. Why don't Maddie and I come up tomorrow, at least we can take your mind off all this?'

A tempting offer when more than anything I wanted his arms around me, but I turned him down.

'Nik, it's pouring with rain tonight, I'm surprised you can't hear it beating against my window, and the forecast for Saturday is no better. Besides, you promised Maddie a trip to the *Harry Potter* story event at the library, and she's so excited about it. Don't change your plans because of me – but I needed to tell you what's going on in case things change.'

'Promise to call me right away if they do,' he insisted.

*

As the tension-filled days passed into the following week with no news, Nik continued to call every night, always full of reassurance, but I couldn't help but be anxious. It was like living under a cloud in that strange greenish light which presages a storm, and the sense of threat which crackles in the air. You can't ignore it, or the heaviness in the atmosphere which makes breathing difficult.

Early on Wednesday morning, Justin sent several panicky texts asking me to call him, but they arrived while we were cleaning the offices (Jim insisted we locked our phones in the broom cupboard while we worked). A couple of hours had passed before I saw the messages and could respond as I walked home.

'Mum? Where the hell have you been? Thank God you've rung – something bad is going on at home. Jerry and Dad had the biggest screaming match last night, and I couldn't help but hear some of it. Dad's got illegal porn or something on his laptop – Jerry found out and went apeshit. He was already sleeping in the spare bedroom, but this morning he packed his bags and left. Dad was white as a sheet at breakfast; I've *never* seen him in such a state. He even suggested I sleep on my girlfriend's sofa for a while in case things get nasty.'

'It might be a good idea,' I said.

'What? Do you know what's going on?'

'No, at least only some of it. Your father is involved in a major sex scandal, a lot more than pornographic photos on his computer, and it's likely that it will all come out in the papers, in which case…'

'He's fucked, isn't he?'

'Probably, yes. As a government minister he could maybe survive an affair, but not something at this level. Your dad is right – if you can get away for a while it might be a good idea.'

'Mum, I can't leave him in this state. He looks dreadful and is scared shitless, but he won't talk to me. All he says is to take care of myself now.'

'He's right. Justin, you're at the very beginning of your legal career and finally getting yourself together. This kind of scandal could cast a long shadow over your life, even though it has nothing to do with you personally. Go to a friend's if you can.'

'I can't believe you're saying this! He may not be Mr Super Dad, but it would be lousy of me to abandon him when he's in trouble.'

'Well, I'm proud of you for feeling that way, but…'

'Forget it, Mum. You don't care what happens to him anyway,' he said and cut me off.

I came to a sudden stop on the pavement, and someone bumped into me, going on past with a muttered "watch where you're going". I had to be honest with myself – how much did I care about Henry's downfall? Dot's assessment that he'd brought it all on himself felt like the right one, and it wasn't him I was worried about but the people who could end up being collateral damage: Justin and myself. Jerry's life had already exploded in his face.

From there everything moved fast – part of me was grateful to be released from the hell of waiting for the axe to fall, but I was mainly overwhelmed by the speed with which things happened.

Kim called at lunchtime on Thursday, just as I was getting ready for the food bank session. 'I'm in London,' he told me. 'Staying for several days because the story will break tomorrow morning, and the tabloids will undoubtedly pick it up in the weekend editions.'

'It's happening then. I guess it's all over for Henry?'

Kim snorted. 'When the sordid details come to light, you won't waste a second on sympathy for him. Jerry finally responded to my messages and the poor guy is so distraught over Henry's betrayals he agreed to cooperate fully with our investigation and told us – the newspaper – everything,' said Kim. 'He even provided a copy of files he'd downloaded from Henry's hard drive before he left the Bayswater house. Your husband is in the whole torture club thing up to his neck, and the fool even kept photographs which include underage boys and incriminate other members. There's no doubt that many of them, including Henry, will be headed for jail. Once the paper has gone to print and the distribution begun, Jerry and I plan to go to the police with everything we have. There are some big names involved who might try and leave the country. I suggest you get away from home over the weekend, as a precaution.'

'It might not be possible. Let me see what Nik says when we meet this evening.'

Kim lapsed into silence for a moment. 'Look, in case you need to find a hotel or other place to stay, I'm sending you some more cash. A friend of mine will deliver it.'

'Kim, no, that's not why I did this...'

He quickly interrupted. 'You think I don't know that? This story is going to benefit me not only financially but in terms of journalistic kudos. You're earning very little from that cleaning job and don't tell me the extra wouldn't be welcome. Put the money aside for a rainy day if you don't need to use it. If the gutter press come after you, make them pay too; it might help fund a new start somewhere else at the very least. I owe you that much.'

I sat on my bed shivering although it wasn't cold, and feeling like someone who'd sent a snowball down a mountain which later caused an avalanche. For better or worse, the thing had been set in motion, and I couldn't stop it even if I wanted to. Henry truly deserved the coming retribution, so why was it me who ended up feeling dirty and sleazy? I took a quick shower and changed my clothes in a futile attempt to cleanse myself.

The food bank was crazy busy, but I managed to pull Nik aside briefly, long enough to explain about the next day's newspaper story.

'Would you mind if we didn't go out this evening? I can't face it, so could we have a takeaway at Sea View instead?'

'Of course, whatever you want,' said Nik without hesitation. 'You know, it might even be better for everything to finally be public. It can hardly be worse than having it hanging over you?'

'Maybe, but I can't be sure until they publish the story.'

When he rang the doorbell in the early evening, I rushed down the stairs to let him in, all but breaking an ankle in my urgent haste to get there and threw myself into his arms.

Startled, he said, 'Frankie, are you OK? Has something else happened?'

'No, but this is me not feeling very grown-up, and wanting someone to make everything better,' I said. 'And you do, simply by being here.'

Later, the two of us ate fish and chips sitting on my bed – I'd have to get the air freshener out or the smell of vinegar would linger. Dot was playing opera loudly downstairs, and it finally dawned on me that this was her way of being tactful, so Nik and I took full advantage of her generosity by making love to the strains of Turandot. I wanted to lose myself in a frantic burst of sensation, but he took it slow and gentle, calming my jangled nerves and then later waking up a few others. Afterwards, I lay beside him with my head on his shoulder, feeling safe and loved.

'My darling, pack a bag and come back with me to Manchester tonight,' he urged. 'Then if anyone should come after you when the story breaks, you won't even be there. Please let me keep you safe?'

'Don't think I haven't seriously considered running away, and it's a very tempting prospect, but I have to work tomorrow. It wouldn't be fair to let Shannon and Doreen down. However, if you were to invite me to spend the weekend with you and Maddie, I'd accept with alacrity.'

'Of course,' he said, 'why would you even need to ask? Maddie has a gymnastics thing after school but if you get on the train, I should be able to pop out long enough to collect you.'

'It's not a problem,' I said, sitting up and resisting the temptation to snuggle deeper into his shoulder. 'If you can pick me up from the station, I'll text my arrival time. Now, you have to leave for the drive home before it gets too late, or you'll be exhausted tomorrow.'

'I wish you'd come back with me now,' he said. 'I do get

it about work; I love how you're so loyal and refuse to let your team down. But, Frankie, please promise me one thing: if the press arrive then don't hesitate; get yourself safe and away. We can figure the rest out as we go along.'

As I waved him off on the doorstep, I asked myself whether choosing not to call in sick for the next day made me an idiot. I couldn't do it, not when my colleagues had been so brilliant and supportive. And anyway, I was lucky to have a job at all after Henry's attempts to get me sacked.

Walking through the quiet town the next morning, my skin crawled with the sense of unseen eyes watching me. Imagining paparazzi hiding round every corner played hell with my nerves, and I had to tell myself not to panic because the papers would barely have hit the streets yet.

The rhythm of our regular office cleaning routine both soothed and distracted me, and my being hyped up on so much adrenaline meant we got done ten minutes early. My colleagues knew the newspaper story was due to break imminently, but apart from hugs of solidarity we just got on with the work. It's not as if there was anything to talk about until we saw what the papers had to say.

Diving into a newsagent on the way home, I looked at the rack of papers and immediately identified which one had the story. The headline "Senior Politicians in Torture and Trafficking Scandal" was a model of broadsheet restraint. The tabloids would be using much stronger language, but the scandal being all over the front of a respected newspaper had more than enough shock value.

I bought a copy to take back for Dot, but she'd heard the worst after listening to the BBC radio analysis of the morning papers.

'I've searched online too – they've even posted a picture of some of them,' she said. 'Frankie, this is damning stuff.'

It gave me the sensation of drowning in the sleazy details and made me feel like I could be sick.

'Kim and Jerry were going to the police last night with all the evidence they had, so I imagine most of the participants will be arrested soon.'

Dot shot me a look. 'Probably already done – a dawn raid before any of them got to see the papers and could make a run for it,' she said. 'Their computers will be seized, everything.'

'Don't, I'm trying not to picture it. Henry has brought this on himself but poor Justin; having the police all over the house will be a horrible experience for him. I did suggest he go to a friend's place.'

'But he didn't want to abandon his father any more than you wanted to let your colleagues down. Don't go out again today, except for work. So far there's no sign of anyone outside, since they have to find you first, and then get someone up here. With any luck it won't be today because they'll be focused on the main players.'

Dot appeared to be right; I saw no sign of activity around the house, and nobody rang the doorbell through the day. She drove me and Buster's weekend holdall to the school shift in the Mini, acting as my close protection officer, keeping me safe from unwanted attention. I hoped she didn't have the gun in her handbag, although I'd have cheerfully let her shoot Henry, or done it myself.

'Keep in touch,' said Dot as she hugged me goodbye. 'I'll text you if anyone shows up here. See you Sunday – try not to worry.'

For once, the girls weren't rushing to get the job done.

'We can skimp it today,' said Shannon. 'You're in a right old state.'

'We've seen the headlines,' added Doreen. 'Your ex sounds like a right bastard.'

I got out my phone to show them the online piece. 'Oh, I can see why you would,' was Doreen's immediate response to the picture of Henry. 'Bit of a silver-fox hunk, but he's got a shifty look.'

We raced our way through the school corridors so that I could get on the train as planned. Settling into my seat as we pulled out of the station, I caught a glimpse of someone running along the platform. It could have been anyone and nothing more than my strung-out nerves, but I hastily turned my face away from the window.

I made a big effort to be calm and think zen thoughts during the journey to Manchester, but panic set in again when I couldn't see Nik on the platform. I sent him a text but got no reply. After fifteen minutes of hanging about in a state of high tension and with no idea what to do, Val suddenly appeared.

'Frankie, I'm so sorry I didn't get here sooner. Maddie had an accident in the gymnastics display. Niko has taken her to the hospital and asked me to meet you instead.'

'Oh God, is Maddie seriously hurt?'

'Maybe a sprained wrist, but her dad wanted to be sure she hadn't broken anything. I'm to take you home to the flat and stay with you until they get back.'

'But shouldn't we go to the hospital too?'

'Not necessary, I promise you. When Niko called me, he said Maddie was absolutely fine and enjoying all the attention. The doctor only wanted to send them to X-ray to rule out a possible fracture.'

Val drove us through the Manchester streets at breakneck speed. As I held tight to the armrest of the little hatchback, I figured she and Dot would get on well. They approached the business of getting through traffic in a similar fashion, although Val's choice of Greek curses was even more impressive, and the horn of her car blasted out much louder than the squeaky beep of the Mini.

Once back at the Salford flat, safe from any possible pursuit, I began to relax. This feeling lasted until Val made us both coffee and sat beside me on the sofa.

'So, now you and I get to know each other better, yes? Niko has told you about the plan for us to buy a house together, but not said how you feel about it?'

I froze. Talk about not being ready to be having this conversation.

Unsure what to say, I managed, 'Nik and I... we haven't discussed living together so far, only the plan you've come up with to sell both properties and pool your resources. We've only been seeing each other for a few months, and I don't want to rush into anything, especially because of Maddie.'

Val leaned forward and took my hand, dark eyes searching mine.

'Niko loves you; any fool can see it because he's fully alive for the first time since Sophie died. I also see you have feelings for him, but if you want to take your time this is wise. If we all decide to live together in the end, we can work things out the way adults should, but it's not easy to take on a daughter *and* a mamma.' She gave me a conspiratorial smile. 'Too many cooks in one kitchen, right?'

'Maybe,' I admitted. 'And there are things Nik hasn't told you about me.'

'Of course, and this goes both ways,' she said, amusement lighting up her face. 'I might have noisy hobbies or habits, take up playing the drums or something. Us retired ladies enjoy keeping busy.'

'No, Val, I mean it... not only is it still early days for Nik and me, but I come with a history you might not welcome.'

Val squeezed my hand as her eyes searched my face. 'I

believe you are a good person, and you care about my son and granddaughter. What else do I need to know? We can be OK together I think – maybe not all the time, but most of it, yes?'

Maybe it was tiredness and stress finally catching up with me, but silent tears I couldn't stop rolled down my cheeks.

'Val, I've been to prison. My husband accused me of arson and lied in court.'

She didn't leap to her feet and show me the door. 'You would not do this, I think,' she said, after a pause. 'Something more subtle would be your style, yes?'

I ended up telling Val a summary version of the whole story – my marriage, the fire, prison, and even the trouble coming for Henry and the others. On hearing this confession, she reached out to hug me saying warmly, 'Poor Frankie, you have had a bad time. This Henry he sounds a total prick.'

This unexpectedly accurate assessment made me giggle and provided another encouraging sign that we were going to get on.

'Val, that's the best description for my ex ever.'

'And now he gets what he deserves; he is deep in the *skata* – shit – yes?'

EIGHTEEN

Val and I continued to bond over a huge, shared portion of take-out fish and chips. We'd reached a place of warm understanding when, a couple of hours later, Nik brought home a weary Maddie with her arm in a sling.

'No bones broken, only a sprain,' he told us, slumping on the sofa and looking equally tired with shadows under his eyes. 'The doctor advised her to wear the sling when her wrist aches, but otherwise we offer painkillers as necessary and encourage her to use it. Good as new in a couple of weeks.'

'Frankie, I did one of my best vaults too, but then I messed up the landing and put my hand out when I fell. It hurt so much,' said the patient. '*Yaya*, I want to go to bed now. Can I have some hot chocolate?'

When they'd gone through to Maddie's room, Nik came across to the sofa and put his arms around me, kissing the top of my head as I leaned into his comforting presence.

'There was a TV set in the waiting room – they had the rolling news on,' he said.

I tucked my head into his shoulder and held onto him the way a drowning person might, and my voice came out muffled against his shirt.

'The morning paper which broke the story is in my bag if you haven't already seen it. Nik, thank you so much for offering me sanctuary – I feel safe for the first time today, but we have to keep Maddie away from the whole Henry debacle.'

'Don't worry – she won't take any notice of the news, she didn't in the hospital,' Nik said. 'Politics mostly zones her out, unless it's something about climate change, which brings out the junior eco warrior. If you stay connected with developments using your phone – assuming you even want to – she'll have no idea what's going on, or that it's anything to do with you.' He tightened his arms around me, before kneading the tension in my neck and shoulders. 'Relax, nobody will find you here so let it all go for now. You have this weekend as a breathing space. If anything changes, we'll deal with it.'

Val went home shortly after with a wink at me, leaving Maddie already asleep, worn out by the day's excitement. We went to bed ourselves soon after, taking with us glasses of a rich red wine and watched a comedy show on the wall-mounted TV.

'I've told Val everything, at least the short version,' I confessed. 'She was very kind and seemed OK, not blaming me for any of it.'

'I'm glad it was you who explained it to her,' he said. 'It would have worked better woman to woman.'

It occurred to me briefly that he'd been too scared to tell Val himself, but I snuggled against Nik's chest as he held me close. After the last few days, I was too mentally and emotionally exhausted to contemplate sexual activity, and he got it without my telling him.

Less than an hour later (or so my brain told me), I struggled to the surface to find full daylight outside. Maddie bounced onto the bed, already removing her hand from the sling to use it, while Nik stood by with a tray which included an aromatic pot of coffee.

'Wake up, sleepy Frankie,' Maddie told me. 'We've been out to get chocolate croissants and Daddy's made coffee. We're going to have a picnic breakfast right here on the bed.'

Nik winced. 'As long as you help me clear up the crumbs, young lady. I'm not sleeping in a bed full of flaky pastry, thank you very much.'

'What time is it?' I managed, sitting up in an overslept fog.

'It's nearly 11.00am, and I had my first breakfast *ages* ago,' Maddie told me, munching a croissant with evident relish, smearing chocolate around her mouth in the process.

'We let you sleep in,' said Nik. 'Maddie and I have been playing board games in her bedroom, anything to keep the little madam quiet.'

'Bloody rude,' protested Maddie.

'What have I told you about using bad words?' Nik frowned at her.

'But you say it, Daddy.'

I tucked into a croissant and took a deep draught of coffee while father and daughter pretended to argue. It ended with them rolling off the bed onto the floor, and Maddie being tickled without mercy until she promised not to say bad words. Someone looking in from the outside would have seen us as a normal family enjoying weekend time. With a sudden lurch of my stomach, I remembered what was going on in London and worried again whether Justin would be OK. Henry was probably in custody, at least I hoped so. The smooth, urbane man who'd been my husband for more than two decades now seemed like a total stranger; even the thought of him enjoying hurting people nauseated me.

Rain drummed on the windows of the flat and appeared to be set in for the duration, but Nik had managed to get us cinema tickets for a lunchtime showing of the latest animated film, which took me far away from my immediate worries. From there we went on to an antique and bric-a-brac warehouse – a surprise because his flat was full of modern furniture, all clean lines. I hadn't imagined Nik liking what he frankly described as "all this junk", and he didn't.

'Sophie adored this kind of stuff, so I figured you might too,' he told me after Maddie and I had pounced joyfully on some doll-sized wicker furniture. 'At least it's out of the rain.'

I had to laugh. 'You don't get it, do you? Yeah, there's a lot of dross in places like these, but it's about hunting for treasure. In among all the "junk" there's always the hope that you'll find something wonderful. Charity shops are the same.' I gave Maddie some money and she headed to the pay booth.

'But why would anyone want this?' he said, touching a well-used Welsh dresser in a dark stain.

'It's a nice shape, good for a small room, and can always be refurbished with chalk paint. You can't furnish the country cottage you're dreaming of with glass and chrome,' I told him. 'It wouldn't work.'

'Ah, well I've been talking to Mamma, and she's not keen on the idea of rural remoteness with nothing to do either. So, a slight change of direction, and we've been looking at properties in St Helens. It's a great place with a good mix of access to town and country; I'll show you the kind of thing when we get home.'

Once back at the flat, Maddie went off with her new dolly furniture to find suitably deserving occupants for it, and Nik opened his laptop.

'I've researched places within our joint budget and come up with an area which has some good schools nearby, not to mention all kinds of amenities such as pubs and shops.'

'But these houses are mainly Victorian. Since you live in a modern block, I assumed that was more your taste?'

'The flat was only ever intended to be a short-term first step on the housing ladder for me and Sophie, but then Maddie came along unexpectedly. What with her arrival, and then Sophie being so ill, we never did get around to the big family house we dreamed of.'

Whose dream? I asked myself. *And if he wants me to be part of this move, where does my own vision of the future fit into the picture?* I hadn't so far been included in the conversation about places to live, and this occupied my mind when Nik set to preparing dinner. Fajitas were his speciality, but he toned down the spiciness for Maddie and said the adults could add hot sauce to taste.

While he got busy creating mouth-watering smells in the kitchen, my phone pinged with a couple of messages: one came from Kim.

Police swooped on Henry and the others around 2.00am; all in custody for questioning. Jerry got called back in to provide some more information. Any sign of the paparazzi? K.

I pictured Henry in a police cell, or being interrogated, and didn't feel sorry texting back: *Managed to get away for the weekend but will hear if anyone comes to Sea View. Congratulations on the newspaper piece. F*

Afterwards, I went back to fretting over the lack of news from Justin, who hadn't answered my many calls and texts. He was probably still furious with me, so I could only hope he'd gone to be with his girlfriend, Betty, and had some support.

The second message was from Dot: *Don't fret about press activity here – nothing much to report. Some guy sat on the church wall opposite for a few hours this morning. I did my batty old lady performance and reported him as "loitering" till he got moved on, but no other signs. Poor bloke might have been innocent but taking no chances. Have a* super *time.*

Her imagination undoubtedly had Nik and me in a lovefest, and we might have been but for my ambivalence about his plans for the future. I wouldn't be able to contribute

223

to the cost, so could hardly expect a full vote in the decision-making process. All the same, this lack of communication made me wonder (again) if it might not be too soon to talk about moving in together.

After dinner when Maddie went to bed, Nik pressed a glass of red wine into my hand and asked, 'Sure you're OK? You've been very quiet, and it must be a huge worry not knowing what might be happening.'

Leaning back against the cushions, I took a mouthful of the rich, fruity wine.

'My immediate concern is for Justin and whether he's all right. Everything else is out of my hands but so far, the news sources are only reporting the same as this morning.'

'I'm guessing nothing will change until after those involved are formally charged, at which point there's likely to be a press conference.'

'Perhaps. There's nothing to do but wait and see. Look, I've been thinking more about us, and how you see me fitting into the plans you and Val have been making.'

It might have been my tone of voice, but he turned to me in immediate concern and put down his wine glass to take my hands. 'Please, darling, never doubt you are automatically part of everything. I want us all to live together, and you already get on so well with Mamma and Maddie. They adore you almost as much as I do.'

'But, Nik, we haven't been together long,' I said. 'Aren't we supposed to be taking things slow and steady, especially with what's happening now? I understand if you want and need to get on with the move because of schools for Maddie. But assuming we decide to move in together, won't I get to have any input on location?'

'Of course, but with so much on your plate right now... I sort of didn't want to bother you.'

I took my hand away. 'You're doing it again; avoiding potentially difficult conversations, such as when you conveniently forgot to tell me I'd be meeting your mum last time I came. Nik, I've heard about *your* dreams, and those you shared with Sophie, even what Val prefers. But at no stage have you asked me where *I* want to live. If this is about a possible future together, then you're excluding me from the decision-making process.'

His dismayed expression confirmed what I'd suspected; this hadn't occurred to him before.

'God, Frankie, I'm so sorry. Do you really feel left out? Sometimes I get an idea in my head and run away with it. OK so let me ask you now – what kind of houses do you like and is there some location you'd prefer?'

'What if I said London, and my old life and friends?'

His face fell. 'I hadn't considered… but in any case, our finances couldn't stretch to it.'

'It's OK,' I said, taking his hand again and squeezing the strong, brown fingers. 'It wasn't a serious suggestion but me trying to make a point. Once, all I wanted were the things I had before, though over my time in St Annes things have changed.' I took a deep breath. 'Nik, you have to appreciate my point of view. I'm very fond of where I live now; walking on the shore brings me peace, and I love how the local people always chat with you. It's also a place where I hope one day to make a real difference, but you're operating on the automatic assumption I'll relocate wherever *you* choose. Tell me straight – is it necessary to live near your work?'

Nik shrugged. 'I suppose it helps – but the Manchester office isn't a place I spend a whole lot of time. The truth is, the territory I cover for Laneways Trust is so big, I could be based anywhere within it. But your present job isn't…'

My temper, already frayed at the edges, finally broke like overstretched elastic. I put down my glass of wine.

'Oh, now we get to it. I'm only a cleaner which is not exactly a career with prospects, so it needn't be given any consideration. You know damn well I'm only doing it because the hours allow me to study and get qualified for the work I hope to do.'

'But, darling, maybe everything that's going on now means it's the right time to move in with us here? If you want to study you absolutely should, and there would be no need to get another job unless you chose to. We could put a desk in the bedroom for you, and there'd be all the time while Maddie's at school for you to give to the course. When I'm away you'd be there for her and building up your relationship. Once we find the right property, we can all begin a new life together.'

His eager face lit up with happiness as he described his vision of a future together. Before I could protest further, he drew me close and kissed me, slowly and tenderly, and then I only wanted to lose myself in being loved. Things weren't as simple as he made them sound, but at that moment, I wanted them to be. Nik carried me through to the bedroom and removed my clothes with infinite care (the fancy underwear had been called into service again). He made me feel beautiful, precious and wanted, and I responded because right then his arms were all I needed; everything else could wait.

The unrelenting rain continued overnight, so on Sunday morning the three of us curled up to have breakfast in front of a film – chosen by Nik this time. Maddie was a little cranky and said her wrist hurt, so we dosed her up with junior paracetamol and more hot chocolate. When offered the last croissant, she brightened even more, while Nik and I ate sourdough toast with my favourite blackcurrant jam. It warmed me to discover he'd bought some in especially, a huge improvement on the sticky red stuff at Sea View.

We kept away from the difficult subject of houses and cuddled peaceably on the sofa before driving to Val's for

Sunday lunch. After we'd eaten, Nik insisted he and Maddie would wash up, leaving Val and me together.

'Let me show you the houses Niko has found,' she said, opening her laptop. 'This is a map of the St Helens area, and you can see in red the location of the best schools, and the areas Nik sees as possible places for our relocation. Here, on street view you can see how nice it is, lots of mature trees and even a park.'

I listened politely, trying to show enthusiasm and I couldn't fault their logic or choices, except for them not being right for me. My heart and home lay somewhere else, back in St Annes where my friends were. Once Nik and Maddie had finished their kitchen duties, the whole family got involved in studying images of the area, but the more the three of them enthused, the more uncomfortable I became.

No way did I want to squelch their excitement, hopes and dreams, or insist I might want something different, especially while still feeling my way towards becoming part of the family. A headache threatened when Val talked about outside space, and how large a plot they would need.

'Are you a gardener, Frankie?' she asked. 'Niko isn't but says he will mow the grass if we find somewhere with space for Maddie to play.'

'I could practise my back flips and everything if we had a garden,' put in Maddie. 'Daddy won't let me do them in the flat, only when we go to the park, and *Yaya* doesn't have room either. Her garden is all lettuces and carrots but no grass.'

'Well, of course, there'd need to be space for a vegetable plot too,' said Val. 'But we also have to consider parking. If Frankie wants a car of her own one day, that would be three vehicles to find room for.'

I'd been checking my phone again, hoping for some word from Justin. Suddenly, all the talk about cars and gardens was several steps too far. Yes, sitting on the time-bomb of the situation in London had stressed me out, but I admit to not behaving very well.

'Since it's been mentioned,' I said, 'what Frankie wants doesn't seem to be the same as the rest of you. So maybe you should leave me out of it?'

As soon as the words were out of my mouth, I regretted them. Maddie picked up on my tone of voice and looked doubtfully at Nik and her grandmother, then back at me.

'You don't like these houses?' she asked in an uncertain voice.

'It's not the houses…' I said, but Val interrupted.

'Frankie, surely Niko has discussed all this with you? Are you saying he hasn't?'

'He's *told* me about your plans, but…'

Val rounded on Nik. 'My son is an idiot. It seems what we are talking about isn't something Frankie wants at all. Niko, how can you be so stupid?'

'I thought…' began Nik.

'Forget everything for now,' instructed Val. 'The two of you need to talk, and there can be no more making of plans until we are *all* agreed. Niko, you should take Frankie home soon; she's worn out and not surprising with what's going on.'

'Have I said something wrong?' asked Maddie in a quiet voice, and I dropped to my knees beside her, taking the small hands in mine.

'Sweetheart, it's not you; please believe me. I have a lot of worries right now, and it's hard to concentrate on anything else. I'm so sorry, I didn't mean to be cross, but maybe we have to talk about all this another time.' She flung her arms around my neck and buried her face in my neck.

'Don't be upset with Daddy,' she whispered. '*Yaya* says he is a big clumsy fool sometimes.'

On the drive home, Nik and I were both quiet until eventually, he said. 'Frankie, Mamma is right; I've messed up. Can we begin again and forget whatever has already been discussed? Tell me about how you want to live – assuming you still want us to be together?'

'Nik, please, I'm sorry if I was short-tempered but I can't deal with anything like discussing property right now. I'm so worried about Justin and what's happening in London. The only thing I'm sure of is that St Annes is somewhere I feel safe, and I don't want to leave the people who've become important to me, even for you, or the place which is the nearest thing I now have to a home. I can't impose those things on the rest of you because it would be every bit as wrong as you expecting me to give up everything and move to St Helens with you.'

'Oh shit, is that how it feels?'

'Yes, it does. Nik, maybe we should cool it for a while, take a step back? I can't deal with all this at once.'

Nik's brown hands clutched the steering wheel as he shot a panicked look in my direction. 'Frankie, please, are you breaking up with me?'

Having been married to a man who dictated all our choices and had expected me to subjugate my preferences without question, no way was I going to let it happen again. In the darkness of the car, one corner of my mind kept insisting Nik and Henry were very different people, and that we could and would be able to negotiate a middle ground. I was about to say so, but then my phone rang.

'Frankie, it's Dot. There are people outside – reporters – they arrived about an hour ago. Not many, but enough. One of them rang the bell but Buster got rid of her. There'll be others by morning. Where are you now?'

'I'm on my way home in the car with Nik, we've not long

left Manchester, maybe forty-five minutes away. Are they paparazzi?'

'They're not selling double glazing, that's for sure. Meet me in Lytham and I'll get us a hotel room for the night, but don't come back here.'

NINETEEN

Following my directions, Nik dropped me off near the pedestrianised square in Lytham where Dot had promised to be waiting.

'Please, let me come with you,' he said urgently as I opened the car door. 'We can't leave things like this.'

I was tired and emotional and didn't want to talk about this stuff.

'I'll call you,' I told him. 'There's too much going on right now so please, Nik, don't add to the pressure but let me navigate my way through all this without dragging any of you into it. I *have* to find out if my son is OK. Everything else can wait, but please make sure Maddie understands nobody is cross with *her*.'

'No, but everyone is mad at me,' said Nik ruefully. 'Let's do what Mamma said and start all over again? No plans or discussions without your full involvement.'

'Not *now*, Nik, I have to go.' I grabbed my bag and fled, not wanting him to see the tears starting. Maybe we wanted different things, but I'd never dreamed of hurting anyone, especially not Maddie.

In the square, I shivered as the evening breeze off the sea

found its way under my jacket. Dot sat on a bench, as promised, with an overnight bag at her feet.

'Good girl,' she said on seeing me. 'Come on, the Mini is parked out of sight and I've got us a twin room for tonight. Raided your room for some clean knickers and stuff, figured you wouldn't mind.'

'Dot, I'm scared and it's all my own fault. Everything is falling apart…'

'It probably will do for a while, yes, but you'll get through it and nothing lasts forever. Helluva cliché, but one day at a time.'

The B&B she'd managed to find was warm and welcoming, with sumptuous deep carpets, designer fabrics and antique furniture. We were shown to a pleasant twin room under the eaves which reminded me of my attic sanctuary.

'Right, stop weighing up what this place costs and don't worry about it,' commanded Dot. 'They have my credit card details which is all you need to know. The only meal on offer is breakfast, so we need to find somewhere to have dinner; it's gone 8.00pm, you must be famished.'

'Not after Val's Sunday lunch,' I said. 'And everything there has gone pear-shaped too.'

'Well even if you're not hungry, I am because with heroic restraint I resisted Sal's dinner and waited for you. It was easy enough to get away from the house because I set off from around the back and accelerated hard. Now they've got my car's registration, but it won't tell them much.'

Dot led the way to a pleasant bistro we'd eaten at before, but I only managed to pick at the food she insisted on ordering for me, while she tucked into her almost-raw artisan steak burger with all the enthusiasm of a lioness disembowelling her prey. By the time we got to the coffee stage, she'd heard the whole story of my weekend, including the Vassos family's moving plans.

'Oh well done for standing your ground with Nik,' said Dot. 'You can't build a future together unless it's based on joint decisions and the things you both want and need. Speaking of which, I'm delighted to hear that your first choice is to stay in St Annes. I would miss you very much if you moved away – life has become infinitely more interesting since you arrived at Sea View.'

'You're a huge part of why I don't want to leave,' I told her. 'Everyone back at home means so much to me. We've become *family*.'

'You're special to me too, like the daughter I once hoped to have, but I long since settled for being Auntie Dot to everyone. No regrets, or at least none I choose to dwell on.'

'Well, you're stuck with me now,' I said as the waiter removed my half-eaten food. 'No way could I have made it this far without you, and I'm counting on Auntie Dot always being part of my life.'

'But does your future lie with Nik and his family?'

'I'd begun to believe it might, but now things are looking shaky or maybe it's just too soon to be making long-term decisions. Why is it so complicated? At my age, shouldn't it be easier than this?'

'That's not how life works,' said my mentor. 'You just get better at pretending to know what you're doing.'

Back in our room at the B&B, I unpacked the pyjamas and underwear Dot had brought for me, more than ready to bring the day to a close. My phone rang and when I saw the caller display, I almost dropped the handset in my haste to answer it, pressing the speaker button for Dot's benefit.

'Justin, thank God, I've been so worried. Where are you?'

'At home, but there's no one else here.' He sounded strung out.

'Your father is still with the police?'

'According to the online news, he's been charged and bailed hours ago pending further enquiries, in which case where the hell is he? When I got home from work, he'd obviously been home this afternoon, because the car's gone.'

'You've tried his phone?'

'The police took it, along with lots of stuff from the study, including his passport and laptop. Mum, you can't imagine what it's been like here. They raided the house in the middle of Friday night, hauled us both out of bed and then they took Dad away.'

'Oh God, Justin, how awful for you.' I tried to picture my boy coping with all this and couldn't. 'They weren't unpleasant to you?'

'No, in fact, the reverse – they did this icy polite thing and called me "sir" all the time. I had to watch while they searched the house and removed boxes of paperwork and all kinds of other stuff. Once they'd taken Dad away, they were here all *day* and kept asking questions I couldn't answer, such as how to open the safe. Even after they'd gone, the press pack were camped on the doorstep, so I didn't dare leave the house. There's a couple of the bloody vultures outside still.'

'They came to Sea View too, but I'm not at home right now.'

Justin's voice cracked. 'Mum, I've got such a bad feeling about Dad being missing, but where would he go? Maybe he's with Jerry – except that snake landed Dad right in it.'

'No, Justin, he did that to himself.'

After a long pause, he said, 'Yeah, that's fair. I can't quite picture Dad involved in… what they're saying he's done. It's too awful.'

'Justin, he never showed either of us his true nature. He fooled me every bit as much as you and for longer.' Fear of the answer made me hesitate to ask the question. 'He didn't ever… touch you, or anything?'

'God, Mum, no. If anything, he fell a bit short in terms of physical affection. All the hugs I got growing up were from you.' He paused again. 'Sorry I didn't answer your calls or messages, but I was pissed off with you and sort of conflicted. All this has been like living in some kind of nightmare.'

I sat on the bed, overwhelmed with guilt. It had been me who first alerted the press to Henry's activities, though from the things Kim had said, the truth was going to leak out anyway via the indiscreet club member.

'Justin, there's something I should tell you…'

'Mum, wait, there's someone ringing the doorbell. I'll have to call you back, it's probably the paparazzi but it might be Dad…'

When Justin put the phone down, Auntie Dot came and held my hand. It didn't take a genius to guess that I was out of my mind with worry.

'Dot, he sounded so scared, and this is a lot for him to deal with – he's only young.'

'It's a lot for *anyone* to deal with, but I'd advise against telling him about the evidence you supplied. I could tell you were about to, but does he really need to know about the part you played? I know it's only 10.30pm but let's be sensible and get some sleep – I won't suggest turning on the news.'

I'd just got my pyjamas out while Dot headed for the bathroom. My phone rang – Justin again, but this time he sobbed and *screamed* down the phone.

'The police are here and they've found… oh God, Mum, please come. I need you!'

I could hear him sobbing again and I said desperately, 'Justin? Are you still there?' Then someone else came on the line.

A female voice said, 'Mrs Wilton? Mrs Francesca Wilton?'

At some primal level, I knew before she told me.

'This is Sergeant Emily Collins. I'm a family liaison officer with the Metropolitan Police. My colleague and I have had to deliver some very bad news to your son.'

'It's Henry,' I said. I'd gone icy cold, ready for what she was going to say.

'Yes, Mrs Wilton. There's been an accident, your husband's car left the road and went into a tree. I'm afraid he died instantly. Understandably, your son is distraught. You should get here if at all possible.'

'Tell him I'm on my way,' I said without hesitation.

The sound of Justin sobbing in the background took me right back into full mama-bear-protecting-her-cub mode. Even when your kids have grown up and aren't little and vulnerable anymore, she's still in there, ready for any crisis. Mine growled inside me, with hackles up and claws out, ready to defend Justin with everything I'd got. Never mind if he could be selfish or annoying – trouble had come to my son's door, and he *needed* me.

Dot waited, alerted by the tone of my voice.

'Henry's dead,' I told her, hearing myself say the words but at another level not taking them in. 'I have to get to London.'

Stress and shock then sent my brain into freeze mode, and I stood there, literally unable to decide what to do next. Dot took charge, entirely necessary because my brain kept supplying images of a dead, cold Henry stretched out on a mortuary slab.

'I'm coming with you,' said Dot.

'Oh but – London? Is it safe for you to go there?'

'There are ways,' she said in a voice which brooked no argument.

We called a sleepy Sal who assured me the paparazzi had given up for the night, so we explained ourselves briefly to the confused manager of the B&B and went home to Sea View. Dot sent me upstairs to pack enough clothes for several days, which took longer than it should have because I could barely manage practical decisions about what might be needed.

When I finally went down to her flat with my case, the only thing I recognised about my friend was her irrepressible smile, and even that didn't look quite right. She'd put on a wig composed of short grey curls, typical of an elderly lady's perm, and the coat she wore might have been fashionable in the 1960s with its ratty fur collar and large buttons. She'd accessorised this outfit with a pair of vintage old lady zip-up ankle boots and a battered wooden walking stick; the full effect of her ensemble was nothing even close to her normal feisty self.

'I've been saving this outfit for a rainy day,' she told me. 'Good, isn't it? I got the coat from a collectables fair.'

'What have you done to your teeth?' I said, hypnotised by the crooked yellow smile she gave me.

'Second-best dentures. Awesome or what? It's amazing how much the small details change your appearance. Now, got your phone charger? Good girl. I've called in a favour and arranged a car for us. This is no time of night for an oldie like me to start driving down to London, especially not with drink taken, and this way we'll arrive fresher in the morning.'

'But, what about…'

'All organised. I went downstairs to see Sal, who is going to tell your work what's happened, and Buster will also inform the probation officer. Given the nature of the emergency, they can hardly object to your absence, or to you reporting in by phone or video call.'

Another of the anonymous saloon cars Dot was able to summon arrived to pick us up. Dot greeted our driver; the man who had taken us to and from the pub.

'Nice to see you again, Norton. Step on the gas please because it's an emergency.'

She had also provided us with a hip flask of her best brandy.

'Good for shock,' she told me. It must have been because the journey is a blur and, against the odds, I managed to sleep on and off much of the way, only waking when we made motorway comfort stops.

'I'm older and need to pee more often,' said Dot with a grimace. 'Pain in the arse, as you will one day discover. Shouldn't have had that second glass of wine with dinner.'

When Dot shook me awake in the early darkness it was 5.00am and I recognised the Bayswater streets which had once been my home.

'Is there access around the rear of the house, ma'am?' enquired Norton. 'There's no sign of the press but still...'

'Yes,' I told him, trying to wake up properly. 'There's a double garage around the back; turn right here.'

The rear gates were locked, but Norton persuaded them to open without apparent difficulty. Another illusion of safety shattered, alongside so many others which now lay in broken ruins.

After a brief conversation with Dot, Norton drove off. From the safety of the small rear garden, I phoned Justin and we stood at the back door until he appeared, bleary-eyed, to let us in, wearing only the shorts he'd slept in.

'Mum? Why didn't you use the keypad?'

'Good morning to you too. I assumed the code would have changed.'

'Nobody wanted to remember a new one.' Behind me, Dot tutted at this lax security.

My jaw dropped as I stepped into the kitchen Henry had redone after the fire. A seating area had cream leather sofas and an enormous TV. The cooking area now had a very different layout with glossy black units, white marble worktops and modern brass handles. Not my taste at all but undoubtedly state of the art. It was also a disaster zone, with that particular smell of bins left unemptied too long, and a litter of unwashed plates, takeaway containers and beer cans on the island.

'Sorry, Mum,' muttered Justin as I took all this in. 'God, I'm so glad you're here, but who is this?'

'It's Auntie Dot, don't you remember her from Sea View?' I didn't blame him for not immediately recognising her; I hadn't myself. 'She's here to help.'

Justin might have been twenty-three years old, but his bottom lip wobbled exactly the way it had as a little boy, and tears welled up.

'Oh, Mum, I can't believe he's dead,' he choked and walked into my outstretched arms.

'Shh, it's going to be OK. I'm here now.' As I held him close, mama bear roared into full protective mode, claws and teeth at the ready.

*

A few hours later, things showed signs of improvement, at least on a practical front. The kitchen had been restored to full function, and we'd all showered, changed and eaten toast with Henry's favourite marmalade from Fortnum & Mason. Something so small as seeing the label on the jar forced me to fully take in what had happened. Henry wouldn't be eating any more of it because he was gone, dead, deceased, as in forever and ever amen. At another level, I simply didn't believe it, couldn't make it seem real.

Justin was a little less fragile with us there if still inclined to sudden tears. He was also reassured by Dot's transformation from a fragile little old lady back into the turban-wearing person in trousers and top he'd met before. She'd put her best teeth back in and blessed him with a wide smile, before sending him to peep around the drawn blinds at the front of the house.

'Those bastard paparazzi are camped outside again,' he reported. 'Not so many as yesterday but a pack of them.'

'We'd best stay away from the windows and leave the blinds down,' commanded Dot. 'Is the back overlooked? Don't want them bribing your neighbours to poke telephoto lenses at us.'

'No, apart from the garage there's a high fence and a couple of tall trees at the rear to screen us from view,' I told her, setting the coffee machine going again. 'Now what are we going to do about food?'

'The fridge is stocked up,' said Justin. 'We put in an online shopping order before the police came for Dad, and it was delivered yesterday morning. I can do another on my laptop any time we need to.' Then he stopped, looking scared. 'It's all set up for his credit card, will that work now?'

'I think we're legally obliged to cancel it,' I told him, realising how many things needed to be done.

'Make a list,' said Dot. 'Then it won't all seem quite so overwhelming.'

Food and company not only strengthened Justin but worked for me too, especially with Dot to hold us together. My son and I were walking blind through a space neither of us had navigated before, without any signposts, just putting one foot in front of another. Dot had already been there and knew the terrain from bitter experience.

Justin's phone rang. 'Hello? Oh, Sergeant Collins. Yes, Mum arrived early this morning.' He listened some more before saying, 'OK great. Let me give you the code for the back door and gate – the tabloid press are at the front.'

The liaison officer arrived in the early afternoon bringing us a couple of the quality morning papers and told us to call her Emily. She had to be around my age but looked like she worked out, dressed in a black trouser suit with odd socks. Dot set to making more coffee, while the sergeant sat Justin and me down at the kitchen table.

'I'm so sorry for your loss.'

She was the first of many to say those words. What did they even *mean*? Just a formula that most people, including me, used when they had no idea what to say.

I put my arm around Justin, and we sat with our heads together. Neither of us yet knew how to respond to the polite cliché, and Emily gave us time before continuing.

'An urgent post-mortem was conducted, and we've just received the results which establish the cause of death as head injury. We thought you'd want to know. Mr Wilton wasn't wearing his seatbelt, there were no drugs or alcohol in his blood and the pathologist says he would have died instantly.' Next to me Justin shuddered, his imagination clearly supplying the same horrific images as my own.

The sergeant produced a packet of chocolate biscuits from her bag. Sugar was such a necessary comfort food, as she must have known from experience.

'An inquest has been briefly opened and adjourned this morning, but I can also tell you that my Scenes of Crime colleagues have conducted a thorough examination of the crash site. From the evidence of tyre marks on the road, it appears Mr Wilton braked suddenly and hard, possibly to avoid an animal. He was driving through a rural area of Kent at the time and veered into a tree.'

Justin put the question in all of our minds. 'Do you think he did it on purpose?' he asked in a choked voice. Dot came up and put coffee in front of him, gripping his shoulder in support. 'It's all over the internet as a suspected suicide and given the newspaper story, he might have…'

I turned to Emily Collins. 'From what you've told us, it sounds as if there's no evidence to suggest anything but an accident, an awful car crash.'

The officer nodded agreement; eyes which had seen too much calm and steady.

'Oh, Mum, for him to die miles away from us and all alone,' Justin sobbed.

Emily leaned forward. 'If it helps at all, Mr Wilton, he wouldn't have suffered.'

I tightened my grip on Justin's thin shoulders. 'Sweetheart, we know he was upset and might not have been concentrating on his driving, but I don't believe your dad would have killed himself.'

Henry had left no letters or any kind of note, so his intentions when he drove to Kent couldn't be known; no use speculating about something which could only hurt his son. Across the kitchen Dot's eyes met mine, while Justin absently dunked a biscuit in his coffee.

*

The time following a sudden death is surreal; everything happens in a kind of slow-motion, and all you can do is keep going through the fog of unreality. Justin's grief for his father was genuine and heartfelt, even if they'd clashed often. If I'd loved Henry at all perhaps my reactions would have been the same, but my emotions were much more complicated. Dot seemed to get it.

'Part of what you're feeling is guilt,' she said, and I recognised this truth. 'Frankie, you aren't responsible for any of Henry's choices, but the son you made together needs you now. That's the only thing you have to focus on.'

But it was more than that; the early years of our marriage had been so wonderful, and those were what I grieved for, even in the face of his later betrayals. Justin and I operated in some kind of sleep-walking state, and Dot held us together, helped

242

along by Emily Collins. The magnificent sergeant also went outside and threatened the paparazzi with dire consequences if they didn't stop constantly ringing the doorbell.

'I know it's awful right now,' Dot told us. 'A loss like this is raw and brutal, rips everything away, but although it's hard to believe you *will* get through it. Take every day, every hour, as it comes and don't expect too much of yourselves.'

'My dad is *gone*,' Justin choked on the words. 'I never said goodbye or told him I loved him.'

'He didn't need to hear the words to know that,' I said, mama bear ready to do battle against the monsters of grief and pain. 'Even when you had those fights, it happened because he loved you and wanted the best for you. I know he didn't show or give affection easily but remember how he'd come home with unexpected gifts rather than *tell* us he cared.'

Justin gazed across the room with an empty expression. 'He always told me to "man up" as a child. What a bloody awful thing to say to a kid. If I ever have a little boy, he'll never hear those words from me.'

'He gave you other good things, including his genes and intelligence,' I said. 'You'll see him again every time you look in the mirror, but it doesn't mean you are the same kind of person. You can be bigger and even better than he was.'

'I want to be,' said Justin.

'You already are,' Dot pronounced, and he hugged his newly adopted Auntie. The two of them got on so well, and typically my son now listened to her more than he did me.

The first shock of disbelief gave way to a kind of gradual acceptance in which we just about managed to function, albeit in a stumbling and clumsy fashion. I put together some simple meals, while Justin got the washing machine on. All of me was focused on providing emotional support for my boy. We followed unfolding events on television, the arrests and revelations, staying away from the more lurid speculative coverage.

'Don't watch the stuff on the internet,' warned Emily. 'I'm here to answer what questions I can, and though I don't have all the answers, you can at least be sure what I can tell you is the truth.'

We probably couldn't have tolerated much more anyway; the details would have been too unbearable.

*

We were idly watching a quiz show on TV while a ready meal from the freezer cooked in the oven, when Justin announced his intention of going back to work.

'I'm not achieving anything here, and it would take my mind off things.'

'But are you sure?' I asked. 'It's only been four days. Isn't it a bit soon to be trying to concentrate on legal stuff?'

'I *want* to focus on something else,' he told me. 'Otherwise, I only go round and round it all in my head. What do you think, Auntie Dot?'

She was contentedly ensconced in a corner of the big kitchen sofa, a large glass of Henry's best malt whisky in her hand.

'Justin, if you want to, then go for it. It's not as if your colleagues won't make allowances if you're not at your best. As long as you promise to come home if it's too difficult, then why not go if you feel up to it?'

'I do. And, Mum... I might go round to Betty's place and hide out there tonight. She's cool with it, and I could do with a change of scenery.'

'And you want to be with her,' I said.

'Yes, we've been talking on the phone, but it isn't the same.'

244

Nik kept trying to call me every night at our usual time, but I hadn't answered. I put my phone on silent through the night, and it stayed in the bedside cabinet. During our overnight dash down to London, I'd sent a brief text to explain where I'd gone and why. He must have seen the news coverage, so he'd know what we were going through. Maybe I'd be ready to speak to him soon; I certainly missed him but had too much else on my mind.

With Justin out of the house at work, Dot and I decided to search through Henry's study. The police had already done so but his constituency paperwork was mostly held at the House of Commons or the local party office.

'The police were bloody clumsy opening this desk,' grumbled Dot, gazing at the offending antique construction, the inlaid drawer front now scarred by forced entry. 'I'd have done a much better job.'

'Justin is upset about the damage because it's a family piece which meant a lot to Henry, but I guess it can be repaired.'

In the slim top drawer, I found Henry's family signet ring. He had never taken it off, even in the shower. With a cold chill, I understood that leaving it behind cast a new light on his state of mind when he'd left the house.

Mutely, I held it out to Dot in the palm of my hand. She understood immediately.

'He wore it all the time? Look, it doesn't prove a thing, but we need to keep this to ourselves if we want Justin, and everyone else, to accept this as an accident. Which it was. Definitely.'

Most of the desk's contents were personal rather than business, and the police hadn't bothered much with them. We took what remained from the drawers and spread them out on the top. Henry's life insurance documents were there, our marriage certificate, Justin's birth certificate and school exam paperwork.

In a folder marked "Home", we found an old will.

'I'm named here as sole beneficiary, but this is from way back,' I told Dot, scanning the contents. 'He had it drawn up when Justin was only a toddler, so there's sure to be a more recent one. It might be in the safe the police took away?'

At Dot's suggestion we made a call to the legal firm whose details were on the envelope to see if they were still representing him. Having confirmed they were, I officially informed them of his demise and made an appointment for the following week to discuss Henry's affairs. Sergeant Collins thought I would receive the necessary death certificate within a matter of days.

Nobody but Dot thought to search behind his public-school photos – I wouldn't have. She undid the tape on a couple and took one out of its frame, to find Henry had fastened a manila envelope inside the back. It contained photographs the police had missed, and they made me feel nauseous. Justin could never be allowed to see them. They only showed people who'd already been arrested so I put the pictures through the shredder and then burnt the fragments later for good measure. The two detectives who'd been to see me had mentioned images found on the confiscated phone and laptop, so they already had plenty of evidence to use. That was when I learnt how even creative passwords didn't necessarily keep people out.

The pictures included a few of Jerry, draped naked across the velvet chaise in the formal sitting room at the front of the house. I had total confidence he wouldn't want them seen either, even if they did bring an appreciative comment from Dot about his muscular body. These went in the shredder too.

'We should search the main bedroom next,' suggested Dot. She'd been sleeping in there because I couldn't face it and had opted instead for the spare room.

'Even though it's been redecorated, I can't. Don't make me go in, it's too much.'

But Dot led me upstairs, saying, 'Frankie, there are no ghosts here. I can see it's not your style at all, though all this black and gold reminds me of my glory days.' I didn't ask.

I stood frozen in the doorway, until Dot said, 'I get how you feel, but let's be practical – this is only another job to be done.'

She persuaded me to step inside, and I focused my mind on a methodical search rather than allowing memory to intrude. All I found were some boxes under the bed which held a selection of Henry's extensive collection of handmade shoes. In the bedside cabinet on what had always been Henry's side, Dot found another will, tucked inside a book.

'This has to be the most recent version,' I said, skimming the document. 'Dated four months ago with everything split equally between Jerry and Justin, so there's no doubt about Henry's wishes.'

'It's not signed.' Dot leant over my shoulder to point at the last page. 'Without a signature or witnesses, it isn't valid.'

'But this is clearly what he wanted to happen,' I protested.

'Then why did he leave it all this time without a signature to make it legal?'

I remembered how often Justin had described terrible rows between Henry and Jerry, bad enough to make him think they were on the verge of splitting up.

'Once Jerry found out about his secret life, perhaps Henry was undecided, and then, of course, they separated. So where does this leave us?'

'Simple; unless there's a signed copy deposited with the solicitors, then the earlier will leaving everything to you is the only valid one under the law. There'd be a kind of justice in that, right?'

I squirmed at the thought. 'Maybe, but it makes me feel uncomfortable. Henry would never have wanted his property to come to me, particularly the family antiques,' I said.

Dot was unimpressed. 'Hmm, but then again, despite the decades of effort you contributed to his career, your late husband behaved with shocking ruthlessness and perjured himself to get you sent to jail. Why should his wishes be treated with respect when he hasn't earned that right?' Her implacable expression spoke volumes.

I thought about the lies and deceit, the betrayal of everyone who believed in him. Henry had even hidden his true nature from Jerry, by all accounts the real love of his life.

'You're right,' I said slowly. 'Henry is – was – indebted to me. What he said in court stripped me of everything, including most of my clothes and personal jewellery, even my friends. Buster told me once that I could sue him for a proper divorce settlement, so he owed me something, though maybe not *everything*.'

'Revenge isn't always sweet,' said Dot. 'Pretty much never, in fact.'

TWENTY

There were reporters outside when we set off to visit the lawyer, but Dot and I made it into the taxi without too much hassle after the warning they'd received from Sergeant Collins. She was only calling in occasionally by then but, knowing of our appointment that day, came and stood on the doorstep to ensure their compliance.

Andrew Hogg's offices were all oak panelling with some good furniture and paintings; horses and dark landscapes, not my thing. We were ushered in as those privileged to enter the Holy of Holies, where a somewhat frosty Mr Hogg awaited us. He had a shiny bald scalp, and, in fascination, I wondered how he kept the gold-rimmed pince-nez glasses on his bulbous nose. He probably wore them as an affectation, along with the waistcoat with its gold watch chain. Against the tweedy fabric of his suit, the overall effect resembled Mr Toad from *Wind in the Willows*.

Far from offering sympathy to a bereaved (if not altogether heartbroken) widow, his body language signalled extreme disapproval of the convicted arsonist showing up to claim her share of the proceeds. No refreshments were offered, and he took his time examining the death certificate and two wills we'd brought.

Dot rolled her eyes at me, equally unimpressed by his attitude.

At last, he said, with visible reluctance, 'I can confirm that your conclusions are correct, and the recent will we drew up for Mr Wilton remained unsigned. We did remind him on a number of occasions that this needed to be done but since he took no action, this earlier document appears to be the only legally valid will. Therefore, despite Mr Wilton's wishes expressed verbally to me, Mrs Wilton will inherit his entire estate.'

'Since you are named as executor, may I then take it you will now apply for probate as soon as possible?' I wasn't going to be polite to this obnoxious man.

He offered no more than a chilly affirmative nod in response, and his expression became even more glacial at my next statement.

'I have very little money of my own, so will be needing access to some cash to tide me over while I settle Henry's affairs. Are you able to help with that?'

Mr Hogg took his time and kept me waiting, studied the paperwork on his desk and steepled his fingers together. Looking at me with evident distaste, he said in a drawling and self-important tone, 'I suppose we can be of assistance in taking care of all the necessary steps, Mrs Wilton, and in a few weeks we should be able to release some interim funds to tide you over the months until probate is complete.'

He appeared to consider this an adequate response, but I didn't.

'I *have* mentioned that I am Ms Douglas these days,' I told him in an equally acid voice. 'But what on earth am I supposed to do for money until then? My stay here in London is stretching into weeks, not days as I'd originally hoped. Such an extended absence means I'll lose my job back up north but have to continue paying rent on my accommodation. With all there is to be done, my son's modest salary won't keep us in the interim.'

I had the money from the sale of my engagement ring, but it was held in an emergency fund not to be used in case I needed it later. No way was I spending it on clearing up Henry's mess.

'Mr Wilton's life insurance should pay out without undue delay since the police have found no evidence to suggest suicide,' suggested Mr Hogg. 'I could chase it up for you and perhaps also draw up a statement for the press. The usual discreet form of words requesting privacy for the family at this difficult time, and so on.' He didn't bother pretending not to be bored.

'Yes, please do so,' I told him crisply. 'And since *I* will be paying your legal fees for this work, if you are to continue acting on my behalf, may I also suggest you revise your attitude towards me and your opinion of my guilt in terms of the conviction for arson. With all the media coverage providing the sordid details of Henry's activities, you can hardly remain in any doubt as to my husband's true character, or the probable veracity of his testimony against me in court.'

Dot snorted and turned it into a cough, as Mr Hogg's porky face went scarlet.

He cleared his throat. 'Ah, well er, just so,' he managed to mutter. 'Mrs... er Ms Douglas, perhaps you would both care to have tea? I do apologise if I have unwittingly caused offence and hope you will continue to repose your trust in our firm.'

Earl Grey tea in the firm's best china duly arrived, along with some very posh biscuits.

'Given your familiarity with Henry's affairs, it does make sense for you to wind up the estate.' I told him. 'However, it is a decision I make with considerable reluctance, and in the hope that you will in future give a better standard of attention to these matters.'

Once we were done, I swept out with my head held high and outside on the street Dot burst out laughing. 'Oh well *done*, Frankie. I'm seeing a whole new side to you now.'

She was the only one smiling. 'I feel so… *polluted* by the whole business. Come on, let's get a taxi back to Bayswater because right now all I want to do is have a good cry and then go home to Sea View. Nothing about London or this life is what I want anymore, but I absolutely can't leave until things are all settled for Justin.'

Since we arrived home late, dinner that evening had to be macaroni cheese with bacon – something I could throw together at speed when we got back – but my son was thrilled.

'How cool is this?' he said to Dot. 'Mum used to make it for me in the boarding school holidays. Nobody ever does it quite the same way – will you teach me the recipe?'

'I'll write it down,' I promised. 'The secret ingredient is Worcester sauce.'

Over coffee, I relayed everything we'd found out from the lawyer, with Dot providing a lively account of my put-down of the unsufferable Mr Hogg.

'Listen to me,' I told my son. 'It's clear from the unsigned will that Henry wanted you to have half of everything, so that is what will happen once the legalities are finally settled.'

Justin pushed his empty plate away and came around the table to wrap me in a hug.

'Mum – seriously? But you were named as sole beneficiary, so you don't have to do that.'

'It's what your dad wanted, and so do I. Nothing else would feel right. This property will need to be sold to realise your inheritance, as long as you're OK with that?'

'I can't say I'm particularly attached to the house, or the area, even if I did grow up here, having been away at school so much,' he said. 'What I really want is to get a flat of my own, maybe persuade Betty to move in with me, somewhere up and coming with interesting bars and restaurants, and in reach of the office.'

'Would you want to keep any of your dad's antique family pieces? Perhaps there are some personal items you'd like to have?' I asked. He was already wearing his dad's signet ring which I'd given him, not correcting the assumption that the police had returned it.

'Only his desk,' said Justin. 'Assuming I can afford a flat big enough to put it in. Wait till I tell Betty about this.'

'If there's anything else, any small mementoes or photographs, take them into your room for safekeeping. Otherwise, we'll sell whatever we can at auction and the rest can go to charity.'

'Speaking of which,' said Dot. 'There are some things upstairs you should see. I'm guessing they used to belong to you, Frankie?'

Justin glanced up from his phone. 'Dad put some of your stuff in the attic too – Jerry gave him a hard time about keeping it.' His face was suddenly stricken, his father's death so raw and recent. 'I guess maybe he sort of loved you after all. In his own weird way.'

This piqued my curiosity since I'd imagined Henry chucking everything I owned into a skip. Dot led us upstairs to the main bedroom, and through into the walk-in wardrobe. There was a space where my clothes used to live, and presumably later Jerry's. All Henry's shirts and suits were still hanging on the other side and below them sat his boarding school trunk, a battered old thing he'd always insisted on keeping. Justin took one look at the clothes, redolent with the scent of Henry's aftershave, went very pale and fled upstairs to his room.

Strange how smells can touch a nerve of memory in a way nothing else can. Kneeling beside the trunk on the carpeted floor, an aroma indelibly associated with my former life lingered around me like some kind of ghostly presence.

'I only opened the lid and took a peek,' Dot told me. 'Sorry, but you know how nosy I am, and the temptation was irresistible.'

Under tissue paper lay a dark pink taffeta dress, ballerina length with a full skirt. It had once been Henry's favourite and I'd worn it to any number of functions. It struck an odd note that he'd chosen to keep it; I'd never have had him down as sentimental, quite the opposite. Below the dress, I lifted out a well-worn flat jewellery box containing a familiar platinum and diamond necklace of art-deco design.

'Wow,' said Dot when I opened it. 'Isn't that gorgeous.'

'I wore it at our wedding because he asked me to. He even chose my Vera Wang dress.'

'You don't care for it, do you?' Dot cocked her head to one side.

'No, I prefer very simple jewellery. It's a family piece – belonged to his grandmother. This is all just weird; I can't imagine why he hung onto this stuff.'

'Well, as Justin said, perhaps somewhere he did have real feelings for you after all?'

The trunk also contained the jewellery box I'd used and inside it all the items I remembered, including some which had belonged to my late mother. The trunk contained a few more bits and pieces of clothing and a couple of designer handbags Henry had bought me as Christmas and birthday presents.

'I'll check with the delightful Mr Hogg, but if my instincts are right and these belong to me personally rather than the estate, then they can be sold to keep us going in the short-term. What a relief.'

'I'd be happy to bail you out,' said Dot. 'I can easily provide bridging funds until you come into your inheritance.'

I smiled. 'Yes, I know you would, but I can't let you do it. You've already been brilliant staying here with me through all this.'

'You could consider it a temporary loan,' she pointed out. 'But I expected you'd say no – some people are bloody difficult to help. Listen, I have a meeting in a couple of days to discuss something I've been consulting on; they're sending a car. After that I should get back home, it's pushing my luck being here at all. Will you be OK if I go back north?'

It would be a massive wrench to be without her, and for a wild moment I wanted to beg her not to leave me. Instead, I managed to say, 'Of course, you must go, especially once I'm able to get some money together. Oh, Dot, thank you *so* much for being here with me, I only wish I could go home too, it's where I want to be.'

Dot raised an eyebrow. 'Shouldn't you be telling Nik that, not me?'

*

I'd been feeling increasingly guilty about not speaking to Nik – avoidance because I didn't know what to say to him. Dot was right as usual, so when Nik rang at his regular time, I accepted the call. My heart was pounding as I pressed the answer icon. Despite occasional texts when I'd first arrived, it had been ten days since we'd had a real conversation. The world had turned upside down since, but what made me nervous was thinking about the way we'd parted.

'Hello...' I said softly.

'Frankie! Oh, thank God; I've been so afraid you were never going to speak to me again. Are you OK? What's happening?'

'Has it been all over the media? We haven't watched the news much, only looked at the BBC on the internet. I've barely left the house except to visit the lawyer's office.'

'It's been everywhere,' Nik said in a rueful tone. 'Mamma and I have been very careful with Maddie's exposure to it, in case there were any photos of you, but she has no idea there's a connection. I saw a picture online of Henry's smashed-up car and all the media talked about suicide at first, but now it's being reported as a tragic accident.'

'I'm encouraging Justin to see it that way too – despite all the speculation. The poor kid has enough to handle, and it's hit him hard, but he's surprising me with a new maturity. His girlfriend is a good influence.'

'And what about *you*?' asked Nik. 'My darling, this must all be so horrible for you, and I've missed you so much.'

Lying in Henry's spare bedroom, I knew I should say that I'd missed him too, but was it altogether true? I'd been so absorbed in the immediate problems that Nik's offer of a whole new life and family had been pushed to the back of my mind. Given the conflicted state of my feelings, could we even have a future together? He made me feel good in the here and now, but would that be enough or only settling for what I had?

'Frankie, please believe how sorry I am for being such a total idiot. Mamma delights in pointing out on every possible occasion how stupid I've been and says I should be down on my knees begging your forgiveness. Even Maddie has had a go at me, and they're both right.'

'Everything that's happened here has kind of put our misunderstanding into perspective.'

Nik gave a huge sigh down the phone. 'It's generous of you to put it in those terms. In these last days I've discovered that there's no imagining a life without you in it, so please, can we begin all over again?'

My bruised heart lifted a little, but I still wasn't ready to commit to anything.

'Nik, if we love each other, we'll work it out, though it may be some time before I can get back home. I'd hoped it would only be days not weeks, but everything this end is such a muddle. Fortunately, Tony at the probation service is being very understanding, so I'm allowed to check in via video call.'

'I wish I could be there to offer support. At least you have Dot with you.'

'She's been amazing, I'd have fallen apart without her, but she can't stay much longer. And you *can* help, by letting me talk like this at the end of the day. I'm sorry, I've been behaving like a stroppy brat and should have answered your calls.'

'No, I get it, you've been overwhelmed by the situation with no time to think about anything beyond your immediate reality. The thing is, I was terrified I'd blown it completely and you wouldn't want me anymore.'

'Nik, I *do* care about you, but right now my feelings are so mixed up. Even when all this London thing is over, I'll need time to work out what I want to do next. I'm just not ready to take on the whole package of the Vassos family. What I need most is some stability in my life, and I can't make any long-term decisions until I've disentangled the mess here. My priority is to secure Justin's inheritance.'

'Darling, I promise not to rush you. What we have is so good it's worth waiting for. Mamma and Maddie send their best, and please know how much I love and need you. I'll be here whenever you're ready, trust me on that.'

This was everything I wanted to hear and as we finally said goodnight, I'd begun to believe that we might salvage our relationship. It could even be very different when half of Henry's estate came to me because I'd be able to bring a contribution to any new home we made together.

*

The police interviewed me again to go through my account of Henry's various extramarital activities, his friends and contacts at the club, and ask some further questions. They assured me the little I'd been able to add all contributed to the picture they were building up.

The media pack outside gradually dwindled from the original dirty dozen. They eventually gave up in pursuit of a celebrity who'd got very drunk and publicly punched her business manager, who promptly made a charge of assault. This made life so much easier since I could come and go from the house without intrusive scrutiny. By the time Dot went north, one of the designer handbags and several items of jewellery had been sold. I also sent with Dot an envelope of cash for Sal, and a note asking her to please keep my attic room open until I could get home again. She sent a text in reply telling me not to be so daft.

Once Dot left, and with Justin either at work or with Betty (who I'd now met and warmed to instantly), I surprised myself by enjoying the quiet and my own company. With mixed feelings, I at last received official permission to dispose of Henry's mortal remains. After discussion with Justin and to avoid press attention, the funeral arrangements weren't advertised, and only private invitations were issued. With the scandal still current, we kept it low-key and hadn't planned for any refreshments afterwards. His formal sending-off took place quietly one morning, at the nearest crematorium, with only a modest number of mourners including Jerry.

It was hard to concentrate on the words – I couldn't stop looking at the oak coffin chosen by Justin and thinking of everything it symbolised. The service wasn't up to much, what I heard of it anyway. The vicar they'd wheeled in to do it knew bugger all about Henry, apart from the career details gleaned from Wikipedia and other sources, but at least he kept it short.

We managed a ragged rendition of "Jerusalem", which had been Henry's favourite hymn from school. After the formal handshaking at the door, Justin went off with Betty, looking glad that the dismal proceedings were over.

'Frankie, can I buy you lunch?' asked Jerry when most of the mourners had gone. 'There are things I need to discuss with you.'

'Jerry, can't it wait… not today, please.'

'I'm sorry, the timing is lousy, I get it. But this is important and affects you. I should have said something before and could potentially get into trouble for withholding evidence. It's important to tell you about it first.'

He had my attention. 'OK then, but not lunch, I couldn't eat. Coffee?'

We went to a small independent coffee shop where we could sit in a back corner and talk privately. My smart black funeral clothes had provided little protection from the chill October day, so the warmth inside came as a welcome bonus. Plus, I was genuinely curious to hear what Jerry had to say. To describe it as a bombshell would have been a massive understatement.

'Here's the thing,' he said, shedding the expensive dark overcoat and smoothing his carefully styled grey hair. 'I know you didn't do it.'

I stared at him over the large gold-rimmed cups the waiter placed in front of us.

'You mean the fire? Well, it makes you one of a very small, select group who do believe me.'

'I don't believe it, I *know*,' he told me. 'Because Henry told me that he did it and how.'

I'd just taken a mouthful of coffee and almost spluttered it all over the table.

When I finally stopped coughing, I said, 'It's a bit bloody

late, isn't it? Henry told you I hadn't done it, but you let me spend two years in prison and lose a chunk of my life I'll never get back. Anyway, why tell me this now?'

'He only told me in January, when he was drunk after a New Year celebration, and by then you were due for release within weeks. He'd persuaded me you deserved the prison sentence, had it coming even. But he also said things about you which somehow never fitted with the person I'd come to respect – you were always courteous and thoughtful to me and the constituency staff.'

'You loved him once, like me.'

'Yes, for a long time, even after I knew... He betrayed both of us. I didn't tell the police about the arson, only the rest. Since Henry's death, I've been feeling I owe you the chance to clear your name.'

'Why would anyone believe you after all this time?'

'Because the proof you need is buried in the garden of your house, along with the petrol can he used and the clothes he was wearing. At that New Year party, he was told by a Home Office colleague about your upcoming release. Henry got appallingly drunk that evening and told me the whole story. Spilled his guts, literally *and* metaphorically.'

'Too much information,' I said. 'So why now, and why haven't you already told the police this along with the rest?'

'Because you inherit everything, right?'

'Yes, but I'm giving Justin half when everything is sold. Then we can both build a new life with the proceeds. The devastation Henry caused means he has a lot to make up for.'

'OK, but here's where I'm coming from. Henry claimed on the house insurance for the damage caused by the fire. The new kitchen, all the redecoration after smoke damage, temporary accommodation for him and Justin, they paid up for all of it, based on your conviction for arson.'

The gears clicked into place in my brain as I finally understood.

'You're saying if you tell the police the truth then my name would be cleared but the insurance company might want their money back?' My calculations were racing ahead.

'Yes,' said Jerry. 'The insurance company would have a prior claim on the estate, before probate, and you'd get the residue. I can't decide for you, either way, but now Henry's true nature and all the lies he's told have been exposed, it's important that I try and make things right. What you do with the information is nobody's business but yours and I won't ever mention it again, whatever you choose to do.'

I finally lifted my gaze from the chaos Henry had left for me and appreciated how Jerry's life had been even more comprehensively devastated than my own.

'We were both fools in love. Having resigned as constituency agent, what will you do next?'

The long fingers fiddled with his coffee cup. 'Part of me wants to get out of London and find something completely different. I sold my flat to move in with Henry, so with the money in my account I could choose to head off to Cornwall or Scotland, anywhere. But I'm a political animal through and through, and now there might be a job at Westminster for me. So, if there is then I'll stay and begin again because it's what I'm good at. And you?'

'You're not going to believe this, but I plan to settle on the north-west coast, a very long way from the London bubble. The place has grown on me, and I have friends there who make me happy.'

Genuine warmth spread across Jerry's face. 'Frankie, I'm so glad. You didn't deserve any of this, and I wish you luck building a new life. Maybe there'll be another Mr Right for both of us one day?'

I trusted his assurance that he would not report the information about Henry and the arson, and because of this we parted friends. In a black cab on my way back to Bayswater, I wrestled with the dilemma presented by this new information. Once, proving my innocence meant everything, and my whole ambition had been to restore something resembling the London life I'd had before. But the inevitable attendant publicity around an appeal would only hurt Justin all over again, and further damage his memory of the father he'd loved. Days passed while I cogitated but in the end, it was, as Justin would say, a no-brainer.

Nothing could ever give me back the years I'd lost. Since the people I most cared about weren't bothered by my criminal record, then proving my innocence would achieve very little beyond a brief personal satisfaction. If I could live without that, there'd be another fifteen months of probation, and then three years further down the line the slate would be wiped clean, one ex-offender rehabilitated, job done.

But what course of action to take? Answering this question kept me awake a couple of times before I came to a decision. In the early evening, as soon as it was dark, I took a spade outside to the narrow strip of town garden, by then distinctly straggly and overgrown although someone had kept the grass cut. Justin was out, having gone straight from work to spend the evening with Betty.

Jerry hadn't needed to tell me where to dig – I guessed as soon as he told me about Henry burying his clothes. They were under a pink flowering shrub which hadn't been there during my marriage. I've never been much of a gardener, only watered the hanging baskets at the front door (delivered by a florist) and planted up a few patio tubs at the back.

The shrub went back into the hole after I'd disinterred the black bin bag, and then I went back inside to sleep on my decision. Nothing changed my mind, so for the benefit of the neighbours I pottered in plain sight around the garden with my secateurs, cutting back some dead stuff and straggly branches. I built a small bonfire with the wood, and Henry's petrol-infused clothes burnt nicely, even the shoes. It was one of those mental snapshot moments, the smell of smoke as the last dead pieces of my old life went up in flames and were consigned to history. I put the empty petrol can out with the recycling, but someone helpfully nicked it before the bin wagon even arrived. There could be no turning back because the evidence had been destroyed, and I didn't have a moment's regret.

TWENTY-ONE

It gave me such pleasure to see how close Justin and Betty had become – nothing like the appalling stress of his father's death to bring a couple together. It came as no surprise when Betty moved into the Bayswater house to be with Justin. The two of them planned to live there until probate was granted in the New Year. As they arrived, Betty was squeaking with excitement and waved the keys to their new flat as I gave her a welcoming hug.

'Justin signed yesterday – the place is ours!'

'That's the power of a cash sale,' I said, starting the coffee machine. 'Even solicitors can move fast sometimes if you push them hard enough.'

'The bathroom is a bit grim,' said Justin, putting his arms around me from behind and kissing my cheek. 'I mean, who actually *chooses* lime-green tiles, even if they are antique? The balance of the life insurance pay-out means we've got funds to get the renovation started. With luck, the bigger jobs like the kitchen will be done before we have to move in.'

'And we still need to choose what furniture we might want to keep from here,' said Betty.

I smiled at their excitement, planning a first home together. I'd never got to do that, having simply moved my few possessions into Henry's house. She and Justin were good together, and I thought they might have a long-term future. After probate was granted, the Bayswater house could be sold, which was expected to happen within days if not hours of it going on the market, there would be a lump sum to divide between us.

'The estate agent thinks we'll be looking at three to four million,' said Justin. 'We talked about it when he was here measuring up – you were at the cinema. Maybe more with the location being so good.'

I almost fell off my chair. 'How much? Seriously?' A house in the same terrace had been sold shortly before I left Henry, and that had gone for close to £2 million and didn't have the garage ours did. Things had moved on since I'd been "away".

He smiled at my ignorance. 'There's been substantial price inflation in the past eighteen months. It's a very desirable address.'

The realisation that I would be comfortably off left me slightly dazed. I didn't even have to think about whether I wanted to work or not. Rev. Ellie's words about lifting the fallen and supporting the weak had made themselves at home in my heart. My one fixed point was that I was determined to help people as much as possible. Before getting too carried away, I sought Buster's advice about counselling roles and talked through all my plans on the phone.

'Frankie, that's fantastic,' she said. 'I'm so thrilled that you want to continue studying, even after everything that's happened.'

'The debt module is almost complete,' I told her. 'I've been working through the stages online and might even get signed off on it before Christmas. That's important because I've signed up for a counselling course at Blackpool College, which starts in late January. It's three months full-time, but I'll be adding a recognised qualification to my skill set and that will be so worthwhile.'

'Wow,' said Buster. 'You're not planning to stand still, are you? I'm already working on attracting funding to the law centre, which might allow me to offer you a paid role in the year ahead. If that's something you'd still want?'

'Buster, that would be a dream come true! Are you sure?' This was more than I'd dared hope for and left me buzzing with excitement.

Buster chuckled. 'Wait until the funding comes through, but I'm confident about getting it. The charity I've applied to understands that people's problems are often complex, and the more support we can offer the better.'

'And you'd be comfortable working with *me*?'

Another laugh. 'I think we know each other well enough by now to rub along OK, right? In the meantime, what would help is if you can put in some volunteer hours here at the law centre – as the course commitments allow – to get the feel of the operation and how you'd fit into it.'

'Absolutely. Looking at the syllabus, there'll be some time to do that. Oh, Buster, I feel so lucky that my ducks are finally lining up.'

'I think we might be the lucky ones, and getting a good deal too. It'll be a pleasure to work with you – but first, let's get that funding package tied down.'

It was thrilling to have a real professional future to plan for and I'd flown my plans for the counselling course past Nik in one of our late-evening conversations.

'I'm giving Justin half of everything, but when I'm ready there will be money in the bank to fund my future plans.'

'*Ours*, I hope,' said Nik. 'No, I'm not going to rush you even though I'd like to, but I do get it that you've been through a lot. Mamma keeps reminding me that you need time and space to think about what happens next.'

'I really appreciate that; it means a lot.'

'You've been so amazingly strong and brave throughout all this, but I miss you like crazy,' said Nik, his deep voice wobbling just a little. 'I can't wait to have you in my arms again.'

*

The train pulled away from Euston Station on a November Friday afternoon, leaving behind so much of my history – mostly things I had no regrets about saying goodbye to. The industrial buildings, yellow London brick and closely built streets gradually gave way to open countryside, and then I relaxed enough to feel the excitement of going *home*. I was travelling with no more than the two suitcases I could carry; the very few things I wanted to keep from the house would be sent by courier in the coming weeks. Justin and Betty had invited me to spend Christmas in Bayswater with them, but for me that would bring too many ghosts out of the woodwork, rattling their chains. I'd politely declined, saying, 'Maybe next year when you're settled in the new flat.'

The train carried me north into the gathering winter darkness, every click of the rails taking me closer to where I wanted to be. The railway coffee was still crap, but I'd made my own sandwiches before leaving the Bayswater house – pastrami to rival even the Lytham deli.

My heart lifted at the sight and sounds of my home, the tang of ozone in my nose and the cries of gulls calling overhead as I walked over the bridge. It had been almost a year since I'd travelled this way with a bin bag full of tracksuits, and pretty much zero in the way of prospects. Even with a criminal record, the real financial security I now had changed everything.

I'd told Dot what time my train would arrive, but turning the corner into Norcross Road, my heart nearly exploded with happiness to see everyone wrapped in coats standing on the top step of Sea View, including Angus. Buster and Sal had helium balloons and a banner saying "welcome home", and everyone wore party hats and tooted on plastic horns at the sight of me. Tears prickled at something so silly and wonderful; a true homecoming in every sense of the word and I couldn't have been more grateful.

There was just time to drop the cases off in my attic room – which Angus told me proudly he'd kept dusted (under Dot's supervision) in the weeks I'd been gone – before joining everyone in the dining room for a celebration buffet dinner.

'Oh, Sal,' I said, looking at the laden table in amazement, 'all this for me?'

'Nah, the rest of us are going to eat it too,' she said.

'Take no notice, she's been planning this for *days*,' Buster told me.

'Well, the pub doesn't do many functions, even around Christmas, and I've enjoyed myself, pushing the boat out,' Sal told me, pink with pleasure at my reaction. She'd even made my favourite sausage rolls, with proper home-made flaky pastry and a touch of onion in the filling.

To my amazement, Angus said he'd missed me (all the while studying the dining table). 'Are you very sad about your husband dying?' he asked. Sal had explained my absence with this basic information.

'No, after the first shock I'm not upset at all,' I told him, biting into a warm sausage roll. 'Turns out he wasn't a very nice man.'

'Oh. Sal said sometimes people are sad and mixed up when someone dies, but if you're not then it's fine, right?'

My real feelings were rather more complex, but I was working on letting it all go. In time, there might even be a kind of reconciliation with the past, and if I couldn't get there on my own, I could afford professional help to achieve closure.

'Come on, Frankie, wrap yourself around some champagne,' said Dot, pressing a glass into my hand.

'God, that's good stuff,' I told her, as the pale golden bubbles slid down my throat.

Buster appeared at my elbow. 'The fizz is Dot's contribution to the party, bless her. I bloody love champagne.' She studied me with care. 'You're thinner. It's been a rough couple of months, hasn't it?'

I didn't waste time on polite denials. 'Yes, but it's almost over, and out of all the darkness comes a hopeful future. I can almost breathe again, and peace will come in time.'

After the party ended – nobody would even let me help with loading the dishwasher – I went upstairs to the refuge I'd been dreaming of for weeks. With the soft folds of my quilt snuggled around me, I curled up in the armchair beside the fire, the helium balloons bobbing against the ceiling in the warmth. Deep contentment flowed through me at being in those safe and familiar surroundings again. The champagne may have contributed to this warm glow of happiness, but it went further and deeper. In the past three years, I'd learnt the painful but essential life lesson of how unimportant possessions and "stuff" are (unless, of course, you haven't got any). The only thing that matters is the eternal truth that it is always and only love that makes the world go round – friends and family, people who have your back no matter what. Since I found myself blessed by those things then I pretty much had everything, including the ability to start again.

I didn't mind being interrupted when Dot came trotting up the stairs carrying her special brandy and a couple of glasses. For the party, she'd worn her favourite black top and trousers and sported a new blonde wig in a short, jaunty bob and pink specs with diamante wings.

'I had laser surgery years ago, so there's nothing wrong with my vision,' she told me. 'But they do make a snazzy accessory.'

'You look divine,' I told her. 'It's a big improvement on the old-lady outfit.'

She grinned, revealing her best dentures. 'Oh, but I rather enjoy that one, though it is revelatory how some people treat you, as if the elderly are persons of no account. Heavens, it's been bloody dull here since I left you in the big city. I want to hear *everything*.'

The following morning, experiencing a slight headache from the amount of brandy Dot and I had consumed, I came downstairs for a very late breakfast of strong remedial coffee and some toast with red jam. These were bringing about a major improvement when the front doorbell rang.

Opening the door with a slice of toast in one hand, I was met by a second welcoming committee. Nik, Maddie and Val stood on the top step with a huge bouquet and yet another helium balloon. Maddie threw herself into my arms and Nik's face indicated he wanted to do the same. Happiness at seeing them all almost banished the self-induced hangover, as tears threatened behind my eyes.

We traipsed upstairs, collecting Dot along the way, and Val admired my attic sanctuary while Nik reached for my hand and squeezed it. He didn't seem to mind that my fingers were a bit sticky from the jam, and the naked love in his face almost made me cry again.

'I want a bedroom *exactly* the same as this when we move to our new place,' announced Maddie.

'Such a gorgeous old house,' said Val, 'though it must be a bugger to dust.'

'*Yaya*, you should not use bad words and Daddy won't let me say that, so you mustn't.'

'A bigger house should mean employing domestic help, don't you think?' I suggested. 'You may intend to be chief cook when the three of you move in together, but it's a tall order to clean the place on top of everything else. You've got better things to do with your retirement.'

Val gave me a sideways glance at this, noting I wasn't including myself in these plans.

'Niko, why you didn't tell me how nice it is here in St Annes? So many lovely old Victorian houses ideal for family living. I can see why Frankie is happy here, it's got everything.'

'*Yaya*, it's at the seaside too,' Maddie said. 'Wait until you see the beach, I love it.'

After the milder climate of the south, I'd forgotten how nippy a November day on the northern coast could be. Making our way down to the seafront, the wind cut through my clothes, and breathing in the arctic air was enough to make my chest hurt and skin tingle. Only Maddie seemed not to notice – children don't seem to feel the cold the way adults do. The mist off the incoming tide also meant you had to use your imagination regarding a view of the sea. Despite these disadvantages, Val appeared to be genuinely taken with everything, perhaps even *over*-enthusiastic. Something felt off.

The wind finally defeated us, whistling around our ears so much that even shouted conversations could barely be heard. Running for cover from the elements, we opted for lunch in a café over a shop.

'But, Daddy, I wanted to have my fish and chips in the paper and eat it outside.'

Nik grimaced towards the rain now beating on the windows. 'Have you seen it out there? If the gulls didn't get your chips the wind would blow them away.'

Tourists being in short supply, we were able to bag a table by the window. As we wandered back down the main street, our bellies satisfyingly full, the rainstorm had moved on, but we all gave off a strong aroma of vinegar and fried food. Val exclaimed over the amenities of the main street and had to be dissuaded from diving into every charity shop on offer.

'Mamma, don't your preparations for moving include trying to downsize some of your clutter, not adding to it?' Nik protested.

Maddie pulled at my sleeve, drawing me and her *Yaya* to the next-door estate agent's window. 'How much?' exclaimed Val, peering at the display. 'So reasonable, *and* this one has a garden flat the same as Frankie's house. We should go in and see the details. Does it mention parking?'

Val and Maddie rushed inside, but I held onto Nik's arm to hold him back.

'Look, this is all a bit premature,' I told him. 'We haven't had much chance to talk about the future or moving in together yet, so we should be clear this family house project doesn't, for the time being, include me. I'm in recovery from… everything, and I've told you it's too soon to commit to anything. Or anyone.'

He blushed and produced a folded sheet of paper from his pocket, which turned out to be a set of details for the house Val had been exclaiming over.

'Mamma told me I would be a bloody fool if I didn't listen to what would make *you* happy, especially after everything you've been through,' he said. 'We started searching online and this place came on the market a week ago. It's easy walking distance from where you live now, a little further from the shops but then the gardens are bigger…'

'I've been set up, haven't I?'

'Um, yes. Do you mind?' said Nik, holding my hands tight. 'If it's not right or isn't what you want, we can forget the whole thing… or maybe we could go and see it this afternoon?'

'You've already made an appointment?'

'Well, we can cancel if it isn't what you want. Maybe you need more time?'

Maddie was giggling with delight and mischief at the surprise they'd made for me, so I could hardly refuse to go along with it. It was impossible to say how the whole project made me uneasy because once again I hadn't been consulted about Nik's plans. It might have been me being unnecessarily prickly or was it perfectly reasonable to want to make my own choices? I thought so.

We went to view the empty house, which was on a pleasant street with trees. Inside, Val and Maddie charged about in excitement, exclaiming over different rooms, and particularly the ultra-modern new kitchen with its granite-topped island. The garden flat made Val's eyes sparkle.

'What do you think?' she asked me.

'It's very similar to Sea View,' I said as we went back upstairs. 'But the developer has managed to strip out much of the character in the "modernisation", along with most of the original features and windows.'

Over time, fireplaces could be reinstated, and the lovely plaster ceilings and covings were still intact if blurred by layers of paint. The bare magnolia interiors would be much improved when populated with furniture and some splashes of colour, assuming Nik was willing to take all that on.

He was frowning as we walked from room to room, so I drew him to one side.

'What is it?' I asked when the others were out of earshot. 'You're not loving the place, are you?'

He shrugged. 'The photos were all right, but actually being here it doesn't have the "feeling" everyone talks about. Am I making sense?'

'Maybe,' I told him. 'It's important you do love it and have a vision for what it could be. There's bound to be something else; this is only the first one you've seen.'

Once again, his guilty flush gave the game away. I walked

over to the window, understanding why I'd had misgivings. Gazing outside without really seeing the street, I tried very hard not to allow the anger bubbling inside to overflow.

'You've found something else,' I said.

Nik crossed the echoing empty room and put his arms around me from behind. 'I wanted you to see this place first, but yes, and it's perfect – there's even a superb high school for Maddie, rated outstanding. Honestly, Frankie, it could be the one. Not quite as big as this but it has a real sense of space and the garden…' He stopped at my expression.

'You've already seen it!' Despite my best intentions, the question came out as an accusation.

'We all went, a couple of weeks ago. From the online photos it looked almost too good to be true, so we *had* to check it out before someone else snapped it up, and you were in London not taking my calls. Maddie and Val adored it, and I know you will too.'

'So why aren't we viewing that one instead of this? You could have sent me a link once we'd re-established communication.'

He wouldn't meet my eyes, like a little boy caught out in some misdemeanour. Then I got it and stepped back from his embrace.

'It's not in St Annes, is it?'

'Well, no. It's St Helens, but I promise you it's perfect. Maddie will be so happy there, and you'll soon make new friends. It could be a *home*, for all of us. Come and see it with me, please.'

'But I *told* you, I don't want to live anywhere but here. I thought you understood?'

I got the full persuasive salesman's pitch; Nik was so sure that I could be talked into seeing things his way. Listening to him, my frustration and uncertainty threatened to boil over, but we couldn't have a row about it in front of his mother and daughter, where all the bad words I wanted to use would be overheard.

'Nik, I'm tired now and more than a little overwhelmed,' I said after a pause. 'You all need to set off home soon but send me a link to the property you've found, and I'll look at it.'

Val came back into the room, her eyes darting between the two of us and taking in the stony expression I'm sure was on my face.

'Frankie knows about the other house,' she said.

'Yes. I've told him to send me the details.'

Nik got out his phone and scrolled through the photos, eager to continue his sales pitch.

'It's everything I always wanted for Maddie,' he said. 'She can grow up on the edge of the countryside instead of being a city kid, see…' He held out the phone and Val saw me take an involuntary step back; she didn't miss much.

'Niko, maybe now is not the time,' she said hastily. 'Give Frankie some space. She's barely back from London. This is all too fast for her.'

He turned to me, opened his mouth, then found something in my face which changed his mind and he put the phone back in his pocket. We straggled back up to Sea View, where Nik had parked his elderly estate car, and I couldn't bring myself to give him more than a somewhat perfunctory hug.

I waved them all off with a sense of relief, but anger simmered inside me as I sat in my window seat, staring blindly into the street and the roofs opposite. Later, as I headed back upstairs after a dinner I'd struggled to eat, Auntie Dot planted herself in my way.

'Something on your mind? I'm getting the impression this afternoon didn't go well.'

Feeling suddenly exhausted and overwhelmed, I stood on

the landing outside her door and gave thanks to whatever gods were out there for having Auntie Dot on my team.

'I'm at the point where I'm not sure whether to cry or be furiously angry,' I told her. 'They set up an appointment to view a house on Regent Road, but I could see Nik was only going through the motions of inspecting the place. He's found something else in St Helens and set his heart on it. I am bloody *livid* with him for not being straight with me, but today has clarified some things at least. There's a lot to think about.'

'I'm available if you need to talk,' she said as I started up the next flight of stairs. 'But may I suggest you focus only on what *you* want, without regard for anyone else's needs and feelings.'

'I plan to do exactly that,' I told her. 'There's some stuff I need to process, and it means asking myself the right questions. Perhaps I can bend your ear in a day or two when I've got my head more organised?'

Wise enough not to press me further, Dot only said, 'You're at probation Monday morning, aren't you? Coffee after lunch then? Text me if you need more time, and don't let anyone else rush you either.'

Up on the top floor, the sight of my room still lifted my heart even after weeks in the relative luxury of the Bayswater house. I fed the meter with coins and sat in the armchair, with Spike's comforting bulk occupying my lap, and spent a quiet hour gazing into the flames. Something which had been itching away at my subconscious suddenly opened like a flower, and things I should have seen earlier came into clear focus. I sat there in my attic, mentally tidying up and getting my ducks in a row, but in a different order and fewer of them. Then my phone pinged with a quick message from Nik giving the link to the St Helens property, and saying he'd ring me later at our usual time.

I'd committed to looking at the website, so I did. The house offered everything he'd promised – a handsome Victorian end of terrace with a large garden bounded by straggly privet hedges. Full of original features, with stripped pine doors and floors, it had been lovingly restored, right down to heritage standard double glazing indistinguishable from the original sash windows. What it *didn't* have was a separate flat for Val, although a huge bedroom right across the front of the house would make a comfortable bed-sitting room for her. Another good-sized bedroom at the back could be Maddie's. The entire top floor had been converted into a superb main suite, complete with its own bathroom and walk-in wardrobe.

I could see why they all loved it, but someone had beaten them to the purchase because a red box next to the listing said "Sold, subject to contract". Nik would be horribly disappointed, but it didn't change the conclusions I'd come to, or how much I dreaded my next conversation with him.

I got myself tucked up in bed with Spike at my side. He had made clear his objections to my being absent without leave and insisted on having all my attention. I fondled his ears while talking through with him all the things on my mind and the ducks I'd been rearranging. He gave a growly rumble deep in his chest when I got to the part about how angry the afternoon had made me feel, and the decisions I'd come to.

Then Nik rang.

'Frankie, are you still talking to me? On the way home Mamma gave me both barrels about what a bloody awful hash I made of today. Good job Maddie had fallen asleep.'

'Val is right,' I told him crisply. 'First you ambush me with a viewing all set up, although I might not have minded that. But then you barely bothered to hide the fact that you were bored and only going through the motions, with your heart already set on something else.'

'I'm sorry, Frankie, but when we found it, you weren't even taking my calls and it's perfect, everything I've dreamed of…' his voice trailed off.

'If it was exactly what you wanted, then it's a shame someone else has snapped it up.'

'So, you did visit the website?' he asked, his voice lifting with eagerness.

'I did, yes, and you're right – the house *is* beautiful, but not perfect. There wouldn't be anywhere for Val to have her own separate space or an office where I could set up my desk. Anyway, how many times have I told you that I don't bloody *want* to live in St. Helens? Why do you never listen to what I say?' Steady; I was letting my rising anger get the better of me.

'But Maddie loves the house so much, and the area has such good schools. She's excited about moving there, especially since we've been for a walk around. When she understood we'd found the perfect place, even Mamma said she'd be willing to compromise on the separate flat.'

'But I'm *not*, Nik. I never signed up for sharing a house with Val. Anyway, this is a pointless conversation since it's already sold.'

A long silence followed. I'm not usually slow on the uptake but then the final missing piece fell into place.

'Oh, shut the front door, now I get it; *you're* the buyer – you've already made an offer on the house!'

'Well… yes, but I haven't told Mamma or Maddie yet. Wait until you hear how it all happened –so definitely meant to be.'

I barely had the patience to listen as the story tumbled out of him; a new colleague at Laneways Trust who needed to buy in Manchester had been keen to purchase the flat if Nik would move out immediately, renting it to him until the sale went through. Such an easy opportunity to sell had been impossible to refuse, so within forty-eight hours everything from the apartment had been put into storage and he and Maddie were already camping out in Val's spare bedroom.

'Then the house in St Helens came up and it was so perfect, meant to be. Yeah, OK, I put in an asking price offer but only because I knew for sure you'd love it too. There's a lot of equity in the flat, so I can afford the mortgage on the new house until Mamma's property is sold. After we put her contribution in, the payments for the new place will be a lot less than what I pay now. It will be so wonderful with all of us together and Maddie will have such a happy childhood.'

'You've got the future all planned out.'

'Exactly, it all makes sense. I knew you'd understand.'

'Yes, I believe I do. You have just overridden and ignored everything I've ever said about where I want to live and why. This is supposed to be about my life too, but I'm expected to just go along with whatever you decide?'

'I didn't mean…'

'Yes, you did!' I was practically shouting down the phone. 'Nik Vassos, you're a fucking coward who avoids having difficult conversations but claims the right to make decisions for other people. Get this straight: I will not be treated that way.'

I'd known Nik wouldn't get it. He tried to talk me round, again, so sure that I would come to see things his way.

'Frankie, I hear what you're saying but *please* don't close your mind because you'll grow to love it there, I'm sure you will. If this is about an office for you to work in, then we can put an extension on the back, or build a garden room, although it would make the outside space smaller which would be disappointing for Mamma and Maddie.'

'Nik, listen to yourself. We've had this conversation too many times. You're a good son and father, and properly concerned for your family's needs, but what about mine?' I was trying to breathe slowly and deeply, control my temper and bring this to a civilised end.

'Are you saying you don't want *me* – is that it?'

'Let me turn the question around. I've come to believe that this is more about you wanting a mother for your daughter than how much you want *me*. I've seen the truth without admitting it to myself, and the time away in London provided distance and greater clarity. This afternoon was the clincher when all my doubts and reservations came together. I'm so much more than a potential substitute mother to complete your fantasy image of a happy family.'

'You can't believe that's where I'm coming from,' protested Nik, his voice a squawk.

'Do you even see me as a real person with needs, feelings and ideas of my own? Because you certainly aren't damn well respecting them. Nik, let me be clear and this time actually *listen* to me. Our relationship is *over*.'

'Have you met someone else?'

I'd been trying so hard to be calm and reasonable, wanting us to part friends. Now I went hot all over with anger that spilled over.

'How *dare* you ask me such a question? I have been 100% straight in all our dealings; I've told you clearly what I wanted, and you've ignored whatever I said. Far from meeting someone else, the absolute opposite is true. What I want and need right now is to be independent and live alone for the first time in my life, and that's what I'm going to do.'

A long pause. 'But why? We were so good together.'

'We were, I'm not denying that, and I did have feelings for you, but now I realise it's not enough. We're not on the same page, not even in the same fucking book, but you've persistently tried to impose your vision of the future on me. I might have tried harder if you'd met me halfway, but you were only ever thinking of Maddie and yourself. Val was trailing in third place, and I came last. London also made me appreciate that I've *done* the family thing and I'm over it, so I'll be buying myself a flat here, where I want to be. I'm ready to embrace my middle years and become a professional woman in my own right.'

'You're really going to do this – break up with me?'

Poor Nik, he'd never understand why I could reject something which seemed so perfect to him. Completely focused on his own dreams, he couldn't begin to imagine my embryonic vision of having a place of my own, everything chosen just because it appealed to me, with no compromises and no having to please anyone else. There'd need to be a cat too, definitely, and Nik didn't like them.

After another long silence, he said, 'You're not who I thought you were.'

'Maybe you constructed an image of me to fit into your ideal family, and I never managed to be what you wanted, even though I tried.'

'Well, I hope you'll enjoy your lonely flat while we live happily ever after in a gorgeous house. I don't understand why you'd turn your back on that, or us.'

He had no idea (because I hadn't told him) quite how much money I would have to begin this new adventure, and it would go a long way in the St Annes property market.

'Exactly my point. You *don't* understand, and probably never will,' I told him sadly, as my anger cooled to the ashes of something burnt out. 'You bought that house kidding yourself you could talk me into accepting your dreams for the future. But I'm going to choose the life *I* want to live because it's my decision. This is goodbye, Nik, but please… let's remain friends?'

He'd already put the phone down.

TWENTY-TWO

Arriving for Monday's probation meeting, I was armed with bank statements and legal papers. Tony offered me vending-machine coffee and drank the vile stuff with apparent unconcern as I outlined my plans for the future, further training and hopes for a paid role at the law centre.

Leaning back in his chair, his smile was approving. 'I'm dead proud of you, Frankie. Everything that's happened might have derailed a weaker character, but you strike me as a strong person with a remarkably practical approach. You like living around here, don't you?' he said.

'It's become home, so I'm going to buy myself a place to live once probate comes through and I've worked out what I want. There's no rush to leave my friends at Sea View.' I'd swallowed two-thirds of the paper cup of coffee but literally couldn't stomach any more. 'Right now, things are fine as they are, provided you approve of my not being in work for a time?'

'We wouldn't normally be happy about that part,' he admitted. 'But you've convinced me that you can support yourself, and you'll be doing a full-time training course, with your future plans solid. I don't see it as an issue, and I'll fight your corner if anyone says different. See you next month and keep up the good work.'

On the bus home, I sat on the top deck and Blackpool blazed with Christmas lights and decorations, the colours catching in the raindrops on the bus windows as I travelled past home to visit the Lytham deli. Perhaps one day an entrepreneur would open one in St Annes.

Back at Sea View, Dot answered my knock decked out in a yellow sweater and a turban-style scarf around her head featuring a banana print.

'I'm early but I brought us lunch,' I said, waving rustling brown paper bags.

'You look *so* much better,' she told me, sniffing appreciatively at the grease-stained bag containing a wonderfully ripe Camembert cheese. 'Do I take it you came to a decision?'

'Yes, Saturday provided the certainty I needed.' Such an understatement; it was hard to describe my emotions, but I felt lighter with a spring in my step and a clear horizon in front of me. Frankie Douglas was free and ready to make her way in the world.

Auntie Dot smiled. 'I can see things have changed. Come in and tell me everything,' she said, holding the door wide.

We munched the cheese with the sourdough rolls I'd also bought, followed by my favourite apricot Danish pastries. She listened as I explained about the ending of my relationship with Nik.

'I'm sad about hurting Val or Maddie,' I said. 'I'll write to each of them, but there's no doubt in my mind – Nik and I wouldn't be right for each other.'

Dot gave her verdict. 'A nice man but not the sharpest knife in the box. I'd back your assessment that what he really wanted was a mother for his daughter and a traditionally shaped nuclear family but failed to understand that need in himself.'

'Yes, and when I challenged him on that, he didn't even deny it. I took a long time to see the truth, but then perhaps I didn't want to. Alarm bells should have gone off when he told me I'd been the first woman to receive Maddie's seal of approval.'

'So, what now? Or perhaps you don't know yet?'

During my enthusiastic consumption of the sweet Danish, I'd managed to cover myself in flakes of pastry and didn't want to decorate the antique carpet with them by standing up. Dot produced one of those hand-held mini vacuum cleaners which solved the problem nicely.

'You know, during the time spent alone in the London house, it came to me that I enjoy living by myself. That leaves me wondering if the single life might even be preferable, at least for now.'

Mischief danced in Dot's face. 'I have never found it a barrier to... interesting encounters. After all these years I am way too stubborn to live with anyone else because they wouldn't let me have my own way all the time. Some would call that selfish, but I feel entitled to make my own choices now, and so are you.'

'I *am* confident it's the right decision for me,' I said, knowing that finally, here, was where my longed-for contentment and peace lay. Settling back in the chair, I continued, 'You get the credit for my blinding flash of insight, Dot, because something you said helped clarify things. You asked me what *I* wanted, and the picture my imagination supplied was a place of my own. Maybe it was seeing Justin's new place that provided the inspiration and got me thinking, but I'd like a flat with a view of the sea, and definitely a cat for company. Once I've bought a home of my own, I'll give some money away, invest the rest and live off what I can earn. It's a matter of pride and self-respect.'

Dot's eyes glowed with pride when I said this. 'That's my

girl,' she said. 'The world is now your oyster, so where will you go?'

'I plan to stay right here in St Annes. I couldn't ever leave you or the people at Sea View who've been with me on this journey.'

'I adore viewing properties,' Dot told me with a wicked grin. 'Please say I can tag along. I promise to keep it zipped if I don't care for what you choose.'

*

Finding my dream home took a long time, not least because of the necessity to wait for probate. The counselling studies kept me *very* busy, and I was putting in volunteer hours at the law centre as a requirement of the course. In the scraps of time available, I began to follow the online estate agencies to get a feel for the market and what might be out there. It was occasionally tempting to buy myself a ritzy place in Lytham – there were some beautiful ones on offer – but it wasn't how I saw my future. Even setting myself a moderate budget (to leave cash reserves for the future) there should be plenty of St Annes flats to choose from.

When my course ended in April, half of Henry's money had just landed in my account, so I could then decide which places I wanted to view. It was all very exciting at first; Dot came with me and (despite promising to keep her opinions to herself) made observations which proved astute, as always.

'Call this a sea view? You'd have to stand on a chair to appreciate it.'

'Frankie, this is poky. You'll go insane without more space to breathe, and the kitchen is no bigger than a cupboard.'

'It smells funny in here and you can hear the lift every time it goes up and down.'

'This place is dark. Whoever did the conversion should be shot.'

The problem was that she was dead right, every time.

Weeks of this left me thoroughly discouraged. 'Dot, what I want is just not out there, is it?' I asked her over a sandwich lunch in the coffee shop – the one where I'd first met with Kim.

Dot's smile was sympathetic under the purple turban. 'Look, I can see you're feeling despondent, but I don't believe that's true. It's not like you're asking for anything ridiculous.'

'Only space, light and character,' I told her, putting down my half-eaten sandwich. The prawns were so bland even the dressing couldn't make them interesting. 'I'm willing to compromise on my preference for an older property, but all the modern ones we've seen…'

'Have been boring, poky, or both!' finished Dot. 'Did you see that agent's face when I asked her where the hell you were supposed to put your clothes?'

I had to laugh. 'Yeah, and the best she could come up with was to suggest that I used the smallest bedroom as a "walk-in closet".'

Dot cackled, but it wasn't funny. That so-called third bedroom had been no bigger than a cupboard anyway.

'Stay with it, sweetheart,' advised Dot, polishing off the last of her beef and horseradish. 'The right one will be out there, and it's not like you hate living at Sea View.'

It was true that I loved my attic, but the siren song of a place of my own kept getting louder and more insistent. Boosted by Dot's words of wisdom, I determined not to settle and hold out for a place which gave me the feeling everyone talked about.

It was already September before a call came from an estate agent I'd left my details with.

'Ms Douglas? I've just taken an instruction for a property which might be perfect for you – it's not officially on the market yet but the owners have moved out and you should see it as soon as possible because it will sell very fast.'

Even without photos (not taken yet), his description of it sounded perfect, so in a state of high excitement Dot and I went to view the place the same afternoon. According to the agent, the vendors were getting divorced and looking for a speedy sale.

The man who did showings for the agency left us to wander freely around the three-bedroom flat, taking in every detail. The property was a "penthouse" on the top floor of a purpose-built Victorian mansion block, another attic with the beamed sloping ceilings I've always adored. The two main bedrooms had en-suites, and the smallest could serve as an office. I had to rein in my burgeoning excitement and stay focused on the practicalities.

'These bifold doors are so great,' I told Dot as we stepped outside onto the roof terrace, which ran the whole width of the building. I was already mentally populating it with plants in pots and garden chairs, maybe even AstroTurf.

Dot squeezed my hand, saying, 'You love it, don't you? I can tell.'

My excited face must have been a dead giveaway. 'After all these months, *finally* a place with a proper view of the sea. I can have parties outside in the sunshine in the summer months, though we'd inevitably have greedy gulls for company.' One perched on the parapet wall as if to illustrate my point.

In the large living room, Dot peered at a long smudge on the wall where a sofa had obviously stood. 'It does need decorating throughout, but this oak flooring is gorgeous, and the white bathrooms are classic, so no major renovations required. There shouldn't be any noise issues up here either.'

'Hmm,' I said as we walked through to the kitchen. 'These units are quite new, but I'm not in love with the dark wood.

Never mind, it isn't a deal breaker because once I've figured out what I want it can all be replaced. Don't have a clue right now.'

Dot beamed at me in happy anticipation. 'We can go and prowl around kitchen showrooms as much as you like. There's a fancy one in Lytham down a side street from the tapas place.'

I made an asking price offer for the flat on the spot, not bothering to haggle because the place "spoke" to me, and already felt like the home I'd been longing for. I'd even begun to plan where the Christmas tree would go, and a bed for the cat. Five weeks later, the deal was done, in what had to be some of the fastest conveyancing ever. It was perfectly possible if you were a stroppy enough cash buyer, and both sides were pressing for a speedy transaction.

I stayed on at Sea View while having the whole flat painted white as a blank canvas to work from. With Dot's assistance, I then went furniture shopping and acquired the bare necessities – an antique brass bed, modern sectional sofa, TV and a lamp. With these items plus my rocking chair and quilt, I moved in with just a basic set of kitchen equipment ordered from IKEA, and finally acquiring towels and bedding from a Lytham department store. It was all a bit bare at first, but I didn't care, determined to take my time over getting the interior right.

There was a huge symbolic meaning attached to owning a property at last – I hadn't understood until then how much I'd craved a space that was mine alone. Throughout my life, everywhere I'd lived had belonged to someone else. There was something soul-deep about reaching this point in my life that I struggled to articulate even to myself, let alone the people around me. The sense of homecoming, both to inmost self and to my very own nest was precious and healing, allowing me to focus on the future rather than being haunted by the past.

*

The flat-warming party was a blast, what I remember of it, with everyone I cared about there to cheer me on into the future, including, of course, Doreen and Shannon. Rev. Ellie turned out to be a wild dancer and I didn't have to worry about noise for the people downstairs because they'd gone to Spain for six months, as they did every year. I had to ask friends to bring garden chairs or cushions and we borrowed a folding table from the church hall for the food – a fabulous buffet supplied by the Spice King restaurant, which remained my favourite place to eat. Auntie Dot generously supplied the champagne and she and Sal were the life and soul of the party. Such a great start to my new life; I couldn't have been happier.

At weekends I haunted the local cat rescue. I'd been imagining a kitten, and they were all incredibly cute, but then a skinny grey scrap of about six months old came strolling over and immediately made himself at home in my lap. When I stopped tickling him under the chin, he climbed up my front and put one soft paw on my face, as if to say "keep going". I was his devoted slave from that moment. The little chap with enormous feet has grown up to be large, heavy and imperious, but a much-loved and affectionate friend. I named him Gus and he adores Dot too, climbing all over her on her frequent visits. Nothing to do with the catnip toys she brings him at all.

*

A year on and Justin and Betty have come up for the weekend, and we're all eating breakfast on the terrace in the early autumn sunshine. Gus is chittering at the birds on the feeding station I set up for them – which he takes as a personal affront. He's much too slow and lazy to catch any of them (thank goodness), but lives in hope.

Everyone is full of enthusiasm for the recently completed kitchen.

'The white is great,' says Justin. 'That room was the darkest part of the flat before.'

'The roof lights help too, and opening up the space,' I say, letting the coffee work its magic. We'd had a late session the night before.

'Knocking the wall through to the living room has made a huge difference,' says Betty. 'Having drawers instead of lower cabinets is such a clever idea.'

'Wait till you see my pantry,' I say. 'The kitchen designer understood what I wanted so well, and the island means being able to chat with people while I cook.

Behind us, the living room is now a restful blend of blues, grey and white with occasional splashes of colour. One wall is home to an eclectic selection of antique blue plates I've collected from charity shops and other places. On the other side, the entire wall is given over to bookshelves – a long way from full but I'm working on it. The aspidistra Buster gave me as a housewarming present is flourishing, even threatening to take over. The grey sofa features a collection of bright cushions; my favourite is the Frida Kahlo one with the pink bobble edging that Dot found in Lytham.

My solitary walks along the beach continue to be a time for reflection. I did have counselling in the end because, I'm not gonna lie, for months difficult memories and some regrets haunted me. Then one day I drew an actual line in the sand with my foot, symbolising everything I wanted to leave behind. I stood for a while before stepping over it, and as I walked back to the shore the incoming tide quickly washed it away. It represented the difference between then and now, before and after, the person I'd been and the one I'm learning to become. It had been my own choice to close the door on being able to clear my name, and because in the end everything led to where I am now, honestly, I wouldn't change a thing.

However, my career as an arsonist is definitely over.

THANK YOU

To the people who were my first readers and were kind enough to provide feedback – my husband Jeff, Marian Hartley, Roy Holden.

To Milla Reed, friend, fellow author and writing buddy who always had time to give me an honest opinion.

To Jericho Writers whose courses, editors and mentors guided me all the way from my first stumbling beginnings to publishable work.

To Phil Downie and Yolanda his trusty assistant for the photographs.

To the Book Sisters just for being there.

To all the friends and family who had my back throughout the long gestation process and allowed me to bore them endlessly with talk about books and publishing. None of them have "unfriended" me yet, but there's still time.